Sandcastles and Second Chances

A Love on Turtle Island Series
Book 1 of 7

Lianne James

APPLEBEE PRESS

This is a work of fiction. Names, characters, businesses, places, events, locales, and incidents are either the products of the author's imagination or used in a fictitious manner. Any resemblance to actual persons, living or dead, or actual events is purely coincidental.

While every precaution has been taken in the preparation of this book, the publisher assumes no responsibility for errors or omissions, or for damages resulting from the use of the information contained herein.

For James

Introduction to Sandcastles and Second Chances

**Sometimes life gives you a second chance
because you weren't ready the first time...**

At forty-nine-years-old, it's safe to say life didn't turn out the way Lucinda Flowers hoped it would. Her husband ran off with her best friend, and her grown children don't come around much. When her sister, Sharon, calls with bad news, Lucinda boards a plane back to the one place she vowed to never return: home to Turtle Island.

Jim Barnes is Lucinda's long-lost high school boyfriend. She doesn't know it yet, but he's been secretly keeping in touch with her eccentric mother, Goldie, for decades. When his estranged wife goes missing in North Carolina, Jim returns to Turtle Island hoping to dodge the web sleuths labeling him a wife-killer.

The Pink Octopus, Lucinda's family's cottage rental business, is in trouble. If it sinks, not only will her mother, brother, and sister be out of jobs, but the entire family will be scattered to the high winds. Can Lucinda and Jim figure out what happened to Camille and clear his name before he's arrested on suspicion of murder? Can they save The Pink Octopus before it goes belly-up? And, will they find their way back to each other, or are some loves too far gone to be rekindled?

PELICAN HARBOR

THE DROP OFF

SALTWATER
REEF

EMERALD ISLE

HAMMERHEAD
WHARF

JELLYFISH
BAY

TURTLE
BEACH

ANGEL
SHORES

TRINITY

PARADISE
COVE

N
W   E
S

Turtle

Island

THE PINK OCTOPUS

Arrive as our guest, leave as our friend

Our Bungalows

1. The Pink Octopus

2. The Yellow Crab

3. The Turquoise Turtle

4. The Tangerine Clam

5. The Green Seahorse

6. The Great White

7. The Blue Dolphin

8. The Purple Starfish

9. The Peach Squid

10. The Lemon Jellyfish

11. The Lavender Walrus

12. The Cerulean Lobster

13. The Ivory Eel

Chapter 1

Lucinda Flowers shifted uncomfortably in her seat while her taxi driver, Arturo, recalled the time he met Frank Sinatra outside of a men's restroom at a gas station in Oklahoma. "Nice guy," Arturo said, opening a stick of gum and throwing the foil wrapper out his window. "Shorter in person, but his eyes were every bit as blue as they say. Man, oh man were they blue!"

Adjusting the rearview mirror to see if Lucinda was impressed, Arturo continued. "My wife sure was taken with old Frankie. She ended up leaving me for a guy that was no Sinatra, let me tell you!"

Lucinda pinched the bridge of her nose and hoped her posture and closed eyes would make it obvious she wasn't interested in talking. She wanted to ask Arturo what on earth Frank Sinatra would've been doing at a gas station in Oklahoma but didn't have the energy to ask.

"I don't have much luck with the ladies," Arturo snorted. "How about you? You lucky in love?"

Lucinda cringed that the conversation had taken such a sharp turn, but pretended she didn't hear him. She asked if he could turn up the air conditioning, but he shook his head and said it was "on the fritz." Lucinda reclined in her seat and tried to mentally prepare for the family reunion to come.

A week earlier, her younger sister, Sharon, called unexpectedly. They didn't talk on the telephone often, and almost never in the middle of the day. Lucinda had hoped all her life that she'd be close with Sharon, the way she'd always seen sister relationships depicted in movies and greeting cards. The truth was, the Perrys were not a close family, and not just because Lucinda married Peter and moved to Connecticut decades earlier. Even growing up, Lucinda, Sharon, and their younger brother, Ben, weren't buddies. They loved one another but were never what one might call friends.

Lucinda was the oldest child. By the time Sharon came along, Lucinda was in kindergarten making friends of her own. She loved her little sister but didn't have time—or the desire—to play baby games. She was in sports and music classes and busy being a social butterfly at her new school.

Ben came along when Sharon was well into grammar school. By that time, it was not only Lucinda with a life of her own. Plus, Sharon was prissy, and Ben was all boy, so they had absolutely nothing in common. Sharon would shriek when Ben brought a toad to the dinner table or forgot to put the lid on his fishing worms, and Ben complained that both Sharon and Lucinda were too bossy.

When Peter proposed, Lucinda didn't have to think twice about leaving Turtle Island. She dreamed of getting a design degree, taking the train into Manhattan every morning with a bagel in her hand and *The New York Times* tucked under her arm. She imagined meeting Peter—who would naturally join his father's law firm—at a café for lunch, somewhere near his office on West 31st Street. Lucinda would order the pastrami and Peter the egg salad. They would split them and discuss current events on their break. *Look at the handsome couple sitting in the window*, passersby would whisper admiringly.

Unfortunately, life didn't work out that way. Lucinda got pregnant during her sophomore year at college. At Peter's insistence, she dropped out, promising herself she'd return the following year, but that didn't happen either. Peter didn't want a nanny raising his children like his parents had done with him. He convinced Lucinda to put her dreams of becoming an interior designer on hold. "Someday when the kids are grown, maybe you can have a career. By then, you'll want something to keep you busy so you don't go stir crazy alone in this big house," he encouraged one night in bed.

Lucinda flicked her bedside lamp off and silently cried herself to sleep. When she awoke the following morning, she quietly gathered her textbooks and put them in a box marked "free" on the curb in front of her house. She never mentioned having a career again.

When Sharon's call came in, Lucinda was scraping the last of her tomato soup from a coffee mug and cursing at the television. She could barely find her cell phone under wads of used tissues and empty candy wrappers. She'd been wearing pajamas for a week straight, letting her newspapers pile up on the front porch, and neglecting her plants. She'd lost count of how many sappy romcoms she'd watched and was growing tired of the guaranteed happy ending they all delivered.

Life wasn't cut and dry—the good guy (or girl) didn't always win at love—and Lucinda knew that better than anyone. "What is it, Sharon?" she asked, brushing cracker crumbs off her robe when she answered the phone.

"Well," Sharon croaked, "the good news is I'm not crazy. The fatigue, the wonky legs, the pins and needles in my fingertips. They finally confirmed yesterday that I'm not nuts."

"So, what is it?"

"MS."

"What?" Lucinda gasped. "Are you sure? That can't be right. No one in our family has that. Maybe you should get a second opinion!"

"I did. Yesterday was my third time sitting in a paper robe and trying to keep it together while a doctor with sad eyes broke the news all over again. 'I'm sorry, Mrs. Klein. The tests are conclusive. You appear to have multiple sclerosis.' I don't know what's worse, Lucinda, the diagnosis or people calling me Mrs. Klein. Should I go back to Perry?"

Sharon sounded a million miles away as she talked about upcoming doctors' appointments, the makeshift cane she fashioned out of their father's old walking stick, and how she'd had to move in with their mother because she was falling too much to continue living alone.

Lucinda got off her chair while Sharon talked and began gathering the dishes that had piled up in the living room over the past seven days. She stuffed used tissues in her robe pocket, sorted her mail into neat piles, and poured an old glass of water with a dead fly floating on its surface into her Philodendron, which was so dry that the water flooded out of the holes and straight onto the floor.

Every so often, Lucinda would say, "Oh, Shaz," to let Sharon know she was still there. She didn't really know what else *to* say. The more Sharon talked, the guiltier Lucinda felt. All she could think of was how she'd abandoned her family on Turtle Island to spend the past thirty years with a man who put cottage cheese on his morning toast and spoke of himself in the third person. "Love the new paisley tie," her husband would say as he dressed for work, "but Peter wouldn't mind if you'd throw in some solids once in a while for meetings with his more traditional clients."

By the end of the call, Lucinda's house was still a wreck, but all she had the energy to do was slip into a hot bath, her go-to medicine for overwhelm. She stared at her legs under the water, and suddenly it mattered less that they were pasty white and a bit jiggly. Sharon's legs were all but giving out on her. At least Lucinda's legs still worked.

A relaxing playlist calmed her nerves, but only until her phone rang, startling her. Drying her hands on a washcloth, she pressed "Accept."

It was her mother, Goldie. "Mom, can I call you back? I've had a rough day and I'm in the tub," Lucinda said wearily.

Goldie asked if Lucinda's front door was locked, recalling a news story where a divorcee was taking a relaxing bubble bath and an intruder walked right in her front door and stabbed her seventy-two times in the tub.

Lucinda groaned, repeating that she'd had a bad day and didn't want to talk. "So Sharon called you then?"

"Yes, and I'm sick about it, so can we talk another time, Mom?"

"Well, I guess since you're already upset, I may as well tell you the rest."

"What could be worse than my little sister having a terrible disease, Mom?"

"Well, when you put it like that," Goldie huffed, "nothing, I suppose. I'll just call you another time."

"What is it, Mom?"

Goldie let out a long sigh and explained the bad news.

When Lucinda could finally get off the phone with her mother, she stepped out of the bath and folded herself back inside her robe. She flopped onto the bed and opened her laptop. After hearing her mother's unfortunate update—the family business was in trouble—Lucinda realized there was no getting out of a trip home. Her family needed her, and, as of a week earlier, her husband no longer did.

Searching the Internet for a plane ticket, Lucinda imagined convincing her sister to move back to Connecticut with her. The hospitals were better in Stamford, and New York City wouldn't be a terrible drive if Sharon needed even more specialized care. They could get Sharon's MS under control and open a bakery together or perhaps take a pottery class. Maybe they could become friends after all.

Lucinda booked her ticket and remembered a conversation she'd had with Peter after Sharon's husband, Alan, died. Lucinda asked Peter if he thought Sharon might move in with them, especially since Jill and Frankie had both moved out. "We've missed out on so many years of really knowing each other," she said, twirling her Spaghetti Carbonara around her fork. "Maybe it's not too late for us to..."

Peter pressed his lips together, held up a hand to silence her, and said he'd been looking forward to the house being quiet again now that they were empty nesters. "We earned this quiet time, Lucinda," he said, sipping his wine. With that, Lucinda laid the idea to rest. When Peter decided something, there was little point in arguing. He was a lawyer, after all, and a pretty good one.

At Alan's funeral, Lucinda squeezed Peter's hand, relieved that it wasn't him being lowered into the ground that day. She knew it was an awful thing to think, but at the time, she couldn't imagine life without him. He was the only man she'd ever really depended on.

Alan was a wonderful man, and Lucinda's heart broke for her sister. Not only had Sharon lost her husband, but her business partner, too. Alan was a prominent dentist on Hammerhead Wharf where they lived. When he died, she was forced to sell the practice that she'd managed for years. That additional loss was like adding insult to injury. Despite the grief she felt for her sister, Lucinda couldn't imagine losing Peter at the time.

No one would argue that Alan was the better man in every way, but even now, despite all the terrible things he'd done, Lucinda still didn't know how she'd get through the rest of her life without Peter. The thought of growing old alone terrified her, which was a paralyzing reality she hadn't come to grips with yet.

With both of their husbands gone, perhaps the trip home to Turtle Island would be a great time to broach the subject of Sharon moving to Stamford.

Back in the bathroom, Lucinda wiped the remaining steam from the mirror and took her hair out of its clip. She studied her reflection, but what she really saw was long walks with her sister, volunteering together at the Stamford Historical Society, and riding the train to New York City to see Broadway shows. The thought brought a hopeful smile to her face. Maybe their most awful traumas would lead to a brand-new chapter in their relationship. "If you want a rainbow, you gotta put up with the rain," Lucinda whispered into the mirror. "So says Dolly Parton, anyway."

Lucinda checked her phone from the back of the cab. There was a message from Peter. It took her seven texts for her to explain the events surrounding her upcoming trip home. She said she didn't know how long she'd be gone and asked him to keep an eye on the house, perhaps water the plants, bring in the mail. He owed her that much.

She hoped Peter could manage this one thing for her and preferably do it alone. The last thing she needed was Peter taking his new girlfriend over to touch things and breathe and leave her powdery perfume stuck to Lucinda's velvet drapes.

Of course, Peter's girlfriend had been in Lucinda's home many, many times over the years already, which only made things hurt that much worse.

All Peter replied was "OK," which Lucinda knew had to be a metaphor for the total lack of effort he put into their marriage. One text in response to her seven.

But, for now, Arturo's microwave on wheels had arrived at The Pink Octopus, the Perry's fifty-year-old family bungalow rental service. The sign was chipped, the potholes had only gotten bigger since Lucinda had last visited, and the giant octopus statue out front was weather-worn and pathetic. She shook her head at the sight of things.

Exiting the cab, Lucinda thanked Arturo for retrieving her luggage from the trunk of the taxi. "Have a nice vacation, doll," he said, sucking on a toothpick and giving Lucinda a once-over. Drawing in a deep breath, Lucinda pressed her lips together, trying to contain a nasty reply. She nodded, braced herself, and walked up the stairs of the office building.

The bells jingled on the front door, and Goldie looked up from her online game of Solitaire. "Well, butter my biscuit and call me Sally!" she shouted, lowering her reading glasses. Lucinda gave a weak smile and set down her bags.

"Hi, Mom."

"Lucinda, you look...healthy."

"Why don't you just say I'm fat, Mom? That's what you're getting at, right?"

"Well, I can sugarcoat it for you, honey," Goldie said, shrugging, "but it might be more helpful if I were honest. You kind of let yourself go, baby. I mean, what gives?"

Lucinda groaned and shook her head when Goldie offered her a drink. She pointed to the clock and showed her mother that it was barely noon—a bit early for liquor by anyone's standards. Goldie quipped, "Since when do we have standards?"

She turned the door sign to *Be back soon*. It had a clock printed on it with plastic hands, but Goldie didn't bother estimating the actual return time. Lucinda followed her into the back office where there was a cot and a fan blowing paper around on a nearby desk.

Sharon was sleeping, curled up tight like a little girl. Lucinda motioned to let her sleep, but her mother nudged Sharon awake, snorting, "Are you kidding? She wouldn't want to miss the return of her prodigal sister!"

Sharon rolled over, rubbed her eyes, and smoothed her hair. Her cheeks flushed, and she apologized for sleeping in the middle of the day. She sat up, slowly lifted her legs to the floor one by one, and let out a heavy sigh.

Looking into each other's eyes, neither Lucinda nor Sharon could stop the tears from rolling down their cheeks. Goldie took that as a cue to return to Solitaire. She spun on her heel and headed back into the lobby.

Sharon ran her fingers through her hair and sighed. "My heart wants to get up and hug you," she trembled, "but my legs are like, 'Eh, it's just your sister, not the queen of England.'"

Lucinda laughed and pressed her palms against the cot. "Will this thing hold us both if I come to you?"

"Sure," Sharon giggled, "Let's try it."

"I don't know," Lucinda said, sitting down. "Mom already told me I'm fat, so consider yourself warned."

"That's okay. She told me I got MS from putting Sweet 'N Low in my iced tea."

For a few minutes, they sat on the cot making jokes about their mother and sharing pictures of their grown children on their phones. "You showed me most of these already," Sharon said, "but I don't care. I love seeing my niece and nephew. How's Jill's business?"

Before Lucinda could answer, the bells jingled on the office doors, and Sharon nervously tucked a strand of hair behind her ear, raising Lucinda's hackles. Ever since she was a little girl, Sharon nervously tucked her hair behind her ear when she was about to get in trouble. Lucinda raised an eyebrow and asked what was up. Sharon glanced at the clock and muttered that it might not be a guest at the door.

When Lucinda asked what she meant, Sharon bit her lip and muttered a long, "Ummm," trying to buy herself some time.

Lucinda peered around the corner and saw a man hugging Goldie. She looked back at Sharon, who was biting her fingernails to nubs, and turned back toward the man. Leaning closer and squinting, she threw a hand over her mouth to keep from screaming. "Tell me that is not who I think it is! It can't be..."

"It's not who you think it is," Sharon mumbled sheepishly. "Unless you think it's Jim Barnes."

Lucinda collapsed onto the cot, its springs jabbing into her back. Her sweaty shirt stuck to her, and she groaned as panic swallowed her up like she'd stepped into quicksand. "Why is he *here*?" Lucinda shrieked.

"Mom asked him to come," Sharon admitted. "She thought we'd need some help around here now that I'm crippled."

"Stop it," Lucinda snapped. "You're not going to get out of this by being self-deprecating. How long have you known?"

"Um..."

"Stop saying, 'Um!' Why would Mom even think to ask my old high school boyfriend—who hasn't been in the picture for what? Thirty years? Why would she even think to ask him to help save the family business?"

Sharon spit a thumbnail into a tissue and revealed that their mother had stayed close with Jim through the years, never letting Lucinda in on the situation. They exchanged emails, Christmas cards, and Goldie kept Jim in the loop with family news. Lucinda's eyes felt stuck open to maximum capacity, completely unable to blink.

Goldie called out in a saccharine voice from the reception desk for Lucinda to come and help her with a guest, still concealing the bomb she was about to detonate. An undigested airplane burrito churned in Lucinda's gut, and she wondered how a month earlier her life was supremely boring and safe. Now, she was back on Turtle Island, bracing for a *Twilight Zone*-worthy reunion with her high school boyfriend.

She stood up, shot her sister a death glare, and tried in vain to smooth her blouse, wrinkled from two flights, a boat ride, and a trip in Arturo's cab. Sharon stifled a laugh, and Lucinda growled at her to shut up.

She pulled the spoon out of someone's cup of tea, shook it off, and examined her teeth in the reflection. "I'm old," she muttered, pinching her cheeks to put some color back in them. Sharon smiled, and snorted, "Well, the good news is, so is Jim."

On her way to the lobby, Lucinda gave herself a silent pep talk. *So I let myself go a little. Who hasn't? I mean, it's been thirty years. Close up, I'll bet Jim's no Hollywood movie star either, right?*

When she reached the front desk, she nodded and smiled, as though it was perfectly normal to come face to face with someone from half a lifetime ago. Though it had been three decades, Jim looked almost exactly the same. No receding hairline, and his belly was flat enough to bounce quarters off of.

She reminded herself to blink and squeaked, "Oh, hi Jim." Jim clutched his ball cap to his chest but didn't say hello back. He just smiled and shook his head. She'd know that smile anywhere, even if someone had shown her a photo with everything covered but his mouth. He still had the chin dimple, but the crinkles around his eyes were new.

Regret settled into Lucinda's kneecaps as she recalled using greasy, processed food to cope with Peter's affair. Had her shirt shrunk in the past five minutes? Suddenly it felt two sizes too small.

When Jim finally spoke, all he said were two words. Only two. "Damn, girl," was all it took, and Lucinda was eighteen all over again. From the fawning look radiating from the front desk, so was Goldie.

Chapter 2

Lucinda hadn't seen her first love in three decades. When she met Peter, the summer after she'd graduated high school, he'd been visiting Turtle Beach with his parents, and asked her to give him a tour of the island. Despite having a steady boyfriend, Lucinda justified spending the day with Peter by telling herself he was a paying customer at The Pink Octopus.

By the end of Peter's vacation, just days after they'd first met, Lucinda was drunk on possibility. Peter was all the things Jim wasn't. He was driven, well-spoken, and had an entire future mapped out for himself. He was on track to become a prominent Manhattan lawyer. He dangled a future that promised to get Lucinda off the island, and one step closer to her dream of being a big-city interior designer.

Lucinda never allowed things to progress past sweet talk during Peter's vacation that summer. She couldn't bring herself to cheat on someone as kind and loyal as Jim. Despite the lack of even a single kiss, though, she knew she'd marry Peter. It was never a question in her mind, but more like something written in the stars that they'd be together forever. She'd go to college in Connecticut, open a design firm in Manhattan, and work minutes from Peter's law firm. No more changing bungalow sheets and gutting fish with her brother and appeasing cranky guests by offering discounts and free champagne.

She ended things with Jim, which was traumatic for both of them. For years after, vivid nightmares of him crying and begging her to reconsider haunted her sleep. Jim was sweet and funny and romantic, but Peter had the means to get her off the island for good, and she took the opportunity for fear there would never be another one.

Island life wasn't terrible, but she dreamed of so much more. A two-story colonial house in Connecticut, summers in the Hamptons, interesting dinner parties with colorful debates between doctors and lawyers and all the elite New Yorkers she'd befriend.

Now, Jim stood before her, his mouth hanging open, seemingly at a loss for words. When he finally spoke, it was a voice as familiar as her son's or daughter's. A voice that time hadn't touched. He said it felt like forever that they'd seen each other. "I know," she replied. "I can't believe we've never run into each other on my visits home."

Leaning in for an awkward hug, she breathed in his cologne. That part differed from her memories. He smelled exactly as he looked now: masculine, steadfast, kind. "I don't live here," he said, confused. "Didn't Goldie tell you I've been in North Carolina for...what's it been, Gold? Oh, I guess twenty-five years now." He looked at Goldie to confirm the time.

Lucinda put her hand on her hip and said, "My mother forgot to mention that you two have stayed in touch all these years, didn't you Mother?" Goldie pretended to be absorbed in something riveting on the computer. Finally, she looked up and tossed a key to Lucinda, asking her to show Jim to his bungalow. "We're putting him in Number 8," she purred, cocking her head and batting her eyelashes at Jim. "Nothing but the best for our Jimmy." Lucinda's mouth fell open. *Our Jimmy?*

Jim blushed, and thanked Goldie, who slid her leopard print reading glasses back in place and lost her flirtatious grin when she caught her daughter's glaring eyes on her.

Lucinda motioned for Jim to follow her to his cabin, apologizing for her mother's lack of discretion. "I'd chalk it up to senility, but Goldie's sharper than I am," she groaned.

"I heard that!" Goldie shouted.

"I meant for you to!" Lucinda called over her shoulder.

The bungalows, small and modest, dotted the shoreline and had long since started showing their wear and tear from years of sea air and strong winds. They were gray with dingy white trim around the windows and doorframes. Lucinda hadn't been home to notice the declining state of things in years. Alan's funeral was on the mainland, which she attended but flew back to Connecticut immediately afterwards to make it to her daughter Jill's college graduation.

After opening the front door of Number 8, Lucinda handed the key to Jim and turned to leave. "We should catch up," he suggested, motioning toward the living room. "Can I interest you in some tap water?" Lucinda smiled, took a seat at the table, and shrugged. "Sure, it'll stall me for a few minutes, hopefully long enough to keep me from committing matricide when I get back to the office."

Jim went to the freezer to get some ice for the water and found it stocked with frozen pizzas, a pint of ice cream, and some vegetables. He opened the refrigerator, and saw milk, butter, eggs, and fresh meat. There was a loaf of bread and a plate of cookies on the counter, along with a note he held up for Lucinda to see. "I wonder if it's from my mother or my sister?" she asked, rolling her eyes.

Jim opened the envelope and read aloud, "Jimmy, you should cook the steaks for a nice dinner with Lucinda, since it wouldn't be heart healthy to eat both yourself. Love, Goldie." Lucinda buried her face in her hands and said it was official: her mother was shameless.

Soon, they were talking like old friends. Had Lucinda heard that Kenny Loomis had died? *Yes, and how shocking for someone so young to have a heart attack.* Did Jim ever get his homemade tattoo removed? Pulling up the sleeve of his shirt and seeing L.M.P., she got her answer. "Bet you regretted getting my initials on your arm a time or two over the years, huh?" Lucinda asked, picking at a cookie from the tray Jim placed before her. He shrugged, grinned, and bit into a cookie.

Lucinda took a bite of cookie, too, and when the strange chemical aftertaste made her tongue tingle, said she'd bet dollars to donuts the cookies were from Food Basket—the most popular grocery chain on the island—but plated to look homemade. Jim chewed his bite and nodded. "Yep, you're right. I think they still use that funky almond extract they used in 1990."

"Blech," Lucinda sputtered, setting her cookie back down on the plate and brushing her hands on her pants. "I think this *cookie* is from 1990!"

They balanced on wobbly kitchen chairs and commented on how the island never really changed, even though the rest of the world did. Lucinda looked around the shabby cottage at the thin, lumpy sofa pillows and faded curtains. "Why did they let it go so badly?" she mused aloud, shaking her head. "Did anyone ever tell you the story of how my mom and dad started this business?"

Jim shook his head and Lucinda recalled the story of Tom winning The Pink Octopus in a lucky hand of poker—though it was called The Whaler back then.

She smiled, remembering her parents retelling the story each year on their anniversary. Tom had gone into a diner in his hometown, Duluth, Minnesota, to get a cup of coffee and saw Goldie sitting there in a wedding dress, sobbing. She'd left her husband at the altar and hopped on a bus to anywhere but Boise, where she'd come from. "Long story short," Lucinda said, "he tricked her into following him to Turtle Island to start a new life."

"Wow," Jim sighed, "Goldie was a runaway bride! Add that to the list of fascinating things about her."

"The place was in shambles when they got here, and they fell in love during the renovation. They put their blood, sweat, and tears into The Pink Octopus and now look at it. Dad would be so upset."

"Foreclosure," Jim whispered. "Goldie told me. I guess that's why you're here."

"She told you?" Lucinda asked incredulously. Well, I guess you two are friends, right? But why did she let the business go to pot? And why didn't Benny or Shaz step in and help?"

"People get tired, Luce. Maybe they're all ready to move onto something different."

Lucinda felt her face flush when Jim called her Luce. He asked some questions about the foreclosure, and for a minute she allowed a seed of doubt to slip in, wondering if Jim had only come back to Turtle Beach to buy the business out from under them.

A few minutes later, when Jim said that he'd lost all his money in a bad investment, she breathed a sigh of relief. She doubted that regardless of how time may have changed Jim, that it would've turned him into a con man.

Lucinda took a long sip of water and noticed that it still had the same metallic aftertaste as always. She placed her hands on the table, as if bracing herself. "I haven't even sat down with my family yet and discussed options. I can't imagine they'd want to close the doors to this place, though. My brother and sister and I grew up here. Every memory we have up to a certain point ties us back to the family business. We can't give it up without a fight."

"When Tom died all those years ago, I wanted to reach out to you," Jim said, staring into Lucinda's eyes.

"Why didn't you? Apparently, my mother could've given you my number."

"She told me Frankie was in the hospital getting a heart transplant, and I didn't think I should pick that moment in time to reenter your life."

Lucinda was taken aback at the sound of Jim referring to her son as Frankie. Only the immediate family called him that. To everyone else, he was Frank Flowers, owner of the most successful privately owned real estate chain in the United States.

Lucinda felt her cheeks flush, and the anger began to well up inside of her. Who did Jim Barnes think he was, spying on her through her busybody mother? All those years, he'd been tracking her? He knew when her father died. He knew about Frankie's heart condition. He even knew about Peter leaving, which made Lucinda feel foolish for some reason.

She stood up quickly, resulting in a loud screech when her chair dragged across the hardwood floor. Jim's eyes widened, and he asked if he'd done something wrong. She told him everything was fine, but she needed to speak with her family. Jim said he understood and hoped they could catch up more over the next few days. Lucinda wondered how long he was planning to stay but didn't ask. She needed to lie down, and to figure out exactly how deep a mess her family had gotten themselves into.

When he walked Lucinda to the door, Jim said, "You really do look good, Luce." No one had ever called her that but him, not even her parents. On the night they broke up, he pleaded with her to reconsider. "Please, Luce. I'm begging you," he said, tugging at her blouse. She apologized and got out of the car, devastated at the thought of hurting him but resolute in her plans to get off the island any way possible.

Jim enlisted in the Army and flew to Florida the next day to stay with his grandparents until basic training began. That was the last Lucinda had ever seen or heard from him.

Even during her long marriage to Peter, he never called her Luce. He preferred formal names and scoffed early in their relationship when she called him Pete. From there on out, they would only refer to each other as Peter and Lucinda, without so much as a *honey* or *sweetheart* between them. Lucinda collected herself, straightened her posture, and said, "I'll see you later, Jim."

"That's the thing with small islands. We're bound to run into each other soon," he chuckled.

Lucinda's eye twitched. Was she really in a *Twilight Zone* episode? She quickly closed the door behind her and set off toward the office building, trying to come up with one good reason not to strangle her mother.

Chapter 3

When Lucinda opened the office door, she was prepared to lay into her mother for bringing Jim to stay at The Pink Octopus without giving her a head's up. Not only that, but the bigger betrayal was that Goldie had been secretly talking with him for decades, filling him in every time Lucinda so much as changed beauticians.

Goldie wasn't at her normal station, and Lucinda let out a long sigh as if she were a balloon being untied. "She went to lunch with a guy younger than you," a familiar voice said from across the room. "It's her second date this week, and it's only Wednesday."

Lucinda spun on her heel to see her brother, Ben, eating a sandwich on the sofa in the office lobby. Her shoulders dropped, she shook her head, and walked over to her brother with extended arms. They hugged, and Ben let go first, just like always. He told Lucinda he was rushing through lunch so he could show a group of prima donnas how to properly clean the fish they caught earlier. "Now that you're here, maybe you can do it for me. As I recall," he said, shoveling a large spoon of potato salad into his mouth, "you're better than I am at gutting fish."

The Pink Octopus mostly attracted couples because nearly all of the cottages were meant for one to two guests. The state of the bungalows wasn't nearly updated or flashy enough to draw in newlyweds, so their clientele was mostly singles and return guests.

That meant Ben's charter guests were mostly older couples vacationing at the beach together or the occasional group of gals sniffing around the island for the notorious bachelor of Turtle Beach, the cute fisherman who refused to be caught himself...or so the rumors said.

Ben offered Lucinda a pickle spear, which she happily accepted. "I can't believe Mom's on an afternoon date. Shouldn't she be manning the desk?"

"We going to talk about Mom? I'd rather hear about my big sister."

"Which one?"

"You, silly. How're things in The Constitution State? How's Petie?"

"How can Goldie be your mother and you don't know that Peter left me?"

"I knew. I just wanted to hear it from you. I consider it *good* news. Maybe we should throw a parade."

Lucinda gave Ben a playful smack. When he mentioned Jim, she shook her head to make it clear the topic was off limits. Instead, she asked him about Sharon, and Ben's neck cracking tick kicked in. He cocked his head from side to side, snapping and popping his joints, and then explained that all he knew was Sharon's symptoms had progressed quickly over the past few months with no official diagnosis until a few days earlier.

Lucinda felt the tears welling up in her eyes, and Ben told her to keep the hysterics to herself, that Sharon needed life to remain as normal as possible. She wiped her eyes, sat up straight, and agreed. "Should we talk about the business, then?" Lucinda asked.

Ben stood up, gathered his trash, and groaned, saying he had to see some girls about a fish. He kissed the top of her head and said, "Besides, there's not much to say. We're tanking. I doubt we have six months left before we go bankrupt." He shrugged and left Lucinda standing in the kitchen with her mouth hanging open like one of the fish he was headed outside to clean. He turned back once to say, "It feels right for you to be back, even if you hop on the first plane out once you put out the fire like you always do. We've missed you around here."

After a few minutes of deep breathing with her eyes closed, Lucinda got up and went over to the front desk where she sat scouring the business records, which were every bit as bad as her mother and Ben had alluded to. The Pink Octopus hadn't seen a profit in six months, probably longer.

Sharon knocked lightly on the edge of the counter to avoid startling her sister. Lucinda smiled, stretched her arms up over her head, and motioned for her sister to take a seat beside her. "So, are you making a reservation or checking to see when they're going to turn out the lights on this place?" Lucinda pressed her lips together and raised her eyebrows. "So, you all know it's bad, then?" she asked Sharon.

Sharon threw her head back and laughed. "I work here, Lucinda, so yes, I know things suck." When Lucinda asked how Sharon could be so glib, she said that they all had a

Plan B if the business failed. "What's that, if you don't mind me asking?" Lucinda said.

"Ben has wanted out of the business for years. If we go under, he'll go do his own thing, whatever and wherever that is."

"Where do you think he'd go?"

"Does it matter? Anywhere but here, I suppose."

"And you?"

"I've been seeing a guy on the mainland for a few months. He said I could move in with him, which, let's face it, would probably be better than living with Goldie. I still own my house, but whatever. I can always sell."

"Wait, you're seeing someone? You don't tell me anything!"

"I was embarrassed. He's kind of young. Besides, don't pretend we're *those* sisters. We barely talk."

Lucinda drummed her fingers on the counter, waiting for Sharon to dish on the guy. Sharon giggled, prefaced what she was about to say by clearing up that Ian was not a *boyfriend*, and then explained that she'd met him at a bachelorette party, of all things, when he was waiting tables at the bar she was at with friends. When Lucinda asked if he was really a stripper, they both burst into fits of laughter. When they'd composed themselves, Lucinda asked, "What about Mom? Where will she go if the place closes?"

"I don't know. Maybe we can negotiate with the owner of Whispering Pines and get Mom put in the same room as Grandma Helen. Worst-case scenario, she can always move back to Connecticut with you!"

Lucinda recoiled. She didn't know which was worse, her mother being placed in an old folks' home or taking

over Jill's old bedroom in Stamford. She buried her head
in her hands, and when Sharon saw her sister's distress, she
rested her head on her shoulder and sighed. "You moved
away and everything went to pot. Dad died. Mom started
going through men like underwear. Ben's depressed. My
husband died, *and* I got MS. When you think about it, it's
kind of all your fault, Lucinda. You're the one who left us
all here to rot."

Lucinda opened her eyes and looked at Sharon, who
couldn't contain a smile. "Gotcha!" Sharon cackled, tossing a paper clip at Lucinda. "Chill, sis. It's only life after
all."

Lucinda couldn't believe how bad things sounded when
Sharon rattled them off like that, even if she pretended to
be joking. After checking some early guests in—the only
ones booked for the entire week—Lucinda asked Sharon
why the link to The Pink Octopus's website was broken.
Sharon casually replied that it became too expensive to
keep paying the website manager, so they took it down.
When Lucinda asked how guests found them without a
website, Sharon pointed to the nearly empty parking lot
and said, "Who said they're finding us?"

Lucinda rubbed her temples and marveled at how non-
chalant her entire family was at the prospect of losing the
business they'd spent their lives building.

Sharon excused herself to get cleaned up for an afternoon visit with Ian. He was taking her to meet his mother.
Lucinda quipped that if Sharon was serious about Ian,
she shouldn't reciprocate, saying once Ian met Goldie, all
bets would be off. Sharon rolled her eyes and said, "Are
you kidding? He loves Mom. It's on the cons side of my
Pros and Cons list of reasons to stay with him. I think she

likes him so much that if I dump him, she'll ask him out herself!" She waved, and slowly made her way out the back door and up to the main house.

Lucinda felt sick to her stomach at the predicament her family was in because of poor business management, bad luck, or something she hadn't yet uncovered. The reason didn't matter. Whatever was going on, they needed help, and fast. She stood up, straightened some papers on the desk, and looked out the window at bungalow Number 8. Jim was carrying brown bags through the front door. His arms looked stronger than she'd remembered, and though they weren't tan yet, Lucinda imagined they would be soon enough if he stuck around for long.

As Lucinda watched Jim move from his truck to the bungalow several times, lifting the bags like they were empty, she had an idea. She knocked on the office window and motioned for him to come over. When she crooked her finger, Jim did what he always did: he came running. No questions asked, no hesitation. And just like that, Jim Barnes was back in Lucinda's life like not a single day had passed.

Chapter 4

Jim stepped into the office, slightly winded from jogging across the lot. He made a joke about being at Lucinda's service, but she didn't smile. Jim leaned against the counter and asked if everything was all right. "I'm not sure my mother called you here to do odd jobs. I think she may be planning to have you help us close the doors on this place."

Jim ran his fingers through his hair and nodded. "I thought maybe she was exaggerating about the possibility of foreclosure. What can I do to help?"

Goldie was coming back from her date, and Lucinda put a finger to her lips. She didn't want to discuss any plans with her mother yet. Besides, she was still intent on confronting her about all the years of secret communication with Jim. Lucinda suggested that she and Jim go to dinner later that night to discuss some things. "Away from here," she said, raising her eyebrows. Jim winked and said, "Pick you up at six?" Lucinda nodded.

He left, and Lucinda saw Goldie hug him in the parking lot. When she came fluttering into the office, giddy from her lunch date and carrying a Styrofoam leftover box, Lucinda wasted no time laying into her. She asked how her mother had the nerve to secretly stay in touch with her old boyfriend for so long without telling her. Goldie sipped a to-go cup of soda and listened while Lucinda vented all her frustrations. Finally, she held up her cell phone and snapped a picture of Lucinda as she was mid-sentence. "What the..." Lucinda hissed.

"I say this from a place of total love and adoration, but you need to lighten up," Goldie declared. "If you don't, your face is going to freeze like this." She turned her cell phone for Lucinda to see the unflattering photo. "If it becomes a habit, I might have to make a meme out of this pic!"

She took another slurp from her straw and clicked across the tile in her kitten heels, plopping onto the sofa, where she began working on a Sudoku puzzle. Clenching her fists, Lucinda stormed out of the building, letting the screen door crack in her wake. She headed up to the main house to unpack her bags and rest her eyes. She walked back to her old bedroom, which was now a home gym with a cot pushed against one wall.

Goldie had a poster of Tom Selleck taped to another wall in front of a treadmill, apparently as motivation to stay fit. Lucinda couldn't help but laugh.

She slid her shoes off, stretched her toes, and reclined on the cot, which was as uncomfortable as it looked. A bungalow would be a much better place to stay while she was on Turtle Beach, but that would mean occupying a potentially profitable piece of the business, something Jim was already doing.

She closed her eyes, hoping to rest her brain for a while.

A groan snaked its way up her belly and out her mouth, thinking of all the times in movies when a counselor told a frazzled patient to close her eyes and imagine somewhere relaxing, like a beach. For Lucinda, imagining a crowded city street or even an amusement park would probably be more relaxing than what was taking place on Turtle Beach, at least in her family.

Back in the office, Goldie answered the phone on the third ring. It was Carl from Island Laundry. Carl was the owner, and he gently explained to Goldie that if she didn't square her account away within a few days, he'd have no choice but to terminate service. "You know I love you, Goldie, but I won't have a choice, honey."

Goldie was so resigned to the business going belly-up that it was difficult for her to get riled up about the situation. Without clean sheets and linens, the business would crumble. They couldn't wash the sheets and towels alone, even with the second washer Ben had picked up at an estate sale. Carl ran the cheapest laundry service on the island, so without him, closing the doors on The Pink Octopus was imminent.

Even though Goldie was ninety-nine percent sure she was going to let the business go, she knew that screwing things up with Carl would be the point of no return. Buying herself a little time, she agreed to give Carl a call by the end of the week after she'd talked to her accountant. Carl didn't need to know Ben was the accountant she was referring to, and not a very good one. She hung up, tapped a pencil on the desk, and thought about what to do.

Within a minute, she was distracted with an invitation to go line dancing with Marvin—a mechanic on Jellyfish Bay. Normally, she'd say no and stay home to figure out a plan to pay Carl. Plus, she knew accepting same-day dates was frowned upon by the authors of *The Rules*.

Deciding that paying Carl would be like trying to stop a sinking boat by using a coffee mug as a ladle, she picked up her phone and started pecking at the keys. Island Laundry was only one of dozens of wolves waiting at the door to collect back payments.

Goldie: Yes to your invite. Pick me up at 8! I'll be the one in the red cowgirl boots!

Marvin: I'll be sure to put on my spurs, then!

By the time Lucinda woke up, it was getting dark. She was disoriented from the nap and forgot where she was until she heard waves crashing outside her window. She groaned as she heaved herself off the cot, which she decided was too low to the ground for a woman her age. Looking at her watch, she saw it was almost time to meet Jim for dinner.

In the bathroom, she splashed cold water on her face, and patted it dry. She brushed her teeth and hair, reapplied her lipstick, and put on a clean top. It was wrinkled, along with the rest of the contents of her suitcase. She poked her head in Sharon's bedroom, but decided not to go in. After all, they weren't teenagers anymore. She wanted to respect Sharon's privacy. She deserved at least that.

She went into Goldie's room instead, where she was sitting at her vanity curling her hair. She was singing a Brenda Lee song and using her foot to pet Ginger, who purred in appreciation beneath her stool. "Mom," Lucinda mumbled, knocking on the doorframe, "can I borrow an iron?" Goldie didn't turn around. Instead, she spoke to Lucinda through the reflection in her mirror. "So, I guess you forgave me?"

Lucinda rolled her eyes and asked what choice she'd had. Goldie motioned toward the closet and said she wasn't sure anything of hers would fit Lucinda but to have a look around anyway. Lucinda bit her tongue and asked again for an iron, but Goldie claimed hers had broken months ago and she'd never gotten around to replacing it.

Thumbing through her mother's closet, Lucinda marveled at how closely Goldie's wardrobe looked like a hybrid of Cher's and possibly a female rapper. The clothes were outrageously young for her mother, and at least a size smaller than what she should be wearing. Lucinda shook her head and thanked her mother, turning to leave empty-handed. "Wait," Goldie said sternly. Lucinda spun on her heel, feeling five years old again, and her mother said, "Peter's gone, Lucinda. I don't know if he's ever coming back."

"Gee, thanks for the head's up, Mom."

"Well," she clucked, drawing red liner on her lips, outside of the margins to make them look fuller, "if you ever expect to land another man, you aren't doing it in that blouse."

Despite vehement protests from Lucinda, Goldie forced her to try on a scoop-neck black nylon top with a rhinestone collar, which made Lucinda feel like a Las Vegas bartender. She groaned when her mother said, "Oh, would you look at that? You have boobs. Who knew?"

"Really, Mother! Could you be more inappropriate?"

"Probably," Goldie teased. "Want me to try?"

The doorbell rang, and Lucinda tried to peel the shirt off, but Goldie fastened a clunky necklace around her and pushed her toward the door. Lucinda said, "Mother, if you think I'm going out looking like this..." but Goldie threw

the front door of the house open and invited Jim inside
before she had a chance to change.

Lucinda would have mistaken her flushed cheeks and
sweaty palms for a hot flash, but she recognized the symptoms as pure rage and humiliation. "You look real nice,
Lucinda," Jim stammered, fighting a smile. "You ready to
go?"

Before she could protest, Goldie was waving them off
and locking the door. Jim helped Lucinda into the truck
and made a joke about Goldie answering the door in a
feather-lined robe. "Stick around for more than five minutes," Lucinda replied, "and you'll probably see a lot more
than that, so consider yourself warned!"

In the truck, Lucinda tried taking the necklace off, but
couldn't unhook the clasp. They pulled into the parking
lot at Clive's Bar—a favorite hangout for locals on Jellyfish
Bay—about ten minutes from Goldie's house. Deciding
to give up, she climbed out of the truck's cab and followed
Jim into the restaurant.

They ran into a few faces from their past, clearly confusing some of their old acquaintances who wondered when
they'd become a couple again. Everyone was nice, but Lucinda could tell they were chomping at the bit to unearth
whatever story brought the two old flames back together
after so many years.

In a booth, Jim and Lucinda sipped iced tea and split an
order of cheese sticks while they waited for their burgers to
arrive. For a while, they made small talk. Lucinda wanted
to save the business talk for after the server brought their
food to the table to avoid interruption.

When she asked what he'd been up to for the past three
decades, Jim answered vaguely. He'd served in the Army,

and then had a contracting business. When he fell off a ladder and needed surgery, he was forced to close his doors. Once he healed, he took odd jobs for a while, but Goldie invited him to the island before he'd had a chance to re-build his clientele. "Do you have a family?" Lucinda said, cutting the last cheese stick in half and pushing the plate toward Jim.

"I did," he whispered, ripping his straw wrapper into tiny pieces.

"Oh," Lucinda replied awkwardly. "I'm sorry."

"It's just complicated, I guess."

That was all Jim seemed to want to say about his family, and he quickly changed the subject by asking if Lucinda had any recent pictures of her children. She pulled up some pictures on her phone to share with him, her hands shaking as she wondered what happened to his family.

It must have been awful, she imagined, if he had refused to discuss it. She wondered if her mother had any insight, seeing that she and Jim were apparently best friends.

Jim looked at the pictures of Frankie and Jill and though he didn't dare admit it, Lucinda could see the light of recognition in his eyes. He'd already seen those pictures thanks to Goldie. "Oh, look," Jim said, "Our supper's here." Lucinda's earlobes grew hot, and she stuffed her cell phone into her purse. She didn't like that Jim had been secretly tracking her all these years. It felt strange, like someone had been peering outside of her window, watching her, observing her children, careful not to step on a branch and reveal his presence.

Chapter 5

During dinner, Lucinda decided to keep the conversation strictly business. When she asked Jim about his family, his entire demeanor changed, so she wasn't going to bring it up again. Whatever happened to them, it was clear he didn't want to talk about it. She figured maybe the memories were too painful to discuss but planned to ask Goldie to fill in the blanks when she got home.

Lucinda pulled a small notepad from her purse, clicked her pen open, and asked Jim to give her some estimates on sprucing up the bungalows since he'd had years of experience as a contractor. He commented that he liked how Lucinda kept it old school with a pen and paper, and they high-fived, proud to be Gen-Xers.

Jim gave Lucinda rough estimates for the cost of paint, repairs to all the bungalows, and landscaping supplies. She'd look online to estimate furnishings, fixtures, and linens for all the cottages later. When Jim asked if Lucinda planned to overhaul the business, she paused.

Finally, she said that Goldie was planning to declare bankruptcy, and that meant the entire family being displaced. "I'm considering a drastic overhaul, yes. It will involve getting everyone else on board, though, and you've met the Perrys. Besides, even if they agree, who knows what a contractor will charge to do the work—or how long it'll take?"

"Do you want to tour all the bungalows with me tomorrow?" Jim asked. "We can see how much of it I can tackle myself, save you all some money?"

Lucinda felt a warmth come over her when Jim used the word "we," as if she wasn't in this mess alone, especially since her mother and siblings seemed as though their bags were already packed for their new lives.

He told her that Bill Xander's family still ran the furniture store on Route 11 if she wanted to refurnish the cottages. He thought Bill might even offer a discount since Lucinda took pity on him in the tenth grade and went to the spring dance with him when his date dumped him at the last minute. "I don't know," Lucinda said, smiling. "If he knows I'm cavorting with you, he may not want to do business with me at all. You did break his shin during the basketball playoffs senior year."

"He got even with me when he dated my sister after graduation, only to dump her for a tourist he met at Crazy Joe's on the boardwalk that summer."

Lucinda remembered Crazy Joe's. It was a now defunct frozen coffee restaurant that was known as the cool place to work when she was in high school. "I'm sure Cindy's better off without Bill. How's she doing, anyway?"

"She's good. Living on Jellyfish Bay. Soccer mom, the works. She gets her furniture online." Lucinda threw her head back and laughed.

Jim excused himself to use the restroom, and Lucinda felt incredibly sad for him. Both he and his sister were dumped for tourists, and then something tragic must've happened to his family from the sounds of it. *Did Jim's life turn out awful?* More importantly, she wondered if the downward trajectory all started with her leaving him.

When Lucinda heard footsteps approaching the table, she looked up, thinking it was the server with drink refills, but saw her brother instead. Ben stood over her, a dumb grin on his face. He wasn't alone. He introduced his date to Lucinda. Her name was Fawn, and she was much too young for him. When her brother couldn't contain his laughter, Lucinda said, "What's your problem?" He pointed to her tight shirt and exposed cleavage, and declared, "Oh, nothing. I just never realized you looked so much like Mom."

Lucinda tugged at the plunging neckline of her shirt, trying to salvage a shred of modesty, and explained to an uninterested Fawn that she'd just gotten to town and all her clothes were wrinkled. "I don't normally dress like this," she clarified, flushing.

Fawn shrugged, and asked Ben for a few dollars to buy a wine cooler.

When she walked away from the booth, Ben's eyes stayed squarely focused on her backside, eliciting a smack on the forearm from Lucinda. "I didn't know you had a part-time babysitting gig, bro," she teased, slurping the last of her Diet Coke.

"Shut up," he replied, and excused himself to catch up with Fawn before someone else caught her attention.

Later on, when Lucinda got home, Goldie was still out line dancing with Marvin. She left a note and said not to wait up. Lucinda groaned, changed into sweatpants and a T-shirt, and opened her laptop. She began creating a business plan to reinvent The Pink Octopus. She outlined exactly what needed to be done, and by whom.

Sharon might be going through a tough time, but she could still be a major asset to the business. She was a gifted artist, or at least she used to be before life got in her way. Her oil paintings could bring in some money, as could some handmade jewelry, if Sharon was up for learning the craft. She thought going with a theme, such as seashells, would make the most sense if they wanted to appeal to tourists.

She didn't want her sister sinking into a depression over her diagnosis, and one way to prevent that was to keep her feeling viable. What better way than to put her creativity to work?

Sharon hadn't painted in years. She got pregnant in high school, which put the kibosh on the art scholarship everyone thought she'd get. The father, a tourist she met while working at the drive-in movie theater, never knew about the baby. He went back home—to somewhere in the Pacific Northwest that Sharon couldn't remember the name of—and presumably continued with his normal life.

Sharon was adamant about keeping Kelly, well before she'd spent thirty-six hours in labor on Thanksgiving Day bringing her into the world. No other option was ever discussed. Kelly was always hers, and only hers.

Sharon gutted it out and graduated high school with honors, smiling at baby Kelly in the audience at gradua-tion. She met Alan a couple of years later while she was taking college courses on the mainland. Alan was in dental school nearby, and they met while standing in line at a newspaper stand. They fell in love, and he was everything a father should be to Kelly. She loved him until the day he died, never calling him her stepfather, but instead, Pops. Alan couldn't have children of his own but considered Kelly his entire world.

Sharon's life only got busier after meeting Alan. She got an associate degree in business administration, eventually helping out at his dental practice by becoming the front office manager. Between work and running Kelly back and forth to her many extracurriculars, there was no time for Sharon to dabble in a hobby, which was all painting ended up being by then.

When the Perry family's patriarch, Tom, died, Sharon dropped to part-time at Alan's practice so she could pitch in at the front desk of The Pink Octopus.

Lucinda created a folder with printouts of beach-themed earrings and barrettes and brooches, along with a list of websites that taught jewelry making. She hoped Sharon would warm to the idea. She'd been feeling guilty that she hadn't been able to keep the hectic pace she normally did around the business, which everyone but Sharon seemed to accept. Being sedentary was driving her nuts, but at least with painting and jewelry making, she could keep her mind and hands busy.

Lucinda hadn't gotten far in the planning process when she realized she'd have to get some money together, and fast. If she was going to present a business plan to her mother and siblings, she needed to make sure the funds were in place to back it up so they couldn't use that as an excuse to throw in the towel. Also, she didn't want to get their hopes up only to have to withdraw the offer when she couldn't finance the upgrades.

She put down her pen and called Peter. Her heart thumped loudly in her chest while she waited for him to answer. He picked up on the third ring and sounded put out by the disruption in his evening. Lucinda explained she wanted to settle their affairs out of court. Though she didn't know exactly what their assets were worth, she estimated her share to be about half a million dollars, probably much more. "If you round up and keep your offer fair," she said calmly, "you can have the house, too. I don't think I'm coming back to Connecticut."

"Lucinda, where do you propose I come up with half a million dollars, never mind buy you out of our house? What's that? Another half a million? You want me to give you a million dollars?"

"Well, I could always hire a lawyer and go for alimony. Sheila, from book club, said when she divorced Greg, her lawyer had all her legal fees tacked onto his bill. Apparently, it's common to make the husband pay for everything."

"Lucinda, you *do* remember that I'm a lawyer, don't you? Besides, why are you so willing to give up your home after thirty years of loving it so deeply? Something sounds fishy here."

"You gave up the right to ask me personal questions when you left me for my best friend, Peter. Besides, shouldn't it be obvious that the house stopped being my home when the kids grew up and left and then you blew up our marriage? I was a good wife, a great mom, and I kept my promises to you. I deserve a million."

Peter sighed and stayed silent for what seemed like several minutes. Finally, sighing heavily, he told Lucinda he'd wire her a hundred thousand in the morning and have the rest to her within two weeks. All Lucinda asked in return was that Peter allow the children to sort through their bedrooms before turning them into a home gym or sewing room for Eve. He agreed, and they hung up without saying goodbye.

Lucinda continued to crunch figures for the next two hours, getting online estimates and choosing color schemes for the office lobby and the bungalows. The dingy bungalows desperately needed a makeover. Plus, they had boring names which were really only numbers—such as Number 1, Number 2, and so on. *How unoriginal*, she thought. She felt a thrill in her belly at the idea of painting the exteriors pastel colors and giving them names like The Green Seahorse and The Purple Starfish.

She'd seen a postcard once with a row of tiny cabins in Germany or some foreign country that were painted rainbow shades of pastels, and the image always stuck with her. The tiny villas looked like tufts of cotton candy dotting the shoreline.

She emailed Jill and asked if she could design a website for the business, if Lucinda provided the pictures. Jill had designed her own site for her organic skincare business and was a natural at website design. Jill answered quickly, saying she could have it live in under two weeks. When Lucinda offered to pay her, Jill replied a single line: "Get real, Mom. We're family."

While Lucinda was looking up software programs for a new reservations system, Goldie came home, laughing and carrying a tin foil swan. "You're still up?" Goldie gasped. Before Lucinda could answer, Goldie held the swan up and said if Lucinda was hungry, she had in her possession the best Arroz con Pollo she'd ever tasted.

Lucinda smiled, asked what happened to line dancing, and Goldie replied, "Marvin blew a knee two dances in, so he took me to a fancy place on Angel Shores as a consolation prize."

Lucinda wanted to ask Goldie about Jim, about the business, so many things. But she decided to hold off until neither of them was exhausted from a long day. She declined the fancy leftovers and Goldie put the swan in the fridge and headed to bed. Better to speak with the whole family together, maybe for dinner the next night. That way, she could present the business plan in a more professional manner.

Everyone needed to be on board for Lucinda's plan to work, and part of getting it to work was being taken seriously. This meant a family meeting, comprehensive notes, and a line-by-line cost breakdown.

Though she fretted about getting her family to agree to a revamping of the business, frankly, it was their only hope if they wanted to stay together. If The Pink Octopus folded, the family would splinter, and never be the same. They'd be lucky to find themselves in the same room once a year at Christmas.

Lucinda texted Sharon and Ben and said to pencil in a family dinner the next evening. Sharon sent back a tense-faced emoji, which made Lucinda chuckle. She hoped it wouldn't be a strained dinner. The facts were clear: If some aggressive action wasn't taken to save the business, it was going to collapse inside of two months. If her family couldn't understand that, Lucinda resolved to get on the next plane out and tell Peter the deal was off. As easily as he agreed to fork over a million dollars, she was certain that wasn't close to half of his net worth anyway.

It pained her to think of Eve getting even a sliver of what she'd help to build over the long years of sacrifice. But it hurt worse knowing her best friend and sister-in-law could betray her in such a pedestrian way. If Lucinda went back to Connecticut, what would she really be returning to?

While she was getting a glass of water, she parted the kitchen curtains and saw the light on at Jim's place. What was so awful that he couldn't talk about it? Did he have a wife and children who died in a tragic accident? A fire perhaps? Wouldn't Sharon or Goldie have told Lucinda something so disastrous? Did he make a huge mistake which resulted in his family disowning him? Drugs? Embezzlement? Tax evasion? None of that sounded like Jim Barnes.

Yawning, Lucinda realized she still suffered from jet-lag. She rinsed her glass, loaded it into the dishwasher, turned the magnet from "Dirty" to "Clean" so her mother wouldn't run it again in the morning, and hit the "Start" button. She shuffled back to the lumpy cot, which still somehow felt heavenly because of her sheer exhaustion. Sleep came almost instantly.

Chapter 6

The morning tide crashing against the shore woke Lucinda from a pleasant dream about rocking Frankie when he was a baby. The longing in her heart for the days when her children were small often found their way into her dreams. She missed Jill and Frank being little, needing her to tie their shoes, to cut the crusts off their sandwiches, edit their English essays. When they needed her for anything, really. Those days were long gone. Both of her children were independent, a lot like Peter in that way.

In the dream, she'd been singing "Hush Little Baby" to Frankie and was getting to the part about the dog named Grover, when a particularly loud wave crashed against the shore outside her window and gave her a start. She buried her head under her pillow and tried not to feel like a teenager again, living under her mother's roof. She half expected to open the bedroom door and smell bacon and cigars wafting from the kitchen. How she missed her father, but not that smell. All Lucinda wanted to do was to go back to sleep again and find Baby Frankie, to hold him and say, *Mama's here, Little Man. You're safe, darling.*

When sleep didn't come, she reached for her cell phone and checked to see if there was a text from her son. Maybe the dream was a sign that he needed her. No message. She let out a sigh, feeling a bit foolish for expecting there to be something from Frankie when there almost never was. Lucinda sent him a text message to ask if everything was all right. He answered, quicker than usual, and said that he was fine, busy, just heading into a staff meeting.

Lucinda set her phone on the floor beside the cot, pulled the covers back over her head and tried one more time to find sleep. Before long, Goldie tapped on the door and asked why Jim was in the office waiting to tour the cottages. Lucinda shot up, pulled on a sweatshirt, and brushed her hair. "About that," she said, yawning. "I am calling an emergency family meeting tonight, so I'm hoping you're free for dinner."

"An emergency meeting? What's this about?"

"We're going to talk about the business, Mom."

"You've been in town, what, less than twenty-four hours and you've already come up with something so big it needs a family meeting to discuss?"

"Yes, and can you make your famous lemon brownies?"

Goldie tutted and made a comment about Lucinda swooping in and trying to take charge of everyone, but as she left the room, she demanded, "You'll need to come with me to Food Basket for powdered sugar. I don't always keep that stuff on hand, you know!"

A few minutes later, Lucinda and Goldie were sitting in the kitchen with Jim—who was eating a bowl of oatmeal Goldie forced upon him. Goldie dictated her grocery list to Lucinda, who wrote the items down on a pad. She cringed, mortified that her mother was taking rollers out of her hair and putting them into a small basket on the table—right in front of Jim. It was just as embarrassing as it had been when Lucinda was ten years old and had a friend sleep over, only to witness Goldie primping over the friend's cereal bowl the next morning.

She took a deep breath and smiled at Jim, giving up on the idea of shielding him from her untamed mother. *If they've kept in touch all these years*, she thought, *any illusions of Goldie being June Cleaver went out the window long ago*. For all Lucinda knew, Goldie FaceTime'd Jim while she brushed her teeth and soaked her partial in denture cleaner. She still had no idea what types of things her mother and Jim talked about on the phone.

Excusing themselves to assess the bungalows, Lucinda scribbled down notes as Jim surveyed the condition of pipes, woodwork, windows, and so on. When they were finished, he offered to go to the hardware store and start picking some things up, but Lucinda said he'd better wait until she learned what the evening's family roundtable meeting produced.

That afternoon, Lucinda suggested to Goldie that they visit Grandma Helen at Whispering Pines. Goldie groaned, saying, "I'll go with you because I'm your mother, but she's probably going to tell us we look a mess, that we need our roots done or something." Lucinda laughed, knowing her mother was right.

Helen hadn't lost her wit or sense of directness at almost a hundred. It always amazed Sharon and Lucinda that Goldie couldn't spot the similarities she bore to her mother. "I'm going to get a shower, Mom. Be ready to go in thirty minutes."

Lucinda smiled and hummed an upbeat song on her way to the bathroom. It felt good to be in the driver's seat of her own life again. She had a purpose and a plan for the first time in too long to remember.

Half an hour later, while getting in Goldie's car, Ben rode up on his ratty ten-speed bicycle and asked where they were headed. Lucinda said they were going to see their grandmother and invited him to ride along. He declined, saying he was taking some guests out on the boat in a few minutes. Lucinda reminded him about dinner at six. Ben opened his mouth to rattle off some excuse or another, but Goldie leaned over and firmly commanded, "Dinner is at six. It's not a request." He backed up, threw his hands up in surrender, and said, "Yes, ma'am." To show his seriousness, he gave his mother a salute.

Whispering Pines was a quaint-looking nursing home on Jellyfish Bay, the main area of Turtle Island where locals went to run errands. The facility was a lemon-yellow ranch-style home with lush landscaping and a cheerful sign reading "Whispering Pines: A tradition of caring since 1965."

Lucinda was gathering her purse and a bunch of flowers she'd picked up at a roadside florist, when Goldie complained about her taking too long.

Lucinda asked what the rush was all about and marveled at her mother's energy level for a seventy-four-year-old.

Goldie had been a lifelong practitioner of yoga, which made her freakishly limber, but as for where she drew her energy? Lucinda wished she could figure it out, and maybe get some of her own.

Grandma Helen was in the common room making a craft with half a dozen other residents and an instructor who talked to the group like she was their kindergarten teacher. She clapped when one resident answered a question correctly and drew out her words as if they were incapable of comprehending simple English. Seeing Goldie and Lucinda, the instructor said, "And who do we have with us today, Miss Goldie?" Goldie rolled her eyes, wheeled Helen toward the door, and said, "We're taking my mother outside for a visit."

Lucinda laughed, remembering all the times her mother had defended her from an unfair school teacher or a neighborhood bully. "I don't know why they have to treat all of you like toddlers, Mom," Goldie huffed, wheeling Helen down the corridor. Helen laughed, resigned to her reality at Whispering Pines.

When they got outside, Lucinda hugged her grandmother, who kissed her hand and said she'd missed her terribly. Lucinda's heart squeezed at the thought of how many times she'd meant to call Helen but got busy with paying a bill or cooking Peter's dinner, or finishing a book. She always planned to call but was so easily sidetracked.

They visited for so long that finally, Goldie ordered pizza and they sat on the veranda eating and laughing and watching the hummingbirds drinking from the Foxgloves. Lucinda observed the banter between her mother and grandmother, wondering if she was getting a glimpse of a future version of herself and Goldie. She wondered if that's how a bystander would view her relationship with Jill but decided against the idea.

Lucinda and Jill didn't speak every day, but they were respectful to one another. Goldie was kind, but self-involved, whereas Lucinda was the type of mother who dropped anything she was doing to be there for her children. She silently confirmed she was nothing like Goldie.

Lucinda studied the faces of her mother and grandmother. Though she found their personalities a bit off-putting at times, she couldn't help but admire their skin. If she aged half as well as the two of them, she'd consider herself lucky. "Grandma," Lucinda said, "you have a big birthday coming up next month!"

"Don't remind me," Helen lamented. "I'm older than dirt!"

"Not everyone can say they've made it to one hundred, Gram!"

"I can't either, yet!"

"Besides," Lucinda said, kissing her cheek, "you're not old. One hundred is just the number of years the world's been enjoying you."

Lucinda asked Helen what she was doing to celebrate the big day, and was disheartened to learn that the home was having a tiny gathering with cake after lunch. Lucinda clutched her chest, asked if that was it, and Helen nodded.

Lucinda was deep in damage control mode when it came to rescuing the family business. Her brain devised a sparkling plan to combine her beloved grandmother's monumental birthday and the relaunch of The Pink Octopus—if her family agreed to fight for it. She suggested a major blowout birthday, with most of Turtle Beach—and maybe all of Emerald Isle—invited. Helen protested, but too weakly to take it seriously. She'd been quietly hoping that if she made it to one hundred, she'd get more fanfare than an extra scoop of pudding from the Whispering Pines cafeteria.

When it was time to go, Lucinda promised Helen she'd be back to visit more often now that she was on the island again. They said goodbye, and Goldie and Lucinda went to Food Basket to buy ingredients for the big family dinner. When Lucinda asked Goldie why she hadn't planned something special for her mother's birthday, Goldie huffed, saying, "I was gonna invite her over to the house, Lucinda. I'm not an animal!"

They picked up potatoes, fresh green beans, and brown sugar and ketchup to make homemade barbeque chicken. "Should I buy wine?" Lucinda asked. Goldie raised her eyebrows, and Lucinda laughed. "What was I thinking? Naturally we cannot have a Perry family dinner without booze!" Four bottles went into the cart.

The afternoon passed quickly as Goldie and Lucinda straightened the house, set the table, and marinated the chicken for the grill. Goldie flitted around the kitchen, singing a happy song and wrapped her arms around Lucinda every so often. She was thrilled to have her daughter home, even if she thought it was dumb of her to leave in the first place.

Tonight, Goldie thought, *all my babies will be here at my table again.* The idea was almost too big and too wonderful to contain in her small body, and as a result, she occasionally broke out in one of her crazy dance moves like the Boogaloo or the Lawnmower as she folded a napkin or pushed more chairs together at the table.

At six o'clock, Ben shuffled in empty-handed, which made Lucinda laugh. Sharon had shown up a little earlier with pasta salad and ice, saying Goldie never kept enough on hand. When everyone was finally there, Lucinda told them to take a seat and help themselves. Ben asked what the emergency dinner was all about, but Lucinda shook her head and said that first they needed to eat. "Let's enjoy this meal together," she said. "It's been too long since we all sat at the same table."

They raised their glasses, and as they clinked them together, everyone smiled and made funny toasts like, "To all of the monkeys returning to the circus," and "To the Prodigal Daughter gracing Turtle Beach with her presence!"

"Hilarious, Benny," Lucinda said, rolling her eyes.

"I'm only joking," he replied, "but pour me another glass of wine, Shaz. I have a feeling Big Sis didn't call us here tonight to tell us how great of a job we're doing with the business."

"Here, here!" Goldie toasted, holding her glass up for a refill. "May as well make mine a double!"

Chapter 7

Over dinner, Goldie, Lucinda, and Shaon chided Ben about the young girl he'd been out with the night before at Clive's. "Hey," he said, holding up his wine glass and toasting his mother, "I learned from the best!" Goldie feigned embarrassment but they all knew she considered dating younger men to be a badge of honor.

The entire Perry family knew that although Ben was closer to forty than thirty, he was the perpetual baby. Goldie doted on him by slipping him twenty-dollar bills or sending him home with leftovers at the end of a long workday. Sharon cut his hair and hung flowering baskets on his porch every spring and stocked his freezer once a month so he wouldn't starve.

Even living far away from Turtle Island for so many years, Lucinda acted—at times—like Ben's personal assistant. It was not out of the ordinary for her to compare meal delivery services for him to see which had the proper macronutrients or remind him when it was time for his annual physical.

With their father dying a decade earlier, Ben probably should've stepped up as the man of the family, the fearless leader. Instead, his mother and sisters kept him as their baby. In truth, Ben filled a need in each of them to feel useful, in one way or another. "Hey," Ben joked, cutting into the lemon brownies, "some of Mom's boy toys are younger than Fawn!"

"Eww," Sharon said.

"What?" Ben replied.

"You're doing that thing people do when they start dating someone. You're looking for ways to insert Fawn's name into random conversations."

"Medical grade cringe," Goldie agreed, nodding.

After another few minutes of chitchat, Sharon and Goldie cleared the table and rinsed the dishes while Lucinda prepared her presentation. Once everyone was handed a cup of decaf, it was time to talk shop. Lucinda thanked them all for clearing their busy dating schedules to meet on short notice, eliciting the expected eye rolls, sighs, and *yeah, yeah's*.

She pressed forward, trying to block out the realization that she was the only one in her family without a love life or a job or a packed social calendar that made scheduling last-minute events difficult.

Lucinda had thought she'd grow old with Peter. Not that they were necessarily happy. They weren't, almost from the beginning. Still, she figured marriage wasn't only about sunshine and daisies. It was hard work. It was juggling kids' schedules, remembering to trim the dog's nails, tipping the mailman at Christmastime and planning vacations that were the perfect ratio of fun and relaxation.

But kids grow up and fly the nest, and when Peter left Lucinda for Eve, he took the last frayed string that tethered her to their house in Stamford. When she accidentally intercepted an X-rated email from her best friend to her husband, 1874 Carriage Hill Lane stopped being home. She could see the divorce unfold like a bad play, the kind without the happy ending.

Peter shattered her dream of bringing all their family and friends together for their silver anniversary party, gray-haired and sporting orthopedic shoes with their party clothes. He squashed the image she'd clung to all those years about a poignant ending like the two of them dying in bed at a hundred years old, holding hands, smiling in their sleep. Now, who knew how she'd learn of Peter's death, or if he'd call out for her in the end? A lifetime of building a marriage, all blown to bits over an illicit affair.

Lucinda swept the heartbreaking images from her mind, cleared her throat, and said, "I brought you here to talk about The Pink Octopus, which I guess is fairly obvious at this point."

"You mean that it's sinking?" Ben said, snorting.

"Yes, Benny," she replied sternly, "and this isn't funny."

"No offense, sis," Sharon said, "but we've had a lot more time than you to adjust to the idea of closing our doors. After all, *we* never left the island."

"I see. Is this how it's going to be?" Lucinda asked, throwing her hands up. "I left the island to pursue a life of my own, so now my opinion doesn't count as much as the rest of yours?"

Goldie shrugged. Ben raised his eyebrows, and his lips drew into a tight line. Sharon just stared blankly at Lucinda. "Do you guys realize," Lucinda said, composing herself, "that Mom plans to declare bankruptcy on the business?"

From the looks on their faces, Lucinda realized they didn't, but was pleased to finally have their attention. Ben dropped his fork on his plate with a loud clink, and the sound sent a chill down Lucinda's spine. "What the hell, Mom? Would you really do that without discussing it with us?"

Lucinda held up a hand to silence Ben, saying she didn't call everyone to the meeting to fight. "The time for finger-pointing is long gone," she said, thumbing through some things she'd printed from the computer. "Now, it's time for damage control, which will require teamwork."

She handed everyone a presentation packet and continued, explaining where she thought things went wrong with the business and how they might fix them. The bungalows were shabby. The website was down. Their advertising was nil. She said it was as if everyone had given up on the place. Ben yawned, and said they were all tired of running the business day after day with no relief.

Lucinda thought for a minute and then clapped her hands together loudly. "Hey," she said, shimmying her shoulders. "What if—and this is if we all agree to my revitalization plan—we create a schedule that allows each of us to take two weeks of vacation a year, plus a week of personal family time? We could have an annual reunion with all our relatives, sleep in, hang out...basically do whatever we want!"

"And who would watch the business when we're all off somewhere sleeping and playing charades?" Goldie asked, tracing circles on the table with her finger.

"Once we're up and running strong again, maybe we could hire a couple of employees, train each of them on every aspect of the business," Lucinda suggested, ignoring the sarcasm.

"Yeah, Sharon replied hopefully, "then we could have a life outside of work. Imagine that!"

Lucinda smiled, pleased to have a partner in battle. She picked at some lemon glaze stuck to the bottom of the brownie pan and licked her finger. She leaned closer to Goldie and asked why they'd all been so willing to let the business go downhill.

Goldie sat back in her chair and looked at a family picture on the wall. She said that once Tom died, she lost her will to continue pouring all she had into the business. It had been her life for so long, their dream, the thing that connected them. "It's not so fun anymore without him," she whispered. After a sip of black coffee, she set her mug down and bit her lip to control the quivering. "But how do you retire when the business is also your home?" she asked tearfully.

Lucinda apologized for being so removed from the business for the past several decades, saying she understood that while she got out and could live a completely independent life, she recognized that no one else had ever taken a break from The Pink Octopus. "I'm here now," she said, looking at everyone around the table. "I have a plan if only you'll all agree to dive in with me and give this place a shot at redemption."

Over more pots of coffee, Ben, Sharon, and Goldie allowed Lucinda to share her big ideas for rescuing the business. Other than the occasional rattling of a candy wrapper—Sharon found an old bag of Halloween candy in the back of the bread drawer—the Perry's dining room was respectfully quiet. They'd committed to giving Lucinda their full attention.

She talked about remodeling, landscaping, and relaunching the website.

Goldie loved the idea of enlisting Jim's contracting expertise to save money, but Lucinda knew she had ulterior motives. Goldie loved matchmaking in general, but when it came to Jim and Lucinda—well, she never wanted them to break up in the first place. She was all in if there was even a one percent chance this project could get them back together.

Lucinda suggested Jim paint the cabins each a different pastel shade. "Instead of boring bungalow names like Number 5, here's a list of possible alternative names, which I'm extremely excited about—so be nice!" She handed them each a list, and they each took a long look.

The Pink Octopus

Arrive our guest, leave our friend

Our Bungalows

1. The Pink Octopus
2. The Yellow Crab
3. The Turquoise Turtle
4. The Tangerine Clam
5. The Green Seahorse
6. The Great White
7. The Blue Dolphin
8. The Purple Starfish

After giving them a moment to read over the new names, she explained, "The Yellow Crab will be yellow, The Green Seahorse will be green, The Lavender Walrus will be..."

"Let me guess," said Sharon, "Indigo?"

Rather than be annoyed, Lucinda allowed herself a laugh. It felt cleansing somehow, or at least like a vent, to expel all the pent-up nervousness she'd been holding onto for days. She also found it inspiring that Sharon could joke despite what she was going through. Stroking the back of Sharon's hand, she made a mental note to take her sister out for pedicures, see how she was really doing.

She wondered if Sharon had considered an action plan that would allow her to stay a few steps ahead of the MS? Maybe there was a holistic doctor on the island who could put her on a raw diet or a physical therapist who specialized in nerve damage. There must be *something* to at least halt the progression if not cure the disease?

Lucinda held a peanut butter chew in her mouth, hoping it would soften. "How old is this candy, Mom?" she asked, trying not to drool.

"A couple years," Goldie replied. "Probably more."

"Mom!"

"They put so many preservatives in those things," Goldie said, waving her hand dismissively. "They'll outlast sharks and roaches if a meteor hits the earth."

Lucinda spit the candy into its orange wax wrapper, wiped her mouth, and got back to business. She discussed adding some recreational activities for guests, such as movies on the beach, a firepit, live music, and even yoga classes.

Goldie's ears perked up at the mention of yoga. "I'd love that!"

"Good, Mom," Lucinda said, smiling, "because you'll be the one teaching it."

Goldie tried to protest, but her children reminded her that she'd been a yogi for forty years. They said that if anyone knew how to lead a class, it would be her. "See one, teach one," Mom," Sharon suggested.

"Yeah," Ben added. "It'll give you a chance to boss people around without anyone questioning your authority. It's perfect!"

Goldie pondered the idea for a while and finally agreed. She shook her head in awe, saying she'd thought they were going to try and inch her out of the business altogether. "I'm glad you're not putting me out to pasture just yet," she said, wiping her nose with a tissue she pulled out of her shirtsleeve.

She was referring to a reservations software program that Lucinda was looking into, which would make things faster and easier for everyone. Lucinda smiled and said that it was time Goldie got to do something she was passionate about, and that certainly wasn't answering phones and making reservations. "I think we should *all* find ways to make work fun," Lucinda added, glancing hopefully at Ben and Sharon, who both had glazed looks in their eyes.

They raised questions about how much the overhaul would cost. Lucinda told them about Peter buying her out of her house, and Sharon began to cry. She said that she hated to see Lucinda lose all that money by bailing the family out from years of poor business decisions. Lucinda handed Sharon a napkin and said it was the least she could do after staying away for so many years. "Besides," she said, straightening her blouse and trying to look like a CEO, "it's business. I fully expect a return on my investment, or I would probably take the money and buy a yacht."

"You obviously haven't priced yachts lately," Ben snorted.

"I'd get a fixer-upper," Lucinda said. "The point is, I know my plan will yield great results, so it's a safe investment in my eyes."

Ben suggested Fawn could design a new website because she was attending night school for an I.T. degree. Sharon mouthed *Eww* again, and Goldie appeared baffled by Ben's suggestion. He began explaining that I.T. stood for Information Technology, and his mother interrupted. "Not that part, dummy. I know what I.T. is. What I need you to explain is who on earth names their kid Fawn?"

Sharon and Lucinda burst into laughter, and Ben sunk deeper into his chair, offended. Lucinda squeezed Ben's hand, thanked him for the offer, but said that Jill had already begun working on some mockups for a new site in case everyone agreed to the relaunch. She'd designed her own site for her natural skincare line, Pure Love 4 Life, along with a few sites for her friends' online businesses, so Lucinda knew she could handle it.

Ben backed down, not wanting to deny his niece a chance to use her design skills, and agreed to help where he was needed but reiterated that he still had dreams that had nothing to do with bungalow rentals and charter fishing.

When Sharon asked what kind of dreams he meant, Ben merely shrugged.

Lucinda resolved to take Ben aside one day soon and see what his dreams were, figuring maybe she could help him if there was any money left over from Peter's settlement. In high school, Ben's only interests were girls, surfing, and fishing, but truthfully Lucinda had no idea who her brother really was anymore. He clearly had dreams, but she couldn't imagine what they were.

By the time things were winding down, everyone was getting excited, but it seemed like Sharon had grown quiet. When Lucinda asked what was wrong, Sharon admitted she was happy about the plans to revamp The Pink Octopus, but it seemed like she wasn't going to serve much of a purpose if she couldn't set up and break down bungalows, and a new reservations and check-in system eliminated the bulk of the front desk work. "I can't do nearly as much as I used to," she said, her voice cracking. "It doesn't seem fair if I get paid the same as the rest of you if I'm not working much."

Lucinda sat down beside her, pulled out a folder marked "Sharon," on the front, and spread out the papers on the table for her sister to view. "You've always had an eye for fashion and design," Lucinda said. "I thought you could create beach-themed jewelry that we could sell to guests."

"Really?" Sharon said, smiling. "I mean, it looks great, but I don't really know how."

"There are so many tutorial videos out there, Shaz. You're a fast learner and so creative. You'll be great at this! I was thinking you could get back into painting, too."

"You haven't had much time for painting since Alan died," Goldie added. "Now, you can take it up again, especially if we get help around here. I have a lot of your old art supplies in the hall cupboard."

"We can display the paintings in the bungalows and lobby with price tags on them!" Lucinda suggested.

Sharon loved the idea, feeling a renewed sense of hope about her future with the family business. When the meeting ended, Lucinda had one more item on her agenda. She said she'd like to fast-track the makeover for The Pink Octopus and have a grand reopening the weekend of Grandma Helen's one-hundredth birthday. "We'll invite the whole island!" she announced.

Everyone agreed it was a good, if aggressive plan since Helen's birthday was only a month away.

Lucinda asked if it would be all right for Jim to stay on in his bungalow during renovations, saying it made sense to keep him on the premises and save time commuting. Ben jokingly asked how else Lucinda was paying him, which resulted in Goldie slapping him on the back of the head like she used to do when he burped at the dinner table as a kid. Lucinda bristled, explaining that she and Jim were only friends. "I'm done with men," she said, and sat down, crossing her arms defiantly.

Before anyone could protest, Lucinda called an end to the meeting, saying she was running on fumes after working all night to come up with the plan. She handed each person at the table a list of priorities, asking them to do what they could, when they could, and preferably in order. There were tasks such as having an electrician inspect the bungalows and give them a clean bill of health, looking into hiring a professional cleaning service, pricing higher quality linens, and so on.

She pulled out her phone and began typing something before setting it back on the table. "OK," she said. "I've started a group text with all of you. Make sure you let everyone know when you're picking one of the tasks, so we aren't all pouring valuable time into the same thing. This is the best way for us to keep from stepping on each other's toes." She finished the meeting by saying she'd like them all to meet back at Goldie's in one week to discuss their progress. "If I'm honest," she said, taking the time to make eye contact with each person at the table, "I really want to instate a weekly family dinner as a new tradition, even if we don't discuss business. Thoughts?" To her delight, no one objected.

Ben and Sharon went home, and Sal picked Goldie up for a late movie in town. Goldie and Sal had been friends –just friends—for years. Though everyone thought they'd end up together, particularly Sal, it hadn't happened yet. When Lucinda asked Goldie outright what the 411 was on the matter, Goldie said, "I had my one true love, honey. That's why I date so many different men. I just try to keep myself distracted from who I really want to be with."

Lucinda smiled a sad smile, looked up at the wall of family photos, and said that she missed Tom, too. She stroked her mother's hair and said that by the time they were done with the relaunch, Tom would be good and proud of all of them. Goldie nodded, kissed Lucinda's cheek, and went to the bedroom to touch up her lipstick for her movie night with Sal.

Lucinda walked along the beach and looked at the stars. She felt hopeful for the first time in months, maybe years. As she turned to go back up to the main house, she heard someone calling her name. Looking back, she saw that it was Jim. He was sitting in the sand peeling the label off a bottle of beer and staring out into the dark sea. "Want to take a load off?" he said, patting the spot of sand beside him.

Lucinda couldn't help but smile when she saw his straight, white teeth glowing in the moonlight. It brought back such fond memories of sneaking out of her bedroom window to meet him on the beach in the middle of the night in high school. "Your mind looks full," he said in a husky voice, "and I happen to be a superb listener."

Chapter 8

The next morning, after getting the green light from Lucinda—along with her credit card for expenses—Jim picked up a truckload of paint and supplies from a hard-ware store on Jellyfish Bay. He was eager to get started with the renovations, feeling a renewed sense of purpose himself—and glad for any distraction that would keep him from worrying about what was going on back in North Carolina.

He began with Number 1, which, moving forward, would be referred to as The Pink Octopus—the business's namesake bungalow. The minute the brush hit the drab cottage, it instantly brought new life to the exterior. It wasn't a Pepto Bismol pink, but more of a soft, flamingo shade that stood out all the way from the main road. Lucinda couldn't wait to see the pastel turquoise, lilac, and mint colors of the cabins. She knew they'd look like a row of dollhouses, or even better, like a miniature version of the Pink Ladies in San Francisco.

She figured that even if all they planned to do was re-paint the bungalows, that alone would be a game-changer for business. But Lucinda had much bigger plans for The Pink Octopus that a few cans of paint.

Ben showed up at ten with a group of his friends, most of whom Lucinda knew from her brother's high school days. They split into groups and began painting the interiors of the empty bungalows while Jim worked on the exteriors. Though the outsides were brightly colored, Lucinda went with crisp white walls inside, allowing for optimal sunlight.

Coughing from the years of dust trapped in them, she stripped the frayed, dingy curtains from all the windows and polished the glass. She'd ordered bamboo mini-blinds and white sheer curtains online, which would be delivered in a couple of days.

Lucinda also cleared the books of all reservations for the rest of the month to get the repairs and remodeling done. She offered discount vouchers for the guests whose reservations had to be canceled, promising when they came back, the whole place would be fresh and exciting, with lots of entertainment and activities.

Charlie Hughes, a family friend, owned a thrift store called Oh, My Vintage! on Jellyfish Bay. He stopped by to haul away the old beds and dressers from the vacant bungalows, along with some outdated art and tchotchkes. Sharon showed him the office furniture, too, which he was thrilled to take. Lucinda knew Charlie from Stamford, where he was Frank's high school history teacher. After Goldie met Charlie at Frank's graduation, she invited him to visit the island and he never left.

When Charlie pulled out of the parking lot, his truck was filled with scuffed, well-worn home goods in dark wood and brass and plaids. He couldn't wait to set them up in Oh, My Vintage! in vignettes, certain they'd sell like hotcakes. Lucinda watched as the last ratty sofa was loaded onto the bed of his truck. Turning to Sharon, she asked, "How did Mom and Dad ever think that stuff was suitable for a beach resort?"

"Not everyone has your keen eye for home decorating, sis," Sharon chided.

"No," Lucinda said, feigning snobbery, "they try, but they can never be me."

They laughed, and Sharon kissed her sister goodbye, saying she had to get a haircut. Before she left, she tugged on a strand of Lucinda's hair that had fallen out of a messy ponytail. "Want me to make you an appointment with Mindy at Magic Mirror? Looks like you could use a new 'do." Lucinda put a hand on her hip and clucked, "Some sister you are!" She told Sharon thanks but no thanks, and that she was too busy saving the business to worry about trying to look like Cindy Crawford. "Really?" Sharon said, confused. "Because your wild hair and unplucked brows are really nailing the supermodel look. All you need is a white tank top and a can of Coke and you'll be stopping traffic!"

Lucinda groaned, examined the errant strand of hair, and told her sister to beat it. "I'm a busy woman. Get lost."

Ben and his helpers left to get burgers, and Lucinda waved goodbye and went up to the main house to see what her mother was doing for lunch. She found Goldie in front of the television painting her toenails a garish shade of red. When she asked if it was called Lady of the Night, her mother didn't miss a beat when she replied, "Nope, it's Saucy Vixen."

Lucinda rolled her eyes, and asked what Goldie was doing for lunch. She said she ate a banana because she was saving room for crab cakes with Sal that evening. When Lucinda cocked her head with interest, Goldie played it cool. "Two nights in a row?" Lucinda asked, waggling her eyebrows. Goldie pretended she didn't hear the question and continued painting her toes.

Lucinda opened a couple of cans of tuna, turned them into a mixing bowl, and added mayonnaise, chopped celery, dill relish, slivered almonds, and salt and pepper. She put the finished product in a plastic storage container and topped it with sliced hard-boiled eggs before snapping on the lid. She grabbed a loaf of bread and a bag of potato chips and went looking for Jim.

He was finishing the first coat of paint on The Green Seahorse—formerly Number 5—and Lucinda whistled, commenting that things were looking good. Jim asked if she meant him or the paint, and she rolled her eyes and held up the bag of food. "I hope you still like tuna salad because I brought lunch."

They went into Jim's bungalow, and he set out a couple of plates and pulled two glasses from his cupboard. He poured Lucinda a lemonade and apologized that it wasn't homemade. She waved him off and thanked him for giving her anything to drink at all, saying she was parched from all her hard work. "It feels good, though," she said, shrugging. "You know? I haven't worked hard—physically anyway—in years."

She sipped her drink and watched Jim move about his kitchen, allowing a thought to creep into her head of what it might be like to live with him. She wondered how things might've been different if Peter's family had never vacationed on Turtle Island all those years ago, or even if they'd have stayed on one of the smaller islands instead of Emerald Isle, where Turtle Beach and her family business was located. Would she and Jim have married, and if so, would it have lasted? "I can't imagine how worn out you must be from all this painting," she finally said, handing him an apple and noticing that his ears were crispy red from the sun.

"Remember, I'm an Army man," he said, biting into an apple. "Plus, I was a contractor for decades. I don't mind hard work. Keeps me from thinking too much."

"Not me," Lucinda said, spreading tuna on a slice of bread. "I've stayed busy, but the work I've always done was more along the lines of management. Home management," she said, sheepishly.

"Hey, don't be embarrassed for a minute about that. I hear you made a nice life in Stamford. Your kids didn't end up serial killers, right? You must've done something right."

Lucinda took a minute to respond, busying herself with cutting the sandwiches and snapping the lid back on the tuna. It was surreal that Jim knew so much about her. He didn't refer to where she lived as merely Connecticut, but specifically mentioned her city.

She took a sip of lemonade and then talked about raising the kids, and volunteering at the elementary school for many years, even after her children had moved on to high school and college. The whole time she was talking, all she kept wondering was, *How much of this does he already know?*

She hoped she wasn't boring Jim, but it felt refreshing to remind herself of how much she'd done over the years. There were the administrative responsibilities she handled for Peter's law firm, and the holiday parties she organized every Christmas. She talked about keeping up on the gardening and the three consecutive years she hosted foreign exchange students.

By the time she'd finished, Jim shook his head and said he was tired just hearing about all she did. The truth was, Lucinda did stay busy, and so did Peter. They just didn't stay busy together. She had her things, and he had his. He golfed and ran marathons. He went on hunting trips with his brother—something Lucinda figured would cease now that Peter stole Stan's wife—and worked long hours. By the time Peter crawled into bed at night, Lucinda was usually asleep with her glasses on and a book lying across her chest. When he left, she was surprised at the depth of her loneliness after all the years of living separate lives.

After lunch, Jim said he needed to run to town for extra supplies. By *town*, Lucinda knew he meant Jellyfish Bay. She offered to ride with him because she wanted to pick up some plants to put in the lobby. She looked at her watch and asked if Jim thought they'd be back in time for a Xander's Furniture delivery. He said he'd be quick, and they climbed in his truck and headed to their first stop.

Jim dropped Lucinda off at a Piccadilly Nursery and told her he'd be back in fifteen minutes. She grabbed a cart and started gathering small potted plants and a few hanging baskets. She was picking bunches of wildflower bouquets when someone gasped, "Lucinda? Lucinda Perry, is that really you?"

She turned to see an old high school acquaintance, Polly March, carrying a large topiary. Lucinda never cared much for Polly. She was the biggest gossip in school. As soon as she opened her mouth to speak again, Lucinda realized nothing had changed. "Did I see Jim Barnes dropping you off outside? I *heard* he was back in town." The way she emphasized the word *heard*, Lucinda knew Jim had been the subject of gossip.

"Yes, that was him," Lucinda said, pretending to be lost in the sea of potted violets before her.

"Be careful there," Polly whispered, looking around. "He's in *all* sorts of trouble back in the Carolinas."

"Wait, what?"

"Yeah, my mother said he's gone and done something awful, but I don't know what. I'm only here visiting. I live in Kentucky now, if you can believe *that*," she said dramatically.

When Lucinda didn't appear interested, Polly quantified living somewhere other than an exciting city like Beverly Hills or L.A. "I mean, my husband is a big-wig vet for The Kentucky Derby, so we sort of *have* to live there. Anyway, how about you?"

Lucinda noticed that Polly still had the same cadence to her voice. No matter what topic she was droning on about, she emphasized one word—usually to brag. In high school, she'd say, "Lucinda, I just got invited to Nate Kennedy's *exclusive* party! Did you get invited, too?" or "Mr. Mandero said my essay on the rise and fall of the Roman Empire was the most *accurate* account he's read outside of a college-level textbook!"

Before Lucinda could say anything, Jim approached them and offered to help carry the plants to the car. Polly's eyes froze open like she'd just seen Bigfoot or Ted Bundy. Swallowing hard, she casually said, "Oh, hello Jim. How are you doing?"

"Do I know you?"

"It's me, Polly March—well, it's Kizinski now."

"Like the Unabomber?"

Polly huffed, and said she was married to Dr. David Kizinski, the renowned horse racing veterinarian for the Kentucky Derby—emphasis on *the*. "So he euthanizes the poor horses when they're run to death or break their necks? Jim asked thoughtfully, scratching his chin and squinting for clarification.

Polly stormed off and carried the topiary outside without paying.

A salesclerk chased her to her car and Lucinda caught enough of the conversation to hear a few colorful curse words. She looked at Jim and said, "There's no way you could have forgotten Polly March. She got our favorite art teacher—Mr. Buzzy—fired for sharing pornography with the junior class when he taught us about the statue of David."

Jim smirked. "I remember her fine, but girls like Polly need reminded that they don't rule the world."

Lucinda rode back to The Pink Octopus with Jim, watching him tap his hand on the steering wheel to the beat of the radio, and wondered what kind of trouble he was in back in the Carolinas. A couple of times, he caught her staring at him, but she'd just smile, playing it cool until she could launch an investigation of her own.

Chapter 9

The next few days flew by, everyone doing their part to prepare The Pink Octopus for its upcoming relaunch. The bungalows all had the first coat of paint on and were glowing in the setting sun. Jim was struggling to tear down an outdated light fixture in The Tangerine Clam, while Sharon and Lucinda kept him company. When he let out a frustrated groan, Sharon suggested the three of them step away from work for a while and get something to eat. Jim looked at Lucinda, who shrugged and said a break sounded good to her, too.

They rode together in Jim's truck, squeezed tightly in the front cab. Lucinda strategically arranged it so Sharon would have to sit by Jim, but made it look casual. She waited until they were both standing by the truck, and said, "Oh no, I forgot my phone. You two get in and I'll be right back." There was no reason for Lucinda to sit by Jim and make things confusing for any of them. They were friends, nothing more. Best to keep clear boundaries.

At nearby Barnacle Bob's, an eighties tribute band played songs that reminded Lucinda of high school. It was

Saturday night, and the place was packed. It felt like the island was a time capsule in a lot of ways, a portal back to being seventeen. People had gained a little weight, and a few buildings were changed from diners to T-shirt shops or from dry cleaners to fudge retailers, but it was still the same old Turtle Island, at least on Turtle Beach, where Lucinda grew up.

Lucinda was staying at her mom's place, and her old high school boyfriend was staying next door. He looked almost exactly like he did the night she broke up with him thirty years earlier. She'd already seen many familiar faces. It was as if even those like Polly, who had made it off the island, kept coming back, getting sucked in by some invisible force. Now, with the thump of Foreigner covers in her chest, she felt all she needed was blue eyeliner and a can of Rave hair spray to enter a true time warp.

When Jim went to the men's room, Lucinda asked Sharon what Polly might've meant by her comment that Jim was "in all sorts of trouble in the Carolinas." Sharon was either playing dumb, or she didn't know what Lucinda was talking about. She brushed off Polly's gossip, reminding Lucinda that Jim was harmless.

Lucinda nodded in agreement, but added, "I've been meaning to ask Mom, or at the very least, look it up online. Something is holding me back, I guess."

From all Lucinda had seen of Jim so far, he wasn't any different than the sweet, loyal boy who spelled out her name in sparklers on the beach for their one-year dating anniversary. "When I asked him if he had a family," Lucinda whispered, leaning across the booth toward Sharon, "he said that he *used* to. I can't get that wording out of my head: 'used to.' What could that possibly mean?"

Jim came back to the table carrying two iced teas before Sharon could respond. He set them down and Lucinda wasn't sure if it was the old, familiar song the band was playing or the dim lighting, but she thought Jim looked like a movie star with his newly tanned skin and black button-down shirt. She bit back a smile, but not convincingly because he asked what she was thinking. Sharon raised her eyebrows in anticipation of her sister's reply, and Lucinda fumbled through her purse as if looking for something important.

Jim let Lucinda off the hook, changing the subject by asking Sharon how she'd been since Alan died. "He was a good man," he said, sipping his beer. "He was a pallbearer at my dad's funeral. Did you know that?" Sharon shook her head, and Jim explained that his father, Angus, was in the Army with Alan's father, Ken.

Ken and Angus stayed friendly after their time in the military. When Angus died, Alan offered to be a pallbearer in his father's place since Ken had dementia. "Alan said my dad once saved his dad's life, and the least he could do was carry his casket. He was a good man, Alan. It's a damn shame what happened. I'm really sorry, Sharon."

Sharon smiled, commented that it's a small world, and added that she'd been doing all right without Alan, minus the uncooperative legs. She seemed always to be making jokes about her diagnosis, which Lucinda figured was a coping mechanism. Jim said Sharon's uncooperative legs were a bummer because he remembered when she could light up a dance floor like nobody's business.

Sharon took a sip of tea, set her glass down hard on the table and said, "Let's show these legs who's boss, Mr. Saturday!" Lucinda nearly spit her iced tea across the table when she heard Sharon refer to Jim by his old football nickname. He laughed heartily and said, "Well, okay then, if you think you can keep up with me!"

"Game on, Jimmy!" she said, challenging him. As Jim led her sister to the dance floor, he turned back and winked at Lucinda, who swallowed a lump in her throat, seeing Sharon strutting like she did in her heyday. The Jim who asked her down-on-her-luck sister to dance so she could feel normal for a night is not a man who could've done something illegal, Lucinda reasoned to herself.

The band played one of the biggest anthems of the eighties, and nearly everyone in the house was on their feet, creating a vibrating effect that shook Lucinda's dangly earrings.

Sharon and Jim danced like they were kids again, laughing hard and tearing up the dance floor like old times. Jim kept a hand close to Sharon the whole time, which Lucinda appreciated more than he could know.

A voice came from behind Lucinda. "Care to dance?" She looked up and saw a handsome man in his fifties wearing a white T-shirt and fitted jeans, smiling at her. She stammered, trying to come up with an excuse. "Aww, come on," he said. "You only live once. Isn't that what the kids say these days?"

"'YOLO,'" Lucinda shouted above the band. "The kids say, 'YOLO.'"

The man invited her to dance again, and Lucinda tentatively took his hand. "YOLO, it is then," he replied, smiling.

The man–Matt—led Lucinda around the dance floor for two songs before the band took a break. When the music died down, she thanked him and started heading back to her table, where Jim and Sharon were drinking beer and keeping a watchful eye on her.

She started to tell them about getting roped into dancing, when Matt spoke up and said, "Hi, I'm Matt Jackson." Lucinda jumped, unaware he'd followed her back to the table. Immediately, she felt heat draping over her from her head to her toes.

Matt shook Jim's hand, and then Sharon's. Sharon gave Lucinda an insistent stare, her eyes as big as ping-pong balls. Finally, Lucinda introduced Sharon, and Matt nodded at her in a gentlemanly way. Jim invited Matt to sit down. "Do you like craft beer?"

For an hour and a half, they all sat and talked, reminiscing about simpler times and inflation and how everything their parents always said about the world going to hell in a handbasket was turning out to be true.

Sharon's easy laughter and hair-flipping clued Lucinda in on how she felt about Matt, though she couldn't tell if he felt the same about her. Jim shifted awkwardly in his seat but remained friendly. Lucinda couldn't tell if he was jealous or suspicious of Matt, or maybe neither. Trying to read everyone's body language, Lucinda dug into her belief that Turtle Island really was like teleporting back to high school. She half expected Sharon to lean over and whisper in her ear, *Do you like him, like him? Because I kind of like him, but only if he likes me, too.*

Sharon asked Lucinda to go with her to the ladies' room, telling Matt, "You know, that's what girls do. We travel in packs." Jim and Matt laughed, and Lucinda realized Sharon must have really liked him to not make an MS joke. The whole way to the restroom, Lucinda anticipated Sharon asking the inevitable question.

In the crowded restroom full of big-haired women fighting to touch up their lipstick at the smudgy mirror, Sharon tried to sound casual when she broached the subject. "So, do you like Matt?"

Lucinda played along, saying that he was nice. "Right," Sharon added, blotting her lips on a piece of toilet paper, "but do you like him, like him?"

"You did not just ask me that, Shaz!" Lucinda gasped. "What are we, a couple of teenagers?"

"Relax! I'm just wondering if you're going to date him. It's no big deal."

"No, Sharon. You can have him. I'll trade you your REO Speedwagon cassette and a pack of cigarettes for him."

Lucinda rolled her eyes and pulled Sharon toward the door. She asked what happened to Ian. Sharon jokingly said, "Ian who?" When she saw the surprised look on her sister's face, Sharon paused in the corridor and explained that everything was fine, but Ian was a transitional man. Lucinda stuffed down her worry, hoping Ian hadn't dumped Sharon when he learned of her diagnosis. Keeping the mood light, she quipped, "Can we call someone his age a *man*?"

After another hour, Jim, Lucinda, and Sharon piled into his truck and headed home. Sharon massaged her throbbing right leg, which hardly fazed her. Holding Matt's phone number in her hand, all she could do was smile.

Lucinda gazed out her window—somehow avoiding sitting next to Jim again—and wondered about his family. He drove along in silence, clenching the wheel so tightly that his knuckles glowed white in the moonlight. He kept his eyes on the road all the way to The Pink Octopus.

When they got out of the truck, Jim said goodnight, slammed his door, and walked up to his bungalow without looking back. Sharon raised her eyebrows and asked what was going on, and Lucinda shrugged. "No idea."

"I think we should Google Jim tomorrow. "See what's what," Sharon suggested.

"Why wait until tomorrow?" Lucinda said, looping her arm through her sister's, and pulling her toward the house.

They scurried inside, opened a bag of pretzels, and sat at the kitchen table, waiting for Lucinda's laptop to boot up. After a few minutes of typing in Jim's name and North Carolina online, there was no shortage of information on the situation.

Jim's estranged wife, Camille, had been missing for nine weeks. *Missing*. It didn't appear that the police suspected Jim whatsoever, but that hadn't stopped people from creating all sorts of terrible scenarios. The story seemed to gain traction quickly thanks to YouTube and Reddit, and Sharon commented that Jim might have come to the island to hide out.

Lucinda closed her laptop and firmly declared that Jim's business was his own, and if he worked hard to help them save the business, she was happy to let the police sort out the truth for themselves. "So, you don't think he did something to Camille?" Sharon said, biting her thumbnail.

"Sharon, no! Of course I don't, and you don't either."

"I don't?"

"No. There was a time when we considered Jim family. He's one of the good guys."

"People change."

"Not that much. He wouldn't hurt a fly. Let's keep our eye on the prize, here, okay? We have very little time to turn this ship around with the business. Please, stay focused."

"Do you think Mom knows?"

"I don't know. The more I learn about Mom, the more I realize I don't really know her all that well, if that makes any sense. But, for now, let's keep this to ourselves."

"What's to know? She's a sixteen-year-old trapped in the body of an old lady!"

Reluctantly, Sharon finally agreed to let the cops sort out Jim's family mess back home. Still, she seemed nervous as she shuffled toward the bathroom to wash off her makeup and get ready for bed. Lucinda missed her sister's place on Hammerhead Wharf. It was so effortlessly cool that it had a name: Sea Rock. It was a Craftsman home with stained glass windows, gorgeous stone fireplaces, and built-in bookshelves. She wondered on a scale of one through ten how much it bothered Sharon to give it up but couldn't bring herself to ask. If her sister wanted to discuss it, she would.

Lucinda had seen news stories of squatters taking over vacant properties and made a mental note to ask Sharon if she'd considered renting Sea Rock out until she came up with a permanent game plan.

The doctors didn't feel she could live on her own anymore, but maybe Sharon would remarry someday and want her own place again. She and Alan had poured so much time and money into their house. It was a shame to let it sit empty. *Would Sharon want to live in her old place with a new man*? Lucinda wondered. Maybe it would be too much to handle. Maybe she'd want a fresh start in a different house?

One night several months earlier on the telephone, Sharon confessed to Lucinda that she hated how quiet it was after Kelly went to Harvard, but that it was still tolerable with Alan there. Once he died, however, it became almost unbearable to live in the house alone. Then, recently the doctors decided *for* Sharon. She couldn't stay there and risk falling, they said, so she boarded the place up and moved in with Goldie.

Lucinda gnawed on a sourdough pretzel and wondered if the trauma of an empty nest, combined with the death of her husband, played a part in the onset of Sharon's symptoms. She knew it didn't *cause* the multiple sclerosis, but maybe it accelerated it?

Lucinda fixed herself a cup of tea and looked out the window at the light coming from Jim's bungalow. After a few minutes of turning the night's events over in her mind, she wrapped a blanket over her shoulders, slid into her shoes, and marched over to Jim's place to confront him.

When Jim answered the door, he invited her in, but she declined. "Look," she said, a hand on her hip, "I don't know what you're mad about tonight or what you and my mother cooked up with you coming here, but the only way this plan to save The Pink Octopus is going to work is if we agree right here and now to be *just friends*, nothing more."

Jim stood before her silently, obviously still upset about something from earlier. Something Lucinda couldn't understand. "What?" she finally said, seething.

"Word has it that you've sworn off men?"

"And?"

"Well, you had no problem tearing up that dance floor with what's-his-name!"

"Are you kidding me right now?"

"No, I'm actually not," he said, stiffening up.

"You don't own me, Jim Barnes. Just because you kept in touch with Goldie doesn't mean you can stake a claim on me."

"Oh, well I think you made that clear three decades ago when you left me for that pinhead and look how that turned out?"

"So we're clear," Lucinda hissed, "We are history, okay? We're coming together to work on this project—this very *important* project—and that's it. Business partners, got it?"

Jim shrugged and said he was fine keeping his focus on business. Lucinda opened her mouth to say, *No wonder! It must be a great escape from wondering when you'll be arrested in the disappearance of your wife!* But she stiffened her postured, extended her hand to shake on the deal, and stormed off.

She crossed the parking lot, breathing heavily and stomping down on the gravel. When she climbed into bed, she buried her head in her pillow and screamed. As far as she was concerned, Jim Barnes was history—and this time for good. "It's not personal, it's business," she repeated into her pillow. It was a line from one of her favorite romantic comedies, but Jim wasn't Tom Hanks and she wasn't Meg Ryan. This was real life, and it was far less funny than a movie. "It's not personal, it's business," she repeated angrily, falling asleep face-down in her pillow.

*

Chapter 10

The following day, Lucinda avoided Jim. It was Sunday and she tagged along with Goldie to church. By the time she'd gotten back, Jim's truck was gone. He stayed out all day, and Lucinda took a break from making calls and working on the bungalows. Her muscles were sore, and she took a personal day and called Jill and Frank to update them on what was going on at The Pink Octopus.

She also watched *The Sound of Music* because people were always shocked when she admitted she'd never seen it. As the end credits rolled, she concluded it was all right, not as over-the-top amazing as most people seemed to think. However, she didn't hate it as much as Christopher Plummer did. She watched an interview after the movie ended, and he'd referred to it as *The Sound of Mucus*.

When she decided to turn in early, she peeked out the kitchen window and saw Jim returning to The Blue Dolphin—formerly Number 8—with a few grocery bags in hand. She wondered where he'd been all day. As she rinsed her popcorn bowl and set it on a towel to dry, she thought,

Maybe tomorrow I'll climb every mountain, ford every stream, follow every rainbow. But for now? I'm going to bed.

Goldie brought Lucinda a cinnamon bun at seven thirty the next morning and waved it over her nose, hoping it would wake her. It did, and when Lucinda complained about her mother barging into her room at such an ungodly hour, Goldie blew out a long sigh and said she'd been on the water since five-thirty a.m. "I get more done by eight than most people do all day!"

"What on earth were you doing on the water at that hour, Mom? That's probably not even safe!" Lucinda wailed, startled at how deep her morning voice sounded with age.

"Visiting with Hercules. What do you think?"

"Oh, brother."

"Say what you want, but I'm not crazy. Maybe if you weren't so closed off to a little magic, he'd reveal himself to you, too."

"Right, Mom. I'll work on that. I'll try to get my head around the idea that a tortoise the size of Rhode Island lives off the coast of Turtle Beach."

Lucinda buried her head under the covers, but Goldie pulled them off, saying it was laundry day. Despite Lucinda protesting that she could do her own wash, Goldie had the cot stripped in record time. Had Lucinda not stumbled to the bathroom, Goldie might have thrown her in the washing machine, too.

While Lucinda was trying to get the last of the shower gel out of the bottle, Goldie poked her head in the bathroom and cautioned her to get a move on or she'd miss Jim without a shirt on. Lucinda groaned and threatened to install padlocks on the doors.

The mention of Jim's name gave her a strange pang in her stomach. She remembered the mysterious news stories she and Sharon discovered about his estranged wife the night before. That, coupled with her tense conversation with Jim before bed, had her feathers ruffled.

She toweled off from the shower and peeked out the bathroom window, ashamed she'd fallen for her mother's schemes. Jim was painting the bungalows a second coat all right, but he had his shirt on. Lucinda laughed that at nearly fifty, her mother still knew what buttons to push.

Wiping the steam from the mirror, Lucinda blow-dried her hair and mentally reviewed her to-do list for the day. First up, Ben and his friends removed the furniture from the bungalow that was occupied the day before and drove it over to Oh, My Vintage! for Charlie. After that, they offered to tape off the lobby so Jim and Lucinda could paint. She applied her makeup, staring at her reflection in the mirror and wondering how awkward the job would be after last night's tiff.

She'd chosen a bright white to paint the lobby, choosing decorative accents in corals, pinks, and yellows to make a cheerful, welcoming first impression. First, she needed to go to Jellyfish Bay and look for paddle boards as one of the entertainment options for future guests.

While reviewing The Pink Octopus's records with a fine-tooth comb, Lucinda was surprised at the lack of entertainment options her parents had offered guests over the years. It wasn't that they didn't care about their patrons. Tom and Goldie made many lifelong friends through the business. People who'd started as first-time guests, ended up being surrogate aunts, uncles, and cousins to the Perrys.

For a few years, they kept two ponies for guests to ride along the shore. But when they died, Tom and Goldie didn't replace them because it hit Goldie too hard watching the horses suffer from illness—first Star, and soon after, Galaxy, who died from a broken heart.

As for other entertainment, when Lucinda asked Goldie questions about it, she was told that The Pink Octopus didn't suffer from a lack of paddle boards. "It takes more than entertainment to run a business like this," her mother sniffed. Lucinda took that as a cue to keep her mouth shut, but now she had more skin in the game. She was investing almost her entire net worth in the business, so she wanted to set it up to be one of the premier bungalow rental businesses on the island.

Many other island lodging establishments offered boat and Jet Ski rentals, live music, and even shuttles to take guests from one attraction to another. Nearly all of them at least offered complimentary breakfasts and paddle boards.

Tom and Goldie seemed content to operate as little more than a motel. Sure, guests had individual cottages, but that was about all The Pink Octopus offered. Lucinda worried that all her grandiose ideas for revamping the business would only get them to baseline, not much more. She wanted them to be the talk of the island, but the level of apathy her family had for so long really put the business at a disadvantage.

In the kitchen, Goldie was pulling a breakfast casserole out of the oven. The smell of sausage and sage reminded Lucinda of Thanksgiving. "Mom, how do you stay so thin eating all your amazing concoctions?" Goldie set down her potholder and stood on her head right there in the kitchen, asking, "How many times do I have to tell you, honey? Yoga!"

Lucinda ate her casserole, wondering why her mother served up such delicious meals every day when she was always on her to lose weight. Her hand traveled to her mid-section. She wasn't *fat*, she assured herself, but it wouldn't hurt to tone up.

Years ago, Lucinda walked two miles a day, and counted that as the time she did her best thinking. When Peter started asking her to handle larger and larger aspects of his business, though, time seemed elusive for things like exercising. Often, she had to eat on the go when she was running errands for Peter's law firm—getting documents signed, serving papers, and so on.

Looking back, Lucinda could see that the things she most often put on the back burner were her own priorities, never Peter's or the kids'. Making Peter, in particular, her entire life had cut her off from the outside world in so many ways. She understood now that she played a role in her isolation. Yes, Peter blew up their marriage, but she didn't need to make herself her lowest priority for so many years, either. Every time a realization such as that came to mind, Lucinda was more and more convinced there was nothing waiting for her back in Connecticut. She'd miss the kids terribly, but they had lives of their own and didn't mind flying. Surely, if she moved to Turtle Beach, they'd visit.

Pouring some tea into a travel mug, Lucinda kissed her mother's cheek and chirped, "See you round like a donut!" Goldie smiled, remembering Tom teaching the children all those funny goodbye phrases when they were little. "Take care, polar bear!" she replied, swallowing a lump in her throat. She missed her husband terribly but felt hopeful that at least now, she and their children could honor Tom by revitalizing the business he'd loved so deeply.

Steve Sorkin was waiting for the green light to replumb two of the bungalows. He'd brought a helper, and they were sitting in his truck. Lucinda approached the vehicle to greet Steve, and was met with the passenger calling out, "Looking good, lady!" She was mortified until she recognized the man from high school. *Don something-or-other*.

"Oh, don't start lying to me now, Don!" she blushed. She leaned through his open window and gave him an affectionate side hug.

"I'm okay," Don sighed, smiling. "I'm married to Cecilia O'Brien now. Got three kids."

"O'Brien," Lucinda said, "Why does that name sound so familiar?"

"She was the lunch lady," Steve cracked.

"Oh, that's right! Ms. O'Brien! Wait, you married our lunch lady, Don?"

"Yes, but when you factor in that I'd been held back a few times in school, it's not so bad," he said, sheepishly.

"It kinda is," Steve replied.

Don punched him in the arm and they both laughed. Lucinda waved Steve's comment off and told Don that what mattered was his happiness. She smiled, remembering the time Don got a pencil jammed in his eye in Chemistry class after a dare had gone awry. Now, here he was, a skilled plumber, a stable father and husband. Life continued to amaze her.

Lucinda shook her head, awestruck. Don married the lunch lady and was happy as a clam. She'd run off with a big-time Manhattan lawyer, and look how it worked for her. Sleeping on a cot at her mother's house didn't exactly make her a success story.

She squeezed Don's hand and said it was good to see him, and it was. Being back on the island was starting to feel a little less like a pair of ill-fitting shoes. Things might still turn out all right.

Lucinda climbed into Goldie's Toyota and was tuning the car radio when there was a knock on the window. *Jim.* She rolled down the window and pursed her lips. "Want some company?" he asked, his nose pink from the morning sun.

"You don't even know where I'm going," she huffed.

"So?"

"What about last night?"

"What about it?"

"I seem to recall a fight."

Jim climbed into the car and said that last night was water under the bridge. He recapped the conversation by saying that he understood Lucinda was only looking for friendship, and that things were to be strictly business moving forward. When she started driving, he added, "Kind of presumptuous of you to assume I want more than friendship." Her mouth fell open, and he added, "Just sayin'!"

When she noticed him stifling a laugh, Lucinda reminded herself to lighten up. She cleared her throat and said, "Well, I'm glad we have an understanding." He nodded, and turned up the radio, singing along in a terrible voice to a song she hadn't heard since 1987.

Suddenly, Jim seemed cool again. Lucinda didn't know if it was the joke he'd just made about not being interested in her, or the nostalgic song, or maybe the relief of setting the record straight. Either way, she found herself with mixed emotions. *Do not look at his biceps*, she warned herself. *Or his five o'clock shadow. Or his thick hair. In fact, just keep your eyes on the road.*

After a few minutes, Jim turned down the radio and looked at Lucinda, who was stopped at a red light. She raised her eyebrows, waiting for him to get to the point. "Sorry I called Peter a pinhead."

"Why?" she said, smiling. "He *is* a pinhead."

The light turned green, and Jim cranked the radio louder. It was another eighties song, which seemed to be just about all anyone played on the island stations. Lucinda stepped down hard on the gas, and Jim let out a raucous laugh. He wound the window down and yelled, "I heart the 80s!" The car next to them honked, and Jim pumped his fist in the air.

Chapter 11

Jim helped Lucinda pick out paddle boards at Kettler's Sporting Goods on Jellyfish Bay. She planned to start with six, hoping to need more in a year due to a major increase in business. She smiled at the thought of too many guests per paddle board, even allowing a humorous fantasy to slip in about two buff young men fighting over the last board, their girlfriends sipping Margaritas on the beach and laughing as they clobbered each other.

After getting the boards, along with two dozen white beach chairs and pink umbrellas she'd had to special order from a store catalog, Lucinda paid for her items and arranged for delivery once the merchandise was in stock. Jim offered to save her the ninety-dollar delivery fee and pick everything up himself in his truck, but she waved him off. She didn't mind paying for delivery. It was worth it to keep Jim at The Pink Octopus as much as possible. There was still a lot of work to do.

On the way home, Jim asked Lucinda to drive through Tropical Smoothie, a small juice bar chain that supposedly had the best kale-mango smoothie on the island. "There's

more than one kale-mango smoothie on Turtle Island?"
Lucinda joked, crinkling her nose. Jim told her not to
mock it until she tried it, but Lucinda opted for the Morning Sunshine, which was mostly fruit and orange juice.
She'd dealt with enough change lately. Adding vegetables
to her fruit juice was a step too far from her comfort zone.

When they pulled up to The Pink Octopus, they sat
in the car listening to music and finishing their drinks.
Lucinda enjoyed the way the two of them easily slid back
into a friendship, the years melting away seamlessly. Jim
apologized again for the nasty comment about Lucinda's
marriage, and she laughed and said it was nothing compared to what she'd said to him. "Which part?" he asked,
confused. "I don't remember you saying anything too terrible." She tapped her temple and said, "It was all up here.
I cursed you out a hundred ways to Sunday in my head."

They laughed, and Lucinda learned that Jim still loved
Jackson Browne and John Candy movies and Swedish
Fish. He still put hot sauce on everything he ate. When he
laughed hard, he still threw his head back, a mannerism
she'd all but forgotten. Each time she started to let down
her guard, though, there was a niggling in the back of her
brain that needed to know the truth about his wife. "Jim,"
she finally said, sipping the last of her smoothie, "What did
you mean the other night when you said you used to have
a family?"

"Oh, I don't know if we need to get into all that," he
said, shifting in his seat.

"It's kind of unfair that you've kept tabs on me through
my mother all these years, but you won't tell me anything
about *your* life."

"That's true, I guess. I wouldn't know where to begin, though."

Lucinda settled back in the driver's seat, watched a seagull pick at a half-eaten bag of potato chips in the parking lot, and said, "I once read about this thing called exposure therapy. One of the things they suggest is jumping into a cold shower. Supposedly it's liberating. The theory is that if you can get in, knowing you're going to freeze your butt off, you'll be more likely to face your fears in life."

Jim scratched his chin, wondering where Lucinda was going with the conversation. "I won't ask you to do that," she continued, "but I'll rip off the Band-Aid for you by saying that I know about Camille."

Before Jim could say anything, Goldie opened the lobby door and headed their way, waving. Her animal print sunglasses and fuchsia handbag made her appear like a young girl on Spring Break.

Jim wriggled in his seat, and Lucinda rolled her eyes. Her mother's timing was impeccable. Before Goldie reached the car, Jim suggested Lucinda join him for dinner at his place. "Come over at seven. I'll explain everything then," he said. She nodded, and Goldie tapped on the driver's side window. Lucinda rolled it down and Goldie said, "I'm going to get my hair did! Wanna come? You could use a makeover."

Lucinda shrank in her seat, remembering a cloak of invisibility she'd once read about in one of Jill's Harry Potter books and wished she had one now. She climbed out of the vehicle, said goodbye to Jim, and prayed he would think her red cheeks were from the afternoon sun. "No purple or pink hair, Mom!" Lucinda said, jabbing a finger in Goldie's direction. In response, Goldie smiled deviously, and thanked Lucinda for the great idea. Then, she sped off in her gold car, which instantly looked sassier than it did when Lucinda was the one behind the wheel.

Lucinda said goodbye to Jim, went into the lobby, and searched online for free templates she could use to design a weekly entertainment schedule, planning on having live music in the evenings and someone to host a weekly round of trivia. If people turned up for that, she'd consider adding a few more activities to the weekly schedule.

She made some phone calls and scheduled interviews with a few bands, a hostess, and someone to take care of maintenance. Jim wouldn't always be around to fix things, and Ben seemed to want more of a personal life, so it made sense to hire an outside person for the job.

Sharon and Goldie couldn't maintain The Pink Octopus anymore, especially with the volume of guests the relaunch would undoubtedly attract. Lucinda planned to hire professional housekeepers as well. As far as she was concerned, the Perry ladies had more than fulfilled their quota of keeping up on other people's laundry.

She crunched some numbers and decided that for about thirty dollars a day, she could offer bagels, cream cheese, fruit, orange juice, and coffee in the bungalows. She thought guests would appreciate having private breakfasts at their leisure instead of rushing over to the lobby before continental breakfast ended. It also made sense because whoever was at the front desk would have one less thing to worry about in the mornings if they weren't juggling breakfast duty and early checkouts.

She went online and ordered thirteen single-serve coffee makers for the bungalows, feeling pretty pleased with herself. She put her pen down and rubbed her eyes. Sharon tapped on the counter, saying, "Knock, knock." Lucinda looked up and smiled. Sharon asked what was up, and Lucinda said she had a mountain of things to do before Jim came by to get the painting started in the lobby.

Sharon listened while Lucinda rattled off her agenda, rubbing her leg to soothe the tingling. She nodded, and told Lucinda she had a lot to do, too. Lucinda's heart ached for her sister. "Let's play hooky for a while and go get pedicures!" Lucinda urged.

"You're on!" Sharon agreed, putting her bags behind the counter.

Lucinda put the "We'll be back at..." sign on the door, set it for two hours later, and locked up. She ran a spare key over to Jim, who was putting the second coat of paint on one of the bungalows. "If you want to tape off the lobby before I get back, you can go ahead inside," she said.

Jim smiled and commented that Lucinda had a mischievous look in her eyes. "Who me?" she replied, batting her eyes. Laughing, she ran to Sharon's car, feeling like a kid skipping school. Sharon turned up the radio, and they sang girl power songs with the windows down. They pretended not to notice Sharon's hand twitching as she gripped the steering wheel.

Chapter 12

Reclining side by side in pedicure chairs at the nail salon, Lucinda and Sharon flipped through beauty magazines like women of leisure without a care in the world. "Should I start wearing a uniform?" Lucinda asked breezily. Sharon stopped reading a Jane Fonda interview and stared at her sister. "What? I'm seriously asking," Lucinda said.

"Why on earth would you wear a uniform? You mean like a waitress, a nurse, what? Are you into some kind of kink now or what?"

"No, dummy!" Lucinda groaned. "Some of the most successful people in recent history have chosen to wear the same outfit every day. To make life easier."

"Wouldn't it stink after a while?"

"Come on! You buy several of the same outfits, not wear the same thing every day! For example, maybe I'd get a white blouse and khaki pants. There. Done. I'd wear it whether I was going to the dentist or out to lunch or to a play. Wouldn't it make life so gloriously easy?"

"Since when do you go to plays?"

"I give up."

Sharon apologized, and said she thought it was a good idea, and that it wasn't the craziest thing in the world to go along with the Steve Jobs and Mark Zuckerbergs of the world. After a few more minutes of learning Jane Fonda's affirmative aging secrets, Sharon looked up at Lucinda. "I mean, it does kind of say you're leaning into the whole no-man thing, though." Lucinda tutted, and replied that men are nothing but trouble anyway.

When Sharon wasn't looking, Lucinda observed her, wondering how bad the MS was going to get, and how else it might eventually rob Sharon of her zest for life.

The more she thought about multiple sclerosis, the more she realized she didn't understand much about it at all. Was it a disease or a disorder? Could it be controlled through proper lifestyle changes? She opened her mouth to ask questions but closed it again and bit her lip. They were having a great time, and she didn't want to spoil it with a heavy conversation.

Sharon picked pastel mermaid colors for her toes, but Lucinda was indecisive. She held up a bottle of creamy beige and asked for Sharon's opinion. Sharon slammed her magazine down on a nearby table and said, "That's it!" She grabbed a bottle of bright pink polish from the shelf and handed it to the nail technician. "My sister will have Watermelon Wishes, Chelsea!"

Lucinda rolled her eyes and said she thought beige was classy. "My sister hasn't given up on men, even if her taste in nail polish says otherwise," Sharon huffed to an amused Chelsea. Lucinda scoffed, and said, "Don't listen to her! I *have* given up on men."

Chelsea shrugged and said, "I don't blame you. None of 'em are trustworthy." Lucinda and Sharon looked at each other, considering Chelsea's statement. Sharon pressed her hands on the armrests of her chair, leaned back, and said, "But they sure can be fun, right ladies?" Lucinda blushed and rolled her eyes. When Chelsea held up the Watermelon Wishes polish with a questioning look on her face, Lucinda nodded, figuring she had nothing to lose.

After the pedicure, Lucinda took a detour to Hammerhead Wharf and treated Sharon to lunch at Vivienne's, a restaurant near Sharon's house on Sand Dune Lane. When Sharon questioned whether they were underdressed for a place like Vivienne's, Lucinda rolled her eyes and promised to leave a big tip to make up for their soccer mom attire.

Over a plate of stuffed mushrooms, Lucinda finally got up the nerve to ask about Sharon's MS. She was surprised at Sharon's accepting attitude toward her diagnosis. She said that while she wouldn't wish it on her worst enemy, the diagnosis was something of a relief. She explained that she'd been experiencing mysterious symptoms for years, if not a decade. "It felt so good to get a straightforward answer," she sighed, taking a sip of peach iced tea. "I cried, but they were almost happy tears, you know? Everyone thought I was crazy! *I* thought I was crazy. Now we can all rest assured I'm not!'"

Sharon said she didn't have a game plan because from the research she'd done, there were too many variables to predict her progression with any accuracy. She explained that there are varying degrees of symptoms, and no real way to know where you fall on the spectrum until you walk the journey for a while. She'd decided after hours of research to close her laptop, lean into the whole mindfulness thing, and take it one day at a time. "Right *now*," she said grinning, "I'm fine. I'm safe. I'm getting ready to hoover the last stuffed mushroom, so I'm all good. Where I'll be in six months? That's anyone's guess."

Lucinda searched her sister's eyes to see if her bright outlook was a front, but it seemed genuine. Sharon seemed okay. *If and when that changes*, Lucinda thought, *I'll be here to hold her hand every step of the way*.

Lucinda touched Sharon's arm and apologized for not writing more often over the years, let alone visiting. She explained, through teary eyes, that getting off Turtle Island was something she needed to do at the time. She had big dreams that wouldn't wait. Sharon nodded and made a joke about how Lucinda used to daydream about designing Nora Ephron's New York City penthouse. They giggled, but Lucinda's face grew solemn, her eyes tight.

She recalled wanting a home with fine art on the walls and expensive furniture, and a life with dinner parties and ski trips and a well-rounded group of intellectual friends. "I wanted the finer things, I guess," she confessed, thanking the waitress for the refill on her iced tea. "A busy schedule, an educated husband, a Labrador Retriever. Mom and Dad's life? *Beach life*? Well, it just wasn't *my* dream."

When Sharon asked if Lucinda had been happy over the years, she swallowed a lump in her throat. "I got the Monet replicas, and an inground swimming pool. I had two beautiful kids who read the classics and chewed with their mouths closed. I've traveled to beautiful places, met Colin Powell…"

"And the Labrador, we know you had," Sharon said, pursing her lips.

"Sweet Bogie," Lucinda cried. "May he rest in peace."

"So, where did it go wrong?"

"Well along with his Ivy League degree and penchant for collecting fine automobiles, Peter never met a woman he found unattractive. Let's put it that way."

"So, Eve wasn't his first?"

"No, not by far. First relative, though, unless there's anything *you* want to tell me."

Sharon pretended to stick her finger down her throat as though gagging. She mumbled something about preferring to be eaten alive by Piranhas than sleep with Peter. "No offense," she said, biting her lip and wondering if her illustration was too much. Lucinda's response was laughter so hard that she feared cracking a rib.

A group of uppity women at an adjacent table looked over disapprovingly, and Sharon leaned closer to Lucinda and whispered, "Can you say Stepford wives?"

They got the check and paid, leaving a large tip like Lucinda had promised. They hurried out of the restaurant arm in arm, laughing the whole way to the car. Sharon suggested they swing by the drive-thru and get a milkshake to take home.

Lucinda knew she should get back to work, but spending a spontaneous afternoon with her sister was too much fun to cut short.

They drove home, and Sharon caught Lucinda staring at her with a goofy grin on her face. "What?" she said, lowering her sunglasses. "I love you," Lucinda replied. Sharon groaned and muttered something about Lucinda being ableist. When Lucinda asked what was ableist about saying she loved her, Sharon replied, "Well, you never said it before the MS, but it's cool. I love you, too." Lucinda threw her head back, exasperated. "You're incorrigible, you know that?"

"One of my many charms," Sharon joked.

Jim was painting the trim on one of the bungalows when the ladies pulled into the parking lot. They sat in the car sipping the last of their milkshakes and watching. Sharon made a joke about Jim being fun to look at, and Lucinda scoffed. "Sharon, really!"

She admitted Jim had invited her to his bungalow later to explain whatever mess he was involved in back in North Carolina. Sharon raised an eyebrow, fished a can of pepper spray out of her purse, and offered it to Lucinda. "Get real," she laughed, climbing out of the car.

Sharon waved goodbye, saying she was headed to Ian's place to pick up some belongings she left there. When Lucinda asked if she was sure, Sharon said that Ian would make a wonderful partner for someone. Before she could finish her sentence, they said in unison, "when he grows up." Saying the same thing at the same time reminded them of their youth, when they'd often have the same reaction to a movie or a joke or start singing a song on the radio at the exact same time. Though they weren't especially close growing up, they thought on the same wavelength.

Watching Sharon drive off, Lucinda hoped with all her might that Matt would call her sister. He seemed like a nice man with a good sense of humor and strong arms to help Sharon if she fell or needed help in and out of the shower.

She called across the parking lot to Jim, saying the bungalows looked great. She emphasized the word *bungalows* this time, a nod to his prior joke. "See you in a few hours," he yelled back.

Lucinda went inside, and was met by a disgruntled Goldie, who complained that with the time it would take her to learn a new computer system, she wouldn't be able to play Solitaire anymore. Lucinda sighed, and said, "You'll be so happy with all the tourism coming through here, that you won't worry about a computer game." Goldie huffed, rested her chin on her hand, and said she doubted it.

Ben walked into the office and leaned against the counter, unwrapping a giant hoagie. Lucinda jabbed a finger in his direction, warning him not to drip Italian dressing everywhere. He smirked and made a smart remark about there not even being any furniture yet. "I have to stand to eat my lunch. What's that all about, Mom?"

Lucinda said the new furniture would be arriving once she and Jim painted the lobby, and that it was never too early to set good habits. Ben asked with his mouth full, why she was making the office so cheerful looking. "All the bright colors you're planning on putting in here will make it harder to mope," he complained, dipping a French fry in ketchup and dramatically eating it over a napkin. "Why are you always wallowing?" Lucinda asked, stealing a fry.

He said that Fawn dumped him, which made Goldie and Lucinda both smile. He asked what kind of woman breaks up with a guy via text message, and Goldie replied, "A teenager?"

Lucinda encouraged Ben to chin up, reminding him that he was the uncatchable hot fisherman of Turtle Beach. "Used to be," he said, picking a piece of shredded lettuce from his shirt. "Now I'm the guy getting gray hair and walking around with Italian dressing on my T-shirt. I lost my hotness."

"Now you sound like Lucinda," Goldie said.

"Don't bring *me* into it!" Lucinda snapped. "Look at my toes! They're hot pink, for Pete's sake!"

"All I can tell you kids is that I'm well into my golden years and I *know* I'm hot," Goldie said, shimmying her shoulders. "If you want to wallow, take it outside. You're harshing my mellow."

Lucinda and Ben burst into laughter, amused at Goldie's constant need to try and keep up with youthful lingo. Ben finally composed himself, gathered his wrappers, and lightly kicked the back of Lucinda's knee, trying to get her to stumble. "You're twelve, you know that?" she hissed.

"Nuh uh," he said, pointing to his hair. "Look at all this gray! I already told you!" He sighed dramatically, then added, "Why are you grouchy, anyway, Lucinda? I hear you have a hot date with Jimbo tonight."

Goldie lit up at the thought of Lucinda and Jim back together again, clasping her hands to her chest as if giving thanks for answered prayer. It's far from a date, Ben. We have business to discuss."

"*Maybe* it's a date," Goldie said. "Do you want to borrow another shirt?"

"Yes, sis," Ben said, grinning. "Do you want to borrow another of Mom's shirts?"

"It isn't a date, Mother, and shut up Benjamin!"

"How do you know?" Goldie asked, hopefully.

"Because," Lucinda sighed, "for the hundredth time, I've given up on men! Feel free to put flyers up all over the island so people stop asking me!"

She left the office and went up to the main house to lie down. She needed to rest after her high-calorie lunch. Reclining on the squeaky cot, Lucinda cursed Ben for being such a brat. She didn't know for sure if it was true or not that she'd sworn off men, but one thing was certain:

The way she hurt Jim all those years ago, he'd never take her back.

Besides, she couldn't imagine passing "Go" in their relationship until Jim provided a rock-solid alibi for where he was at the time of his wife's disappearance. Judging from the online web sleuths, plenty of people were hedging their bets that Jim did something terrible to Camille before disappearing from Wilmington without a trace.

Chapter 13

At seven o'clock, Lucinda carried a raspberry lemon cake over to Jim's bungalow. Goldie raised her to always bring something to a dinner party—no matter how small the guest list. She found the recipe online and was thrilled to see her mother had all the ingredients in stock.

Approaching the freshly painted bungalows, Lucinda felt a flutter in her belly. They looked exactly how she'd imagined in her mind's eye. Often, when she tried to make a recipe or craft she found online, it fell into the "fail" category, never looking as good as the picture or video made it appear. The cottages, however, looked like an assortment of cotton candy against the beautiful sunset.

She imagined how nice the photos would look and couldn't wait to send them to Jill, who was busy at work on the new website. She smiled to herself, feeling hopeful that her plans were going to turn out all right. She knocked lightly on the door, and Jim opened it, grinned, and said, "Right on time."

Lucinda set the cake on the counter and accepted the glass of wine he handed her. "Maybe just the one," she said, "but only water after this." She resolved to keep her head clear for their impending discussion. When Jim made small talk about something he'd seen on the news, Lucinda stopped him. She said she was sorry to be abrupt, but that he needed to explain some things before she could continue with the evening. Either that, she joked, or she'd push him into that cold shower she'd mentioned earlier. Jim took a long pull on his glass of Merlot and motioned for her to take a seat at the table.

He began explaining. Years earlier, he was devastated when Lucinda left him for Peter. He said it took him a couple of years to even date anyone seriously. After a few tries, he finally met Camille while he was stationed with the Army in Louisiana. She laughed at his jokes, was an obsessive cleaner, and respected his need for solitude from time to time. They married inside of nine months and started a family shortly thereafter, having a son named Max and, a couple of years later, a daughter, Savannah.

Lucinda cut a meatball in two, speared it, and popped it in her mouth. Jim had made spaghetti, which was surprisingly good. She didn't know he could cook. Listening intently to his story, waiting for the part where Camille went missing, Lucinda noticed that Jim had all the same mannerisms he'd had as a teenager. He still ran his fingers through his hair when speaking about something painful, still drummed his fingers on his knee or the table when trying to articulate a thought. "Savannah was a Daddy's Girl," he said, smiling. The way he spoke of Savannah, Lucinda would've thought she'd died, except she knew better from her online investigating with Sharon. Savannah was alive and well and living in Manhattan.

Jim continued, saying that Camille didn't like military life, especially when he got called to duty in Afghanistan or Iraq. He'd be gone for up to a year at a time, and sometimes came home to find another man in the house watching television or cooking macaroni and cheese for the kids as if he lived there. Every time Jim threatened to divorce Camille, she would tell him he'd never see his children again. Finally, he turned a blind eye to her infidelity and the two became nothing more than roommates. "Then," he said, leaning back in his chair, "last year, I finally left. The kids had grown, and I figured she'd declare a national holiday when I walked out the door."

"But she didn't?"

"It was nonstop harassment. She'd see me driving down the road and make an anonymous call to the police, reporting me for drunk driving, even though I hadn't had a drop to drink. Sometimes, she'd show up at my apartment and pick a fight. Then, she'd wait until the neighbors were gathered and yell, 'You said the last time you hit me, you'd never do it again! Why, Jim? Why?'"

"I won't ask if you ever hit her. I know you wouldn't do that."

Jim put his chair back down on four legs, pushed his pasta around with a fork, and groaned loudly.

"So, what happened the night she went missing?" Lucinda croaked.

"I can honestly say I have no idea. Savannah called me and said she couldn't reach Camille for a few days and was getting worried. She wondered if I'd seen her. I said I hadn't, but when days stretched into weeks, then a month, people started pointing the finger at me. It's always the husband, right?"

Jim said that he'd been called into the police station three times for questioning. When Lucinda asked if he had a lawyer, he shook his head and joked about whether Peter would give him a discount. Peter was a corporate lawyer, but Lucinda didn't correct him. She pursed her lips when Jim explained that he couldn't afford an attorney once Camille bled him dry with the divorce. "So, you didn't really lose your money in a bad investment?" Lucinda asked sadly. Jim laughed, pushed back in his chair again, and said, "Well, depends on how you look at it. One could say getting mixed up with Camille was the worst investment I ever made. But yes, the money is gone because she took it all."

Finally, he said, even the kids started looking at him suspiciously. Once he left North Carolina for Turtle Island, Max and Savannah considered it an admission of guilt. "And now you're here," Lucinda said, breaking the last piece of bread and handing Jim half of it.

"Now I'm here."

"Making me spaghetti."

"Making you spaghetti."

"How long will you be here?"

"Until...I don't know. Until they find her and officially clear my name, or until someone on this island gives me a reason to stay, I suppose."

Lucinda fidgeted in her seat. Was Jim flirting? She knew if she didn't come right out and ask if he killed Camille, she'd never fully trust him. She hated that reality, but admitted to herself that there was no way around it. She couldn't move forward, as business partners or friends or anything else without directly asking the question that felt like gravel in her mouth.

She'd ask him and get it over with. If he admitted something heinous, or if Lucinda didn't believe his response, she'd pretend to get an urgent text from Jill and hightail it out of his bungalow. "Jim," she said, tearing her napkin into shreds, "I have to ask."

"You want to know if I killed my wife."

"I'm sorry, but I need to ask, or I'll always wonder. I know you'd never lie to me, so whatever answer you give, I'll believe you. I mean, maybe you two had a big fight and things got out of control? I don't know."

Jim looked her right in the eye for a long time, unblinking. Reaching for her hand, he said, "Lucinda May Perry—I'm going to leave off the Flowers part since you finally dumped that jackass—I swear I had nothing to do with my ex-wife's disappearance. I have never physically hurt anyone in my life. I give you my word, and that's the most valuable thing I have to give."

Lucinda wadded up the remnants of her napkin and set it in a ball on her empty dinner plate. The chair screeched on the floor when she stood up. Jim's stomach lurched, fearing he'd somehow chased her off a second time. He couldn't imagine losing her twice in one lifetime. He nervously cracked his knuckles, swallowing a lump in his throat, waiting to see what she was going to do next.

She bit her lip, pulled her laptop from its zippered carrying case, and sat on the sofa. "Well, come on," she said, patting the empty cushion next to her. "This mystery isn't going to solve itself, now is it?"

Jim let out the deep breath he didn't realize he'd been holding. He walked over to the couch, sat down, and answered Lucinda's questions. All the true crime interrogation programs she'd watched over the years made her sound like a real detective. Jim had been through multiple police interrogations, but the Wilmington detectives seemed straight out of Mayberry compared to Lucinda's detailed line of questioning.

After thirty minutes or so, she turned to Jim and said, "The good news is, I believe you 100%. The bad news is, you need to jump in the cold shower." When Jim scratched his chin, she pushed his cell phone across the coffee table and added, "We're going to need to get Max and Savannah on board if we're going to crack this case. Start dialing."

Chapter 14

When Jim's kids ignored his calls, Lucinda asked for their phone numbers and programmed them into her cell phone. She sliced and plated dessert, joking that although detectives normally ate donuts, all she had was lemon raspberry cake. The moment the words escaped her lips, her face flushed. "I'm sorry," she said, sitting down. "I guess I shouldn't joke at a time like this." Jim shrugged, turned on the television and searched for a movie to distract them while they ate.

He stopped at an old black-and-white film neither of them had seen before. It was half over, but they settled in and watched anyway. It was a well-known film with Claudette Colbert and Clark Gable, and it made Lucinda long for olden days that she wasn't even alive to miss but somehow did anyway.

During a funny scene, Jim laughed and slapped his knee. When he put his hand back down, it grazed Lucinda's hand, and her mind traveled back to a time when they couldn't stay away from each other. Even now, there was a familiarity between them that wouldn't have made it awkward if either of them reached for the other's hand, finished the movie with their fingers interlaced. But they watched the film with their hands in their laps, eyes on the screen.

Right about the time the end credits began rolling, Lucinda gathered the dessert dishes and asked if he was still up for getting the first coat of paint on the lobby's walls. He nodded, said he could go all night if she had the stamina to keep up with him, and raised his eyebrows waiting for her answer. Lucinda laughed, hung the dish towel over the stove's handle, and made a joke about being able to paint Jim under the table.

The truth was, she was exhausted and had no idea where he got his energy. Jim reached up and grabbed the trim above the doorway, exposing a sliver of his belly. She looked away quickly, wondering if it was quick enough. "Hey, Luce?" he said, squinting.

"Yeah?"

"How can you be so sure I didn't do something to my ex-wife?"

"Because I know you, Jim Barnes," she said, shrugging. "That's how."

Once they'd painted the entire office and lobby with one coat of Snowstorm paint, Lucinda said goodnight and headed home She was surprised to see Ben and Goldie sitting at the kitchen table playing cards. Lucinda shook her head and remarked how strange it was that neither of them had dates for a change. Ben teased it was even stranger that Lucinda *did*, and ducked when she threw a saltshaker at him. "How many times do I have to tell you, it wasn't a date? And by the way, while you sat here playing cards, I painted the lobby!"

Goldie dealt Lucinda in and pushed a bowl of corn chips in her direction. The game was Rummy, and Ben explained they were playing for a car wash. "You're actually going to make your seventy-four-year-old mother wash your car if she loses?" Lucinda asked, incredulously. "She won't lose," Goldie deadpanned without looking up from her hand.

Lucinda smiled, gathered her cards, and started playing. After a few minutes she cocked her head, raised her eyebrows, and nudged Ben's arm. "I don't have a car! What happens if *I* win?" Goldie and Ben responded in unison, "You won't."

An hour later, Goldie abandoned her hand mid-game. She took a call from someone whose voice made her blush. Ben grabbed the empty corn chip bowl and pretended to wretch. Lucinda made kissing sounds.

She marveled at how quickly she reverted to a petulant child in her siblings' presence, which sent her into a fit of giggles. She doubled over, held her belly, and winced when her mother shot her a stern glance. "Prepare to lose," Ben cried in his most evil laugh.

Goldie had been winning at Rummy, but when she left to take the phone call, she forfeited her position, sliding Ben into the number one spot. With eighty points between them, Lucinda called "Game," and begged Ben to let her out of washing his car. "Nope," he said, yawning. "Fair is fair. I'll bring her by tomorrow."

"Her?"

"My Charger. I call her JoJo. She's the only female in my life who doesn't bust my chops."

"Come on, Ben!"

"You should wear a bikini while you wash her, too. Give old Jim something to look at while he paints."

Lucinda threw her cards at Ben and stormed off. He yelled, "Mom! Lucinda hit me!"

In her room, Lucinda dialed Jim's daughter's phone number, but hung up before Savannah had a chance to answer. It was almost eleven o'clock, which Lucinda deemed too late for an introductory call. She washed her face, brushed her teeth, and crawled under the covers. She'd try again in the morning. Hopefully Jim had raised a reasonable young woman. Without Savannah's help, Lucinda wasn't sure she could solve the mystery. Who would know Camille better—and be most likely to track her last known footsteps—Lucinda figured, than her own daughter?

She propped herself up in bed, browsing the Internet on her phone. She found Savannah's social media accounts, but Max's were anonymous or nonexistent. Savannah was an art curator at the Museum of Modern Art in New York City, loved biographies, and had a little white dog named Wonton, who had an impressive collection of bowties and his own successful Instagram account. Savannah appeared to be single, and she had Jim's blue eyes.

Lucinda's heart squeezed at the thought of Jim's children believing he'd murder their mother. Not only must they be terrified that they never knew their father, but it must also be excruciating to picture their mother dead in a ditch somewhere. Even though she felt compelled to ask Jim directly about his involvement in Camille's disappearance, deep down she never suspected him. How could she?

How could anyone? Jim was a white hat kind of guy. She set down her phone, turned off the lamp, and rehearsed the next day's conversation with Savannah in her head until she slipped into a deep sleep.

Lucinda made strawberry and banana muffins for breakfast in the morning. She sat with Goldie in silence until finally Goldie placed a warm, soft hand on her cheek. "He's telling the truth, baby." Lucinda dropped her butter knife and stared into her mother's eyes. "How do you..."

"We know him. He's family. He'll always be family, and he didn't do it. I know it in my bones, and so do you," Goldie urged.

Lucinda smiled, squeezed her mother's hand, and told her she was scary sometimes. That her mind-reading skills were way too advanced for comfort.

After a few more minutes, Lucinda rattled off a few ideas she'd come up with for advertising the relaunch. Goldie suggested an airplane banner, but Lucinda thought a feature on the local news would significantly broaden their reach. "Those banners are always too high to make out what they're advertising," she said.

"Why would Channel 6 be interested enough in our business to haul their cookies from the mainland to rinky-dink Turtle Beach to do a story on our business?" Goldie argued, adding a spoon of honey to her Chamomile tea.

"Mom, the business has been around for fifty years! Don't you think that alone is worth celebrating?"

"I guess so."

"It is! In this day and age, not many businesses can last that long. Especially in the hospitality industry, with the big companies taking over and putting hotels up and people renting out their homes on sites like Airbnb."

"They'll show up in droves to see my mother. She's older than dirt after all. Maybe we should contact the Guinness Book of World Records?"

"Mom!"

"What? You heard her say it herself! Her exact words were, 'I'm as old as dirt!'"

"You love Grandma, Mom. Why do you always pretend you don't?"

Goldie brushed Lucinda's concerns off, saying she and Helen had always exchanged witty banter. Lucinda raised her eyebrows, questioned her mother's phrasing of *witty banter*, and continued eating. She figured whatever type of relationship her mother and grandmother had was between them. She loved them both and knew neither old dog was about to learn any new tricks at their stages of life.

After breakfast, Lucinda went back to her room, shut the door, and dialed Savannah's number. A clear, confident voice answered on the second ring, saying, "This is Savvy." *Savvy? Cute.* Lucinda introduced herself as an old friend of Savannah's father. When she did, Savannah's voice tightened, and she made an excuse about being on her way out. Lucinda asked her to please give her five minutes. "Just five minutes, Savannah," she said, "and if you still want to hang up, you can. I won't bother you again."

Twenty minutes later, Savannah was still on the line, telling Lucinda that all her parents ever did was fight, until one day they stopped. "It wasn't that they started getting along," she said stiffly. "It's that they stopped speaking altogether. Imagine family dinners and holidays? Not much fun."

"How long ago was that?" Lucinda asked.

"Five years ago. They stayed together for four years without saying anything beyond, 'Did you pay the gas bill on time? And 'We're out of milk.'"

Lucinda listened while Savannah recounted how wonderful Jim was as a father, but said that the past several years, he had become something of a shell. He stuck to himself, didn't attend important functions, and even stopped going out to play pool with his friends on Saturday nights. Savannah explained that when he left Camille, both she and Max were living on their own, Max in Chicago and Savannah in New York City. "My aunt Becky called me one morning and said that Mom hadn't checked in with her in a couple of days. She went to the house and used the spare key to get in, but no one was there except Penelope, Mom's cat."

"What do you think happened to your mom, Savannah?" Lucinda asked, chewing on her cuticles.

"I don't know. People are saying that Dad had something to do with her disappearance. I hope that's not true for several reasons, the main one being that if it is, that means my mother is dead."

"Do you think your dad's capable of hurting someone?"

Savannah didn't answer, and Lucinda could hear her crying on the other end of the line. She waited a minute and apologized for having to ask. Savannah took a deep breath and whispered, "When I was in seventh grade, my father wrote a note to my biology teacher citing all the reasons that frog dissection was barbaric and completely unnecessary. He was *that* dad, a total pacifist. But I don't know. My mom really knew how to press his buttons."

She continued, saying that when Camille got mad, she thought nothing of keying Jim's car or maxing out his credit cards. She said that one of the last straws that led to Jim leaving, was when Camille had his truck painted pink while he was on a hunting trip with his friends. "Her unhinged behavior would be enough to infuriate anyone, even someone as patient as my father," Savannah continued. "Once, he slammed a power tool on the table and charged at her in the kitchen when he'd had enough. He stopped short of grabbing her, maybe because I walked in the room. He had a look...I don't know. It wasn't my dad. Like I said, she's always had a way of stirring things up."

Lucinda told Savannah she'd like to stay in touch if that would be all right. Savannah agreed and promised to reach out with any updates. Lucinda wanted to suggest that Savannah call her father but didn't want to overstep her boundaries. She promised to stay in touch, and they ended the call.

Lucinda thought about calling Max but was a little upset after speaking with Savannah. Without so much as an online profile picture of Max, she was intimidated. What if he didn't respond as kindly to a stranger meddling in his family business as his sister had? She knew he must be incredibly upset at his mother's disappearance—and the inability of the police to find her—probably imagining all sorts of worst-case scenarios, so she opted to wait and call another time when she could think of something helpful to say.

She pulled her hair back, put on some headphones, and decided to go for a walk on the beach. Sitting with Jim and watching the movie the night before, got her thinking that at some point she'd inevitably get back into the dating pool again. She knew that first, some changes were in order. Perhaps coloring her hair, buying a few outfits, shedding some weight. Either way, she knew she'd have to skip the personal uniform idea. She couldn't show up on multiple dates with someone wearing the same white blouse and khakis week after week.

She played a happy song and walked briskly along the shore. Less than a week ago, she'd been living on canned soup and tubs of cake icing she'd hidden all over the house. She'd sneak a spoon or two while changing the laundry from the washer to the dryer or talking to her friend, Rachel, on the phone. She was depressed and most days didn't have the energy to get out of her pajamas. Now, she had an active missing person's case to solve, a family business to rescue, and a sister who needed a game plan for dealing with a major illness. There was no time for cake icing.

As she walked and felt the sand give way under her sneakers, Lucinda saw a couple snuggling under a beach towel. They had just come out of the water, and the man was kissing the woman's face and tucking a strand of wet hair behind her ear. *Lovebirds*. She wondered how they'd met, how long they'd been together.

She didn't miss Peter. The truth was, they fell out of love long before he fell for Eve. They were little more than roommates toward the end, sort of like Jim and Camille. Peter was a dolt. Her friends and family had been telling her as much for years. She simply didn't want to be alone. The more space she had from him now, the easier it was to see that.

Working up a sweat felt fantastic. Lucinda had forgotten how much she missed her daily walks. *Maybe being on my own for a while is a good thing,* she thought, *but then again, maybe I was alone long enough during those miserable, lonely years with Peter.* She picked up the pace, sucked in her tummy, and fell into a light jog. Cher belted out the million-dollar question through Lucinda's earbuds. "Do you believe in life after love?" She smiled, shrugged, and thought the question was at least worth considering.

Chapter 15

Turtle Beach was filled with tourists much of the year, so Lucinda couldn't help but feel relieved that her family crisis occurred during the island's off-season. She needed some things at the market and found herself meandering up and down the aisles of Food Basket, comparing prices and listening to the oldies radio station playing over the sound system.

She saw a mother bargaining with a misbehaving toddler in the cereal aisle. She helped an elderly man reach a bottle of karo on the top shelf in another. She smiled, shook her head, and wondered what he was planning to do with the karo. In the bakery—which smelled of vanilla cookies and fresh strawberry—she watched two sisters arguing over whether to put their mother's face on her birthday cake. One sister said it was a beautiful tribute; the other argued it would serve as a reminder of how old their mother was when the frosted photo highlighted their mother's many wrinkles.

After forty-five minutes, Lucinda's cart was full, and her mind was empty for the first time in a week. It felt heavenly, like good medicine for a tired brain. She stood in line reading the ridiculous claims on magazine covers about how to lose fifty pounds in twelve days, and ten secrets to make men beg. *Beg for what?* She laughed, marveling at how gullible some women must be for tabloid rags such as these to stay in business.

While Lucinda was loading the back of Goldie's car with groceries, she looked around the parking lot and thought it strange that she hadn't run into any familiar faces. If people on Turtle Island didn't remember Lucinda, or had left to pursue dreams of their own, maybe it could offer her a fresh start. Perhaps she could reinvent herself like some of the celebrities she'd seen interviewed after their high-profile divorces?

The thought made her laugh again, and she got in the car and looked in the rearview mirror, imagining a radical new hairstyle or becoming a Botox Betty as Sharon called women who overfilled their laugh lines. She pulled all her hair back, piled it high on her head, and puckered her lips. "Reinvent myself," she said to her reflection. "Who do I want to be, anyway? Rita Hayworth?" She snapped the visor back in position and headed toward home.

Back at Goldie's, Lucinda spent hours putting together three casseroles and two stockpots of soup. She also made several dozen breakfast burritos. When Goldie came into the kitchen, carrying a purple yoga mat, she stopped dead in her tracks. "Who died?" she said, filling her water bottle. Lucinda asked what her mother was talking about, and she replied that the only explanation for the volume of food on the center island was that someone must've died. "I'm making meals to freeze, Mother," Lucinda replied drily, separating the burritos into piles and labeling them. "If you don't like spicy food, steer clear of the ones with the orange stickers, okay, Mom?"

"We don't really eat all that heavy food down here, baby," Goldie said, chugging her water. "It's too hot. Surely you haven't been away so long that you've forgotten?"

Lucinda looked around the kitchen at the spilled pasta, the congealed bacon grease on the griddle, and the thin layer of flour, coating everything like a dusting of fresh snow. She sat down on a kitchen chair and buried her face in her hands. Goldie poured Lucinda a cup of blood orange tea, sat beside her, and sighed. What's going on, honey?" she said softly.

"I'm scared, Mom."

"Of what?"

"Are you kidding? Of the business crumbling. Of being alone. Of getting old. Where do I begin?"

Goldie stood up and started rinsing spatulas and frying pans in the sink. She turned on the radio, tuned it to something upbeat, and told Lucinda that if she took on all those things at once, she'd implode. She said it was best to take things one day at a time. "We're all here, alive and kicking, aren't we?" she asked Lucinda. Lucinda nodded, wiped her eyes with a napkin, and rested her cheek on her palm.

Goldie said nothing else. She loaded the dishwasher, sang along to Elton John on the clock radio, using a wooden spoon as a microphone, and acted as though the conversation was complete. Lucinda watched her mother clean up the mess she'd made and wished she had a giant sponge she could use to mop up the mess her life had become.

Finally, after Goldie threw a fresh rag in Lucinda's direction, she peeled herself off the kitchen chair, and took her mother's lead. She began cleaning up the cooking mess, gathering eggshells and apple cores and coffee grinds into paper towels, and tossing them into the trash. She wiped off the countertops and snapped lids onto freezer dishes, admitting to herself that cleaning up was somewhat cathartic.

Soon, she was dancing in the kitchen with her mother like they'd done when she was a little girl. Lucinda watched Goldie do a botched version of the Macarena dance and shook her head in awe of her mother's upbeat attitude.

Could it be as simple as Goldie was always saying? That living in the moment—giving all your focus to the task at hand—was the key to contentment? She tried focusing on one thing for the time being, which wasn't hard to do since the egg whites were so dried on the counter that she needed a chisel to pry them loose. After a while, she looked up and said, "What are we going to do with all this food now? Should we still freeze it?" Goldie shook her head and told Lucinda to take it to Harry Beechwell across the road.

She said his wife died a few weeks earlier and that by now, all the old bitties on Turtle Beach would have stopped taking him food, and he may be fixing to starve. "I can't take all this over myself," Goldie sighed. "Good Lord, he'll propose on the spot! Harry's nice and all, but I don't want 'em."

When they were finished, Lucinda went into the bathroom to tidy up for the day. Changing into clean clothes, she stood before the full-length mirror on the bathroom door and examined her figure. In truth, she knew she was considered a standard American size for a woman, especially a woman pushing fifty. Still, she knew that putting on a nice dress or shorts would produce the level of dread usually reserved for major dental procedures.

Now that she was facing the possibility of reentering the dating world, she couldn't help but wonder what it would be like for a man to hold her close, run his hands along her bare skin. Would she enjoy it, or instead be petrified that he'd linger a little too long on a dimple or surgical scar?

Back in her bedroom, she was gathering a few things when Jill texted. She had some ideas about the new website. She sent a link that only she and Lucinda could see since the site was in maintenance mode. Everything looked good. It would really shine once Lucinda sent Jill the pictures of the freshly painted bungalows, the paddle boards lined up behind the office building, and, of course, the row of white beach chairs and pink umbrellas dotting the shoreline.

Jill had tabs on the site for entertainment, pricing, and an availability calendar. She even had an "About Us" section that showed a picture of Tom and Goldie standing next to the gigantic pink octopus statue they'd had custom made by an artist friend on the mainland. Lucinda texted Goldie and asked if she still had the name of the artist who created the statue, suggesting he could revitalize *it*, too, for the relaunch. Goldie replied that Mackenzie Mackenzie was hard to reach when he was alive, so good luck now that he was dead. She told her she'd have to ask his son, Mack 3, to recondition the statue.

Lucinda: Please don't tell me the son's name is Mackenzie Mackenzie Mackenzie?

Goldie: Boy, living in Connecticut has made you a real snob.

Lucinda: Mackenzie Mackenzie Mackenzie???

Goldie: He's a nice boy, Lucinda! I'll text you a link to their website. Get off your high horse and call him.

Lucinda texted Jill and said she would take the pictures some evening in the next few days after the beach chairs and umbrellas arrived. She'd found an amateur photography channel online that said early evening was the optimal time for taking outdoor pictures, something about there being fewer shadows.

Jill suggested Lucinda photograph a few guests, even their profiles or backs, to show people enjoying the amenities. Lucinda had cleared the puny reservations schedule for the next few weeks to get things decorated and organized, so she'd have to be creative if she were going to include people in the shots. She didn't think it would be hard getting Goldie to agree to lying on a beach chair sipping a daiquiri, though.

After finishing the chat with Jill, Lucinda tucked in her blouse, adjusted her collar, and went back into the bathroom to stand before the mirror. "I'm not tragic," she whispered to herself. "What I need is a little exercise, a lot more water, and maybe a good old-fashioned makeover." She knew just who to ask for help.

Chapter 16

Sharon was sitting on the sofa in the office, talking to someone on her cell phone. Lucinda busied herself at the front desk, drawing up a mock entertainment schedule. She wondered if six a.m. was too early for Goldie to teach the yoga classes. She knew her mother was an early riser, but didn't know if guests would show up at that time of the morning for a workout, particularly while on vacation.

Sharon's call was taking longer than Lucinda had anticipated, so she got on the computer and searched for used shuttle buses. She thought it would be a huge selling point for the business if guests were offered pickup service at Turtle Beach Port, where all visitors to Emerald Isle were dropped off after ferrying from Pelican Harbor. They had to take a taxi or rideshare from Turtle Beach Port to their lodging or shopping destinations. Unfortunately, many of these companies gouged terribly for the short rides, and yet it was just a bit too far to walk.

Turtle Island was essentially three separate islands: Pelican Harbor, Angel Shores, and Emerald Isle, where Turtle Beach was located. All travelers arrived via puddle jumper from the mainland, getting dropped off at the welcome center on Pelican Harbor. Before the mainland, they flew in from all over the world, each traveler touching down on Turtle Island for a very specific purpose. There were the Spring Breakers headed for Saltwater Reef, the families looking for a kid-friendly tropical vacation on Turtle Beach, and the spa-seekers escaping to Angel Shores for R & R, a writers' retreat, or sometimes celebrity rehab.

Taxis and rideshares across all three islands cost travelers a fortune, something that didn't necessarily hurt The Pink Octopus, but didn't make for happy check-in guests. By the time they'd taken multiple planes, a ferry, and an outrageously expensive taxi, they were disgusted and drained when they arrived to check-in.

Lucinda figured if The Pink Octopus could offer free shuttle service, it would be a massive feather in their cap. Tourists would appreciate the savings, which could easily amount to hundreds of dollars by the end of the trip.

Lucinda found a decent-looking shuttle bus for sale on Jellyfish Bay that would mean trimming another area of the business's budget to afford it but would pay off in positive reviews. She emailed the seller, who responded right away and invited her to drop by around seven p.m. for a test drive.

Since Sharon was still on the phone, Lucinda stepped outside and looked for Jim in hopes of roping him into accompanying her to check out the shuttle. She didn't want to meet a stranger alone and risk the possibility of ending up the subject of a true crime podcast. The thought of search crews finding her rotting corpse in the back of the shuttle on a back country road made her cringe.

She shuddered at the thought of poor Jill and Frankie hearing the gruesome details of their mother's demise and instantly thought of Camille. Crazy or not, Camille probably didn't deserve whatever heinous thing happened to her. Her children would never be the same once the truth was revealed. It was all too much to think about.

Jim was out front planting flowers around the perimeter of the office building. "Hey, how's it going?" she asked.

"Good, but I'm getting hungry."

"How do you feel about casseroles?"

"Goldie told me you cooked enough to feed an entire Navy fleet."

"Isn't 'Navy' a forbidden word in your vocabulary? I thought the Army and Navy hated each other?"

"You watch too much TV."

"Well, anyway, if you accompany me to Jellyfish Bay tonight, I'll pay you in Cowboy Casserole."

"Don't know what that is, but it sounds intriguing. You're on!"

Jellyfish Bay was only a ten-minute drive from Goldie's house, and Lucinda could drive it in her sleep. However, she was thrilled that Jim would be with her while she test drove the vehicle. The more she thought about the hundred ways something like an online meet-up with a stranger could go south, the more she thanked Jim for tagging along.

When he asked why they were headed to Jellyfish Bay, Lucinda told him about the shuttle bus. He asked who was going to drive it once she bought it? "I'll hire a driver," she said. "I'll have to squeeze it into the budget like I do with everything else, I guess."

Sharon opened the door to the office and yelled out to Lucinda, asking her why she'd been lurking in the office like she needed something while she was on the phone with Matt. Lucinda felt like her mother when she clasped her hands to her chest and said, "Matt? Really?" Sharon blushed and said to take a chill pill.

She asked again what Lucinda wanted, and Lucinda held up a finger for her sister to wait. "Bye, Jim," she said, hopping up the steps and pulling Sharon back inside the office building. "See you tonight!"

Lucinda confided in Sharon, saying she wanted to re-vamp her look. Sharon laughed, and Lucinda punched her lightly in the arm. "Sorry, continue," Sharon said, "and don't hit the differently-abled girl." Lucinda rolled her eyes and leaned on the counter. She tapped excitedly on the Formica and explained that she didn't hate her appearance, but admitted it was probably time for a makeover. Sharon laughed and said Lucinda had been doing an awful lot of "revamping" lately.

After thinking it over, Sharon grabbed her car keys and said, "You know what? I'm always up for a makeover montage!"

They went to Alice's Closet first. Lucinda had never heard of it, but Sharon said it was considered fashion for mature women. She used her fingers to put air quotes around the word *mature*. Lucinda rolled her eyes and said, "How did this happen? Yesterday, we were making out with boys at Rocky Point, and now we're 'mature.'"

"Who did you make out with at Rocky Point? You said 'boys,' plural?"

"Focus, Shaz! I need a new look!"

"Jim will be pleased."

"I'm so not doing this for Jim."

"Uh huh. Keep telling yourself that, sis."

After a few minutes of browsing, Sharon's legs started wobbling so she sat in an overstuffed chair and watched her sister try on outfits, feeling like they'd stepped into the part of the romcom where the divorcee picks herself back up to start a brand-new life. She smiled, happy for her sister.

It was hard not to think about Alan, though. Sharon and Alan didn't have nearly the perfect marriage everyone thought they did. After he died, she didn't see any reason to set the record straight, figuring she'd allow her family and friends to keep Alan on his saint-like pedestal. Still, she missed their easy routine. Missed having someone take out the trash and bring her flowers on her birthday. Though she dated now, it wasn't anywhere near the same as what she and Alan shared. Seeing Lucinda hopeful about starting over got Sharon's wheels turning, too. Maybe she'd build a new life, too. Someday.

Lucinda decided on neutral colors but promised Sharon she'd experiment with daring nail polish shades to offset the safe wardrobe palette.

The last time Lucinda came out of the dressing room, she saw Sharon wiping her forehead with a tissue. She was sweating, but the store was air-conditioned. Lucinda knelt beside her and asked if she needed anything. Sharon waved her off and said, "I need you to buy one sexy dress. Something that shows you have a waist somewhere under all those clothes."

"Sharon..."

"Come on! I'm serious. We're not leaving until you get a date night dress."

"I don't have a date, though."

"If you build it, they will come, right?"

"You're quoting a Kevin Costner movie now? Is this what my love life has become, a baseball metaphor?"

Seeing that her sister wasn't going to back down, Lucinda grabbed a black dress off the rack, and threw it on. The fabric was silky and felt cool against her skin. She gave herself a once-over in the mirror and went back out to get Sharon's critique. When Sharon applauded, Lucinda knew it was the one. She gathered her new findings and headed for the cash register.

Lucinda offered to drive on the way home, fearing Sharon's legs would go numb and they'd have an accident. They'd planned to go to a few more stores, pick up some jewelry, perhaps a new signature fragrance, but Lucinda faked a headache so Sharon wouldn't feel bad for cutting the trip short.

They said little on the drive back, and Lucinda was thankful for the Motown radio station she'd found when they got into the car. She drove along the main roads, across the bridge, and back home, stealing glimpses of her sister when she could get away with it. Sharon was staring out the passenger window, her head on the glass, impossible to read.

When they pulled into the parking lot, Lucinda turned the car off and handed the keys to Sharon, who shook her head and wouldn't take them. She pushed Lucinda's hand away, saying, "I've been thinking." Her voice cracked on the last word, and she busied herself digging through her purse, pretending to look for something. She cleared her throat and said, "You need a car, so I'm giving you mine."

"What? I would never take your car. Get real!"

"No, really, I insist."

"What would *you* drive? How would you get around?"

Sharon looked at her hands, folded on her lap. She paused for a long moment, trying to work up the courage to speak. Finally, she cocked her head, looked into Lucinda's eyes, and said, "Who are we kidding?" She continued, explaining that the reason she was staring at her hands so much was to remind herself that they were still there because she kept losing feeling in them. She said she hadn't felt like a safe driver in a while, and now that she was living with Goldie, there'd be no reason to keep putting herself behind the wheel.

When Lucinda protested, Sharon reiterated she was trying to give her sister a gift. "So, would you please just let me, Lucinda?" she said, her lip quivering. "Spare me a shred of dignity?" With that, she managed a giggle, but it was obvious by the tears welling up in her eyes that the whole thing was excruciating. Lucinda pressed her lips together, racked her brain for a fitting response, and settled on, "You're a real mess, you know that?"

Sharon's head quickly pivoted to see her sister's face, and when she noticed Lucinda fighting back a laugh, she couldn't help but feel relief. Then tears. Then they both cried. Not only about Sharon's MS, but about the business, Alan dying, Peter leaving, Eve turning out to be the world's worst friend, Camille possibly being stuffed in a duffel bag somewhere...lots of things. Though neither of them said a word, they both sobbed, staring at their family business, the chipped sign, faded octopus sculpture, and a future that was entirely uncertain.

Finally, Sharon interrupted the crying jag when she said, "That damn octopus statue looks like crap." Lucinda sniffed, straightened up, and took a deep breath. *This*, she could control, if nothing else. "Mack 3 is picking it up tomorrow afternoon to restore it. The octopus is getting a makeover, too!"

"Who or what is Mack 3?" Sharon said, laughing and reaching into the glovebox for more tissues.

Chapter 17

Jim knocked on Goldie's front door at six o'clock. When she answered, the first thing she said is, "Well, you clean up nicely!" Jim blushed, thanked her for the compliment, and began nervously cracking his knuckles when Goldie inquired about his cologne. "That's what a man *should* smell like, Lucinda," she said, leaning into Jim's shoulder for a closer whiff. "Come smell him, honey!" Lucinda groaned, kissed her mother's cheek, and ushered Jim outside, apologizing all the way to his truck.

On the way to Jellyfish Bay, Lucinda thanked him for going with her on short notice. Jim shrugged, saying he didn't have much of a social life on the island, and was happy to get out for a bit. She shrugged and asked what a social life was. "Saturday night and we're going used-vehicle shopping. Aren't we a couple of wild and crazy kids?" he joked, tuning the radio.

After a few minutes, Lucinda cleared her throat and said, "I called Savannah. She's a really nice girl, Jim." Never taking his eyes off the road, Jim drove in silence. Lucinda scrambled to fill the dead space between them, rambling about weather, her dead dog, Area 51, and anything else to defuse the awkwardness that resulted from mentioning Savannah.

When she paused for Jim to interject but he remained quiet, she kept right on talking. She recounted the day Peter stood outside the shower while she shaved her legs, and casually admitted to falling in love with someone else. Lucinda had confronted him on the phone, saying she found Eve's disgusting email, and pieced together a timeline of their affair—which she estimated to be at least a year long. Peter got home from work a few hours later and caught Lucinda in the shower after she'd gone on a five-mile walk to clear her head. He spoke to her through the steamy shower glass. "I don't know what to say, Lucinda. We're in love."

Lucinda spoke softly, recounting the horrible incident to Jim. "I lost a good friend, a sister-in-law, and a husband in one fell swoop," she whispered, cleaning her sunglasses with a Microfiber cloth. "He never even apologized. It should've killed me, but it didn't. Somehow, I'm still here to tell the tale."

"Did the woman—your sister-in-law—apologize?" Jim finally asked, breaking the painful silence.

"Not really. I mean, she sent me an email explaining that she didn't plan it, that it just *happened*. People always say that. She said she was sorry, but that she needed to allow herself to be happy for once...whatever that means." Jim shook his head and mumbled something about life eventually kicking your behind if you live past the age of twelve.

When the navigation system said they'd arrived at their destination, Lucinda let out a long sigh. She figured Jim was mad at her for meddling, but all she wanted to do was help. He cut the engine and turned to face her. "I can't believe you called my daughter," he said, shaking his head.

"I'm sorry," Lucinda cried. "But..."

He held his hand up. "That was real nice of you, Lucinda. Thank you." He rested his hand on the back of hers, and she smiled. His palm was calloused from all the painting, but his skin was warm, comforting. He opened his mouth to say something, but someone playfully tapped a horn several times in a row, almost as though greeting them. They looked up and saw a young man hanging out the driver's side of the shuttle bus they'd come to see. He was smiling and waving. "We better go," Lucinda said.

Blaze was a twenty-something young man with a lengthy pink scar down his right cheek and greasy, unkempt hair. He looked like he'd seen a lot for his age, and yet somehow retained his boyishness. Blaze was selling the bus, which he referred to as "Marla," for his grandpa who went into a nursing home and had to give up his shuttle business. It had eighty-thousand miles on it, but Jim said that for the make and model of the bus, that wasn't bad. Blaze suggested they take the bus for a test drive, and Lucinda, intimidated, motioned for Jim to get behind the wheel.

It was a smooth ride, and Blaze sat in the back seat and told them all about his Grandpa Dale, and how he'd run the shuttle business for twenty-five years after serving in the Marines during two wars. Dale had worked right up until the stroke. "Grandpa made a good living off the business," he said. "Enough money to haul my ass out of trouble a time or two, if you'll excuse the language."

"You didn't want to take over the business?" Lucinda asked.

"Oh, I made some bad decisions a while back," he said sheepishly, "and I don't currently have a driver's license to speak of."

Lucinda looked at Jim, who sucked in his cheeks to keep from laughing. Blaze picked awkwardly at a spot of acne on his chin, apparently embarrassed about his admission. She nodded, and changed the subject, trying to spare the boy further humiliation. When they got back to Grandpa Dale's house, Lucinda asked Blaze for a moment of privacy to speak with Jim. He agreed and went into the house to fetch the extra set of keys. "What do you think?" Lucinda asked Jim.

"It's a fair price. It looks like it's in good shape, and he's providing records for the last inspection report and oil change. I think it's the best deal you're going to find."

"Would you be willing to drive it home if I say yes?"

"Sure. You'll have to drive my truck. I'd ask if you know how to drive a stick, but I'm the one who taught you."

"On your dad's old Buick!"

"You remember," he said, running his hands through his hair and smiling.

When Blaze returned, he handed Jim and Lucinda each a cold bottle of water. Lucinda asked if cash was all right, and Blaze's eyes lit up. "Cash works for me!" he said, enthusiastically. They drove to the local notary to transfer the title, and afterward, Lucinda told Blaze she hoped his luck would turn around.

She agreed to meet Jim at home, and he asked if he could take the shuttle to his cousin's place to let him look under the hood first. "I didn't know Lenny still lives on the island!" Lucinda gasped.

"Yep, still here. Still married to Rita."

"OK, sure. I'll see you at home then. Tell them I said hello."

"I should be back in a couple of hours."

Lucinda drove Jim's truck back to Turtle Beach, which she determined was only marginally less intimidating than it would have been to drive the shuttle bus. She hadn't driven a stick in decades.

She pulled into the driveway and saw Ben sitting on their mother's porch steps. He asked what she was doing driving Jim's truck, and when she told him about the shuttle, he buried his face in his hands. "Please don't ask me to drive guests around the island."

Lucinda set down her bags and took a seat next to her brother, who chided her for smelling like cologne. "Benny," she said seriously, "what would make you truly happy?" He backed up, furrowed his brow, and said, "Get serious!"

"I've only been here a while, Ben," she said, nudging him with her shoulder, "but I can tell you're unhappy. What would it take to change that?"

Ben made a joke about anything that involved him not smelling like fish every day would help immensely. He kissed the top of Lucinda's head and got in his car. He rolled down the window and said, "Don't forget you owe JoJo a bath! That would make us both happy!"

Lucinda waved goodbye to her brother and wondered to herself why so many men insisted on naming their cars. Ben, Blaze...she looked at Jim's truck and wondered if he had a name for it. Maybe something like Brandy or Autumn? She laughed to herself and made a mental note to ask him about it.

A few hours later, Sharon got back from a walk on the beach. "Jim says we have a new addition to The Pink Octopus," she said, dangling a set of car keys. I just ran into him outside. Goldie looked out the window at the shuttle and shrieked. Lucinda told her to calm down, explaining the high return they could get from having a shuttle service. "Besides," she said, folding a load of fresh towels, "I think we're the only place on all of Turtle Island that doesn't offer shuttle service, Mom. We needed to get on board."

Tasking Goldie with placing an ad in the newspaper for a driver, Lucinda winked at Sharon. Goldie agreed to place the ad the next day. For now, she went back to her game show on the television, muttering something about the finances going in the wrong direction.

Jim unlocked his bungalow and was taken aback when he saw a casserole on the table, a battery-operated candle, and one place setting. He picked up a card that read, "Thanks for all you've been doing for us lately. Enjoy your dinner. Two minutes per slice in the microwave should do the trick."

He heated his food according to Lucinda's instructions, sat down at the table, and ran his finger over her handwriting. It was exactly as he remembered it.

The cowboy casserole was delicious. It had been a long time since Jim had tasted home cooking. The whole scene—quiet cottage, pretty table setting, savory meal—seemed almost perfect. His mouth twisted into a melancholy grin. He shrugged and took another bite, loving the combination of barbeque, garlic, and cheddar. *Per-*

fect, he thought, chewing his food, *would be if she had set two place settings.*

Chapter 18

Lucinda was poring over her business plans the next night when she couldn't sleep. She was at the kitchen table, and it was nearly midnight when she got a text message from Frankie. Her son was notorious for sending late-night texts, often well after Lucinda was asleep for the night. She often wondered if he did it to avoid a two-way conversation.

He said he'd closed on a big real estate deal, started a new workout plan, and was doing all right. It seemed to be little more than a pleasant wellness check. He asked Lucinda when she was returning to Connecticut, which twisted her stomach in knots. She wasn't sure he'd take the news well that she sold the family home to Peter and might not be returning to New England at all.

As always, it was easy enough to distract Frankie, who was always multi-tasking during their chats. She asked if he'd seen the latest interview with Jeff Bezos online, to which he scoffed and went into a long diatribe about all the reasons Amazon is not really a monopoly like the media tries to portray it. Her return plans to Connecticut never came up again before they ended the call.

As Lucinda sent back a few surface-level texts—too tired to get into all the details of her situation—her heart ached for the days of Frank being a little boy. She remembered a time when he couldn't wait to get off the school bus and fill her in on every detail of his day. Now she was lucky to get a phone call once a month, and even then, he kept things mostly superficial.

When she heard a noise outside, Lucinda looked out the window and saw Jim getting something out of his truck. They hadn't seen each other all day. He was gone for most of the day again, and she couldn't help but wonder about where he was always disappearing.

She tapped on the glass and waved. He waved back, and she motioned for him to come over. She wrapped a blanket around her shoulders and stepped onto the porch.

They sat down, and Jim thanked her for the previous night's dinner and asked why she was still up. "I was working on the business plan," she said, shrugging. "Trying to give us the best chance at hanging onto this place."

"How's things looking?"

"We'll see," she said, pursing her lips.

"I remember when your dad used to have the ponies for guests to ride along the shore," Jim said, staring at the old stable behind the office building.

"Star and Galaxy," Lucinda smiled. "Funny, I was just thinking about them, too."

"I remember that year your mom had a tiny carnival on the beach. You threw up on the Ferris wheel and it spilled onto Jerry Orwell's head. That was a gas!"

"Wow, you seem to remember a lot."

"I remember *you*," he said, his eyes reflecting the moon.

Lucinda made an excuse about getting some sleep to be up in time for an interview with a band. Jim felt foolish and wondered if Lucinda was nervous around him because his wife was missing. She patted his shoulder and told him to get a good night's rest. "Lots to still do around here!" she said, her eyebrows dancing.

Jim nodded, waved goodnight, and stared up at the black sky long after Lucinda disappeared inside the house.

While she was washing her face to get ready for bed, she wondered if her reluctance to get closer to Jim was because somewhere, on some deep, subconscious level, she had reservations about what really happened to Camille. It certainly wasn't because she hoped to win Peter back. If anything, the time apart continued to shed light on what a disappointing husband he had been throughout their entire marriage.

She shook her head in the reflection. Jim would never hurt anyone. She concluded that the issue was she didn't know if she was ready to dive into another relationship. All she'd known in her romantic past was Jim and Peter. Neither union worked out. She thought maybe it was time to consider her options, even if it meant being alone for a season.

She sat on the cot and made a list of things she needed to do before getting into a serious relationship again. She added things such as getting her teeth whitened, coloring her hair, and starting to journal. She'd heard it was therapeutic, and she thought it would do her good to weed through her feelings about the divorce and the kids growing up and getting their own lives.

Finally, she added one thing to the list before turning out the light. She wrote *Go on a couple of dates with people who didn't witness me throwing up on Jerry Orwell.*

Lucinda folded the paper, hid it between the pages of the tattered mystery novel someone had forgotten on a plastic seat at LaGuardia Airport, and turned out the light. She fell asleep smiling, only allowing a minute or two of worry over the possibility of her dying in her sleep and Jill or Frankie discovering her embarrassing *New Me* list.

The next afternoon, three bands were set to audition for the staff entertainment position at The Pink Octopus. Lucinda enlisted Sharon, Ben, Jim, and Goldie to give their opinions. Goldie made jugs of tea, and Sal showed up unexpectedly with two dozen donuts, so they invited him to stay and take a vote on the bands as well. Looking for any excuse to be in close proximity to Goldie, Sal happily obliged.

As the first band was unloading their equipment and setting up, Goldie thanked Jim for what he was doing around the property. "We like having you back around, Jimmy," she gushed, pushing the box of donuts in his direction. He smiled, nodded, and said he was happy to be back, to be a part of the business's metamorphosis.

Lucinda smiled, and looked at the office building, visualizing it restored to its former glory. The siding was going to cost a fortune to replace, so she planned to power wash it instead, add new shutters, and overstuff the perimeter with lots of lush hydrangea bushes. When it was finished, it would be good as new. *Almost*. And maybe almost was good enough, especially compared to foreclosure.

After hearing the bands, the consensus was that they were all good, which made Lucinda bristle. "Of course they are good. Otherwise, why would I have auditioned them?"

Everyone nibbled on donuts and listed the pros and cons of each band. They had lively debates over the uncanny resemblance of one guitarist to Steve Buscemi, and whether the drummer of another band was silently flirting with Sharon.

Lucinda finally put it to a vote. Goldie liked Golden Oldies, a barbershop quartet that incorporated modern songs in a humorous way. Sharon liked Cheeseballs in Paradise, a (mostly) Jimmy Buffett tribute band who infused stand-up comedy between numbers. Ben liked Hair Me Out—an 80s tribute band—which surprised no one. Sal and Lucinda thought for a while and agreed with Sharon that the Jimmy Buffet numbers were funny and would encourage a lot of audience interaction. "What do you think, Jim?" Goldie asked.

"I'm just visiting. I better leave the big decisions up to you Perrys," he said.

"Come on!" Ben said, throwing a hunk of powdered sugar donut at him.

"Look, no one loves the 80s more than me," he told Ben, "But, if we're going with what the guests would like best? I'm going to go with the Buffett dudes."

"I take it back," Ben huffed. "Jim shouldn't have a say."

Lucinda laughed, and ultimately agreed with Jim, citing that most of the tourists were from places that didn't have beaches nearby. They saved up all year to go someplace tropical, and part of the fantasy that got them through the long months of saving and enduring gray winters, she said, was the idea that everyone on the island wore tropical shirts and conducted their lives with the sound of steel drums playing in the background. "And saying things like, 'Yeah mon,'" Sharon added.

"And everyone lies in the sun all day but never gets burned," Sal joked.

"And all the beaches have lifeguards who wear red bathing suits and look like Pam Anderson!" Ben cried.

"You wish!" Lucinda groaned, rolling her eyes at him.

"I have one," Goldie interjected, clinking her glass of tea with a pen.

"A red Pam Anderson bathing suit?" Ben cringed. "The image is burning my eyes, Ma!"

"A falsehood about island life, smart mouth!" Goldie shot Ben a threatening glance and continued. "If you don't show up on the island in love, you'll leave having found your soulmate!"

Ben mouthed the word *falsehood*, snickering. Lucinda looked at Jim, who was smiling brightly and staring at her. She cleared her throat, stood up and announced the decision was made. She'd call Cheeseballs in Paradise and ask if they could start in three weeks—on the condition that they include some eighties and nineties songs for Ben. Plus, it might be nice to add a little variety rather than pigeon-holing the music by only playing Jimmy Buffet—as beloved as his music was.

Goldie asked if she should get working on invitations for the "relaunch-slash-Grandma Helen's birthday," but Lucinda suggested they think bigger. She said they could hang flyers all over Turtle Island and asked Goldie if she'd scheduled the news piece.

Goldie nodded, told Lucinda the date and time the WTIX news crews were visiting to begin interviews. "They're going to break the segment into three," Goldie explained, "airing the last part live at the relaunch in front of the whole crowd."

Ben suggested that rather than catering, they invite all the island food trucks to the party and ask them to offer a limited free menu to guests. When Goldie asked why they'd agree to something like that, Ben suggested the exposure would more than makeup for the cost. "Yeah," Sal agreed. "They'll get to look philanthropic, but in exchange probably see a three-hundred percent increase in revenue when the busy season hits."

Lucinda admitted she hadn't thought of that and was nodded enthusiastically at Sal's business savvy. "It beats us having to pay thousands for catering," she said, looking to Goldie. "What do you think, Mom?" Goldie snorted, held up her iced tea as if toasting the idea, and said it was the first time she'd heard any talk of saving money since Lucinda had arrived on the island.

Ben high-fived everyone, said he thought they'd all made significant progress, and excused himself to tend to his online dating profile. Apparently, he'd had enough of the single life. "I'm lonely," he scoffed. "Someone as handsome as me should never be lonely."

"Fawn only dumped you two days ago, Ben!" Sharon said.

"That's more than I've ever gone without a steady lady," he said, putting an ice cube down the back of Sharon's shirt. "I told you, I'm too hot to be alone! Ask Mom!"

Making their way inside, Goldie excused herself to go to an evening church service. Sharon took a cup of tea and headed for her bedroom to FaceTime with Kelly in Boston.

When it was just the two of them in the kitchen, Jim fidgeted with a potholder, sticking his finger through the loop, and swinging it in circles. Lucinda raised an eyebrow, and he set it back on the counter, taking a deep breath. "Can we talk?" he finally asked.

Chapter 19

Lucinda and Jim walked along the shoreline, neither wanting to be the first to speak even though it was Jim who initiated the conversation. Every so often, he would pick up a smooth stone and skip it in the water.

Finally, he cleared his throat, and said that he wondered if Lucinda had ever thought about giving him a second chance. She smiled, touched by his shyness, and replied that he wasn't the one who screwed up and needed forgiveness. "You were wonderful back then, Jim," she said, nudging his shoulder. "You still are. You can rest easy knowing I think very highly of you."

"Oh no," he said, running his hands through his hair. "Please don't say, 'It's not you, it's me.'"

"No, I wasn't going to say that."

"Then, what is it? Are you still hoping to reconcile with Peter?"

"A thousand percent no. Not in this lifetime or the next."

"Is it the situation with my ex?"

"No, it's none of those things. It's me."

Jim threw his hands up and grabbed the sides of his head, groaning. "No, listen," she said, pulling his hands down. "I went from living under my parents' roof and dating you, to marrying Peter and raising kids. Now I'm back under Mom's roof and sleeping on a squeaky cot in her spare room that's not even a bedroom. I seriously think the mattress is stuffed with steel wool or possibly horsehair—something incredibly prickly. Nothing makes sense right now."

"So, you need some time to figure out what you want?"

"Well, yeah," she said, squinting into the sun, "and who I *am*. I look at myself and see a middle-aged, tired version of who I once was. And let's face it—nobody wants to date Frumpy Mommy."

"I'd give 'er a go," he said, chuckling.

Lucinda smacked his arm, and told him to get serious. She quickly changed the subject, not in the mood for compliments.

She asked Jim if he needed to run errands or shower before they started painting the second coat on the lobby. He sighed and said he'd meet her back at the lobby in an hour after he'd walked a bit on his own. Lucinda nodded, said goodbye.

She started up to the house to change clothes but stopped partway there. She turned back to Jim and asked if he had a name for his truck, immediately feeling silly mentioning it. He nodded, told her it was Dolly, and she doubled over in laughter. *Men are toddlers*, she thought. *Naming their cars like little ones naming a toy*.

She waved and headed back home. Jim called out and asked where she was going, and she rolled her eyes. Throwing her hands up as if surrendering, she yelled back that she was making good on a bet.

At her mother's kitchen sink, Lucinda filled a bucket and took it outside where Ben had parked his car. She began washing it and got to the tires when someone whistled. She stood up and saw Ben leaning against a beam on the porch of the office building. "Looking good sis," he chided.

Ben wasn't alone, and Lucinda ignored him, not wanting to be introduced to someone new when she was covered in soap suds and her shirt very well might have been see-through. Ben walked down to the car, along with his buddy, and said, "Scott, meet my sister. Told you she was hot."

"Ben, knock it off," she hissed, pretending she was going to hose him down with cold water.

The man extended his hand and shook Lucinda's, saying he was Scott Turner and had known the family for years. "Well, all except the mysterious sister that flew the coop," he said, playfully. "You're quite the legend around here. Almost like a unicorn."

"No, like Hercules," Ben said.

Turtle Island had a legend akin to the Loch Ness Monster, but on a much smaller scale. Depending on which islander a visitor asked, Hercules—the supposedly whale-sized sea turtle—was everything from a magician to a prophet to the ruler of an underwater kingdom off Turtle Beach...a land so magnificent that it rivaled Atlantis.

Lucinda rolled her eyes and sighed, blowing a strand of hair out of her face. Scott had short, salt-and-pepper hair and working hands. When he smiled, he had a cheek dimple and put off the vibes of a mischievous boy keeping a secret. "How do you two know each other?" she asked.

"We met about seven years ago, right bro?" Scott said to Ben.

"Maybe even eight," Ben replied.

"We were on the water," Scott said, "I run charter for my uncle's motel on Saltwater Reef, so we'd run into each other pretty often. Finally, we decided to start running into each other on purpose at Clive's, where I mop the floor with him at pool."

"Hey, I never said I was good at pool," Ben said, punching Scott's arm. "I only befriended you to get to your sister."

"Yeah, too bad Claire went and married Doug, huh?"

"I'll wait for her," Ben joked. "However long it takes for her to come to her senses."

Lucinda chatted for a while, and thought Scott seemed like a nice guy. He was a few years her junior, and she wondered what Sharon would think if she witnessed them talking, especially after how much Lucinda joked about her dating Ian.

Despite being younger, Scott liked *The Brady Bunch* over *The Partridge Family*, agreed that Jell-O shouldn't have discontinued Pudding Pops, and sided with Lucinda that David Lee Roth made the better front man for Van Halen over Sammy Hagar. When there was a break in the conversation, Lucinda excused herself to change so she could get to painting the second coat in the lobby.

She locked her bedroom door and dialed Jim's son, Max. He answered with, "This is Max," and Lucinda immediately wondered which of Max and Savannah's parents taught them to answer the phone that way. Something about their similar greeting made Jim's kids more real to her, though she couldn't articulate how or why. It was as if she could tell they were related without ever having met them in person.

Lucinda introduced herself as a friend of Max's father, and asked if he had a moment to chat. Max asked if his dad was all right, and Lucinda immediately assured him he was. Once he knew Jim was okay, Max stiffened up. "How can I help you, Miss Perry?"

"You can call me Lucinda, and I wanted to let you know your dad's here—here being Turtle Beach—and that he misses you."

"Anything else?"

"I know it's none of my business, but your father's an old friend of mine. For what it's worth, I don't believe he would ever hurt anyone."

"Miss Perry–er, Lucinda–my dad knows I love him. But I can't go about business as usual until my mother's found. When he skipped town in the middle of the hunt for my mother, he kind of painted himself in the worst light."

Lucinda spoke for a few more minutes with Max, trying to explain that Jim wasn't hiding on Turtle Island, but rather helping old friends with their business. Max remained polite—if a little guarded—throughout the conversation but ended the call when an important business meeting was scheduled to begin. She worried Max thought she was a romantic partner meddling in his father's family affairs but didn't have time to clarify since Max had to run.

She sat on the edge of the cot and bit her lip. She felt terrible that Jim had to endure such an ordeal alone. She put on some dry clothes and went up to the office building to paint, figuring by now Jim had started without her.

When she dropped an earring, she knelt on the floor to check for it under the bed. Prying a box of photo albums loose from underneath the cot, she flipped through them and laughed at the outdated hairstyles she and her family had retired decades earlier.

Ben knocked on the door. He came in and said that Scott was asking if Lucinda was single. "I told him yes, but that you're desperate so he should act quickly before you run off with a carnie on Saltwater Reef."

"Lovely, Ben."

"Seriously, though," he said, sitting on the floor and grabbing a stack of photos, "He's into you. I personally think he needs his eyes examined, but whatever. You should go for it. Scott's a stand-up guy."

"If he's so wonderful, why's he single?"

"Couldn't he ask the same of you?"

"Touché."

A few minutes later, Lucinda joined Jim in the lobby and began painting. After an hour or so, Scott texted Lucinda. She climbed down from her ladder, leaned against the counter, and shook her head in disbelief over how quickly he was moving.

Scott: Hi, Lucinda. It's Scott, your brother's friend. I was wondering if you wanted to grab some dinner tomorrow night? We could go to Clam Palace, or to Clive's and shoot some pool? I'll go easy on u.

Lucinda looked at Jim, who was precision painting around the perimeter of the ceiling. She had no expectations with Scott but had read about the importance of casual dating after divorce. She forgot the exact theory, but it was something that alluded to not wasting good emotions on the first guy who came along. The advice was

to date around a bit, try a few men on for size, and figure
out what you really wanted before getting serious again.

Lucinda laughed to herself at that thought. *It makes
sense*, she reasoned. *If I'd have really known what I wanted
the first time, I never would've gotten stuck with a narcissist
like Peter.* She began texting Scott back, prepared to lean
into the quote she'd taped to her bathroom mirror years
earlier when she considered skydiving for her forty-fifth
birthday. It said, "Everything you want is on the other side
of fear."

Lucinda: Sure, why not? Does eight work for you?
Scott: I'll pick you up then!

Lucinda set her phone down on the counter and picked
up her paintbrush again, feeling proud of herself for stepping out of her comfort zone. Scott seemed to like emojis,
particularly smiley faces with sunglasses, which for some
reason amused her.

Jim observed her behavior and thought he recognized
the look as someone smitten. He hoped he was wrong,
especially since Lucinda had just told him she wasn't ready
to date a couple hours earlier.

As the evening continued, Lucinda began to worry.
Why *was* Scott still single? At least she'd married, settled
down for several decades, committed to one person until
he blew the relationship to pieces.

Either way, she figured she'd go through with it. It was
just dinner, not a trip to Tuscany. She'd play some pool,
have a few laughs, and be back in her prickly cot by ten.
No big deal. She could handle it. When she finished the
second coat on her side of the room, she sat down at the
counter, and texted Sharon.

Lucinda: You're not going to believe this...

Sharon: You'll love Scott. Not much going on upstairs, but he's smokin' hot!

Lucinda: How do you know about this already? I swear all anyone on the island needs is The Perry Gazette!

Sharon: Oh, relax! Most of the women on the island have cycled through Scott. He's the divorcee whisperer. It was only a matter of time till he got to you.

Lucinda: I'm going to be sick.

Sharon: Breathe. Go out and rip the Band-Aid off. Get yours, sister!

Lucinda rolled her eyes, stuffed her phone in her back pocket, and glanced at Jim, who was putting the lid back on a gallon of paint. He told her the walls needed to dry for a while between coats and asked if she wanted to grab dinner while they waited. She agreed and asked for an hour to clean herself up.

In her bedroom, Lucinda peeled off her clothes, and drew a bath.

Knowing she didn't stand a chance at solving the mystery of what happened to Camille Barnes that evening, she took solace in knowing she was quickly approaching resolve in her thriller novel.

She climbed into the tub, feeling a shiver of excitement as she cracked the yellowed paperback, its spine near collapse after being well-loved by someone in its former life. Everything but her face and right hand were immersed under the healing bubbles. "Chapter sixteen," she muttered aloud.

Detective Kat Greenleaf sips her Diet Coke, tapping the steering wheel to the beat of a cheerful song on the cruiser's radio. She vibrates with excitement over being part of her town's biggest unsolved murder case in its hundred- and

fifty-year history. She's been sent to follow up on an anony-
mous tip that might lead her a step closer to cracking the case
once and for all.

The tipster claimed that while he and his dachshund were
on an evening walk, they'd stumbled on a most gruesome
discovery near the Baptist church on Chicken Dinner Road.
"I was texting my ex-wife," the caller gasped. "I was telling
her in no uncertain terms that I'm not going to give her the
boat. I paid for that myself with my pizza delivery tips. You
know how awful it was to work all day as a plumber, only to
have to deliver pizzas right up till bedtime? She ain't gettin'
that boat, I tell you."

When Bev, the Bloomsbury P.D. dispatcher, tried reeling
the man in, he cleared his throat, took a deep breath and
continued. "Right," he said, trying to calm down. "Anyway,
we was caught up in a heated argument and I dropped the
leash for no more than a minute. Next thing I know, Pick-
le—that's my dog—is gnawing on something, really going
to town, you know? I went over to the firepit by the church
to take a closer look. Turns out, I think it's a human hand,
sticking right up from the ash pile!"

Bev relayed the message to Kat, who agreed to drive over
to the church and check out the lead, asking Bev to in-
struct the man to pry his hound off the corpse's finger. It
could be another prank. There'd been enough of them since
the last victim—twenty-six-year-old kindergarten teacher,
Piper Shields, was discovered hanging from a flagpole at
the elementary school. Suddenly, people were seeing dead
bodies everywhere. Kat never understood the public's need to
muddy the waters on an active murder investigation.

She pulls up to the church and is greeted by a portly man
wearing a bucket hat and holding a barking wiener dog.

She exits the cruiser, shakes the man's hand, and follows his finger—which is pointing to the potential crime scene. She points her flashlight at what appears to be a greyish human hand protruding from the mound of ashes, just as the tipster—who introduces himself as Gunther Dupree—described.

Trying to maintain decorum, Kat leads Mr. Dupree to the cruiser, where she asks him to wait inside with Pickle until they have a chance to dig up the rest of the victim and clear the scene.

Relieved that she's probably located the missing Candy Jo Pillsbury, the pretty bartender who has been missing for twelve days after clocking out of her shift at Smokin' Joes, Kat phones for backup.

While she waits for backup to arrive, Kat nods, and pumps her fist, congratulating herself on a job well done. She'll be the youngest detective promoted to sergeant after this one, no doubt. Her mother will be so proud. Maybe she'll invite the family over and they'll take turns reading the newspaper clipping.

Poor Kat. There won't be much time for basking in her outstanding detective work. Things are about to take a very dark turn for Detective Greenleaf. Very dark indeed.

She is exactly seven seconds from leaning in closer with her flashlight and noticing a tattoo she recognizes on the chewed left pinky finger of the victim. It is a word in black ink.

She is sixteen seconds from taking off her glove and holding up her own shaky right hand, aligning her pinky with the victim's only to see that the tattoos, when held next to one another, spell out "Best Friends."

The discovery will mean the body about to be unearthed outside of Glory Bible Baptist Church is that of Kat's twin sister, Natalie, who talked her into getting matching tattoos on their sixteenth birthday. The rest of Natalie lay beneath the ash, rotting, cold, and alone, instead of basking on a beach in Hawaii where she is supposed to be honeymooning with her new husband, Victor Collins.

It will take until right around the sixty-second mark, for Kat to call Natalie's phone, only for Victor Collins to answer and claim Natalie is lying down with a migraine. "She's sleeping off a headache," he'll say, "but we're having a blast in Oahu, Kat! Wish you were here!"

Through stifled sobs, Kat will play it cool and end the call without giving away her grief. But at precisely ninety seconds, she'll collapse in the dirt and need oxygen from the back of the Kent County ambulance parked a few feet away. She'll have a hard time catching her breath as she mentally connects all the dots in the case and realizes that her sister's new husband—the mysterious Dr. Collins—has not only killed Kat's twin but is almost certainly the notorious Bloomsbury Butcher.

Instead of whisking her off on a romantic honeymoon, Collins has turned Natalie into victim number eleven.

The only thing that will make matters worse is at fourteen minutes and two seconds when police pull a note from Natalie's pocket that reads, "Kat, Natalie is number eleven. You can find number twelve—Candy Jo Pillsbury—by searching the one place in her home you forgot to look. Here's a hint—since we're family now—she's in a place fitting for a girl who worked in a bar called Smokin' Joe's. Whew, is it hot in here, Kat, or is it just Candy Jo? In the meantime, your next task is to catch me before I strike again, because I will stop at nothing but the 'best' for lucky number thirteen."

At this point, Kat will grab her pinky and look at her tattoo: Best. Her blood will run cold, but she'll have the wits to call her partner, Detective Douglas Ciglianni, and tell him to go to Candy Jo Pillsbury's house right away. "You'll find her in the chimney, Doug," she'll stammer, before passing out in the dirt at sixteen minutes and ten seconds.

Kat will regain consciousness in the hospital in a few hours when she hears a scraping sound outside her door, but because it will be three o'clock in the morning, the other officers will have gone home for the night. Her hospital room lights will be off, and Kat will initially feel safe knowing a guard is positioned at her door. However, when the scraping sound doesn't let up, Kat will creep to her door, open it, and see the guard being dragged around a corridor—a pool of blood trailing behind him.

She'll instinctively reach for her gun but realize she's in a hospital gown. In the seconds Kat searches in vain for her uniform—and in particular, her holster—the killer is mere feet from reaching her room. She will run toward the door to lock it, but the killer will get there first, swinging the door open, and standing face to face with Detective Kat Greenleaf. "You," she'll gasp, realizing the person holding an ice pick over her head is not Victor Collins at all, but to her shock, it is...

The bathroom door swung open, and the overhead light clicked on, causing Lucinda to release a bloodcurdling scream. "Good grief,," Sharon shouted, clutching her chest. "Sorry! I saw the light off and was coming in to get some Advil."

Lucinda used one arm to cover her bare chest and the other to fish her novel and book light out from under the water. Looking at her waterlogged copy of *The Case of*

The Bloomsbury Butcher, Lucinda glared at Sharon, who muttered, "I'll come back later for the Advil," and backed out of the room, closing the door behind her.

Chapter 20

Just before sunset, Lucinda finished drying off from her bath, put on some makeup, and scrunched her partially wet hair. She walked outside with her camera to take a few pictures for the new website while she waited for Jim to join her for dinner.

When she approached the common area between the backs of the bungalows and the shoreline, she noticed that Jim had aligned all the chairs and set up the umbrellas, which looked wonderful. She'd been too engrossed in her novel to hear the delivery van drop them off.

After she'd gotten a few shots, Jim opened his bungalow door and motioned for her to come over. When she did, he pointed to the spot underneath the porch light. It was an address plaque that read, "The Blue Dolphin" and featured two cute painted dolphins playing in crashing waves. "Where did you get this?" Lucinda shrieked. "It's adorable!"

"Surprise! I ordered thirteen of them when you told me the new names of the bungalows. Rita is making them as we speak, but I wanted to give you a preview. Each one will have the name of the bungalow and the animal they're named after. Wait'll you see The Great White! It's my favorite."

"Lenny's Rita? Is this why you stopped over there after we got the shuttle?" Lucinda asked.

"Yeah, I didn't really need Lenny to look under the hood of the shuttle. He doesn't know jack about cars."

"Well, I'm amazed, Jim Barnes. Delighted and amazed. Thank you."

Lucinda saw Jim had the television on, and asked if he was watching another old movie. When he nodded sheepishly, she laughed and suggested they order takeout rather than go to a restaurant. Jim patted the sofa cushion beside him, and an hour later they were eating tacos and watching an old James Dean film.

Every so often, Lucinda would catch Jim looking at her, and when she turned to face him, he would smile, but somehow, it didn't reach his eyes. She knew she needed to help him resolve the disappearance of his wife. To help clear his name. It felt like the least she could do after all he was doing to help her family's business.

When there was only one taco left, Jim and Lucinda played Rock, Paper, Scissors for it. When Jim won, he still gave the taco to Lucinda, who ate the whole thing with a smile on her face.

The next day was productive. Everyone continued doing their part with cleaning, painting, decorating, and getting their items checked off the list in preparation for the upcoming relaunch. Ben and Jim replaced fixtures in the bungalows, while Lucinda and Goldie shopped online for new bedding, curtains, rugs, and towels.

The lobby was looking fresh, too, though there was still much to do. The new vending machine was delivered in the afternoon, and everyone took turns putting their dollar bills in and buying a drink. When they each had one, they all toasted. "To fifty more years of The Pink Octopus!" Ben said, and Sharon added, "Here, here!"

Sharon had been busy for days creating oil paintings to hang in each cottage. She could be found sitting outside by the shoreline, on the front porch of Goldie's, or even in the office lobby, blissfully caught up in getting a set of eyelashes just right or blending the curve of a scoop of ice cream to make it look like it was melting down the side of a cone.

It seemed there was nothing Sharon couldn't portray with stunning accuracy. Whether it was sea life, children building sandcastles on the beach, or glorious summer desserts, the time away from painting hadn't dulled her talent in any capacity.

She planned to put price tags on the paintings, offering tourists a chance to take a little piece of the island home. Goldie suggested pricing the pieces high enough to offer guests free shipping, which Lucinda thought was a fantastic idea since everyone enjoys feeling as though they got a bargain.

Lucinda marveled at her sister's artistic ability. Sharon had always been the most creative Perry, being involved with a theater troupe, getting poems published in national magazines, and possessing a natural painting ability that none of the others had.

Inspired by artists like Edward Henry Potthast, Degas, and Renoir, Sharon was a self-taught painter who missed her calling when she decided to partner up with Alan at his dental practice. Lucinda was thrilled to see Sharon with a paintbrush in her hand again.

When Sharon caught her sister staring at her, she rolled her eyes and joked, "I know I'm pretty, but it's not nice to stare."

Lucinda and Goldie stole away for a quick trip to Kettler's for yoga supplies. Goldie embraced the idea of finally being an instructor instead of a student after decades of daily practice. On the way there, she waved a fifty-dollar bill in the air. Lucinda lowered her sunglasses and waited for the punchline, before finally saying, "OK, Mom. I'll bite. What's up?"

"Sal gave me some money for yoga supplies. He's very supportive of this new endeavor."

"That's sweet. It might come to a little more than fifty, though."

"I know that!" Goldie snapped.

Lucinda's cheeks flushed. Why had she downplayed her mother's excitement at the gift from Sal? She bit her lip and said, "I'm sorry, Mom." Goldie huffed, crossed her arms, and stared out the window. Lucinda hadn't meant to put a damper on the outing.

She pulled into the parking lot, turned off the car, and said, "You know Mom, Sal has the kindest eyes, doesn't he?" Goldie lit up and started rambling about Sal being the child of poor, immigrant parents who worked hard to come to America from Sicily. She added that Sal rose from nothing to become the go-to butcher on Turtle Island. Lucinda didn't know if that was true, but she nodded anyway, saying, "He's fantastic, Mom."

"Did you see those steaks in Jim's fridge? That was all Sal. I offered to pay for them, but he told me any friend of mine is a friend of his. He's very sweet, and I dare you to find gristle in one of Sal's steaks. You can't do it!"

Inside the store, Goldie picked out twelve pastel yoga mats, and added to her cart yoga bricks, straps, and neck pillows for guests who couldn't lie flat on the ground. Goldie suggested they go to another store and buy a portable radio, which made Lucinda laugh. "Mom, I'll do you one better and get you a portable speaker. Then, we can connect your phone to it and play any music you want with no need for a clear radio signal, or worse, cassettes."

"What's wrong with cassettes?"

"Nothing, Mom. But this way you won't be so limited. You can change up the music anytime you want without having to buy another tape. If you want to do a funky session, you can easily toggle between Stevie Wonder and Eminem with no muss, no fuss."

Goldie beamed. She was so happy by the time they left the store that she insisted on treating Lucinda to ice cream. Lucinda wasn't in the mood for sweets, especially since she was trying to shed a few pounds, but she didn't dare say no. They went to a place Goldie hadn't tried before—a new creamery called Motown Scoops—with a sign depicting four cows singing into ice cream cone microphones. A Marvin Gaye song blared from outdoor speakers and the line wrapped around the block. "Long lines must mean the ice cream's good," Lucinda whispered, trying to lean into her mother's excitement.

Goldie nodded, looped her arm through Lucinda's, and began swaying to the beat. "I sure love you, honey." Goldie beamed. "Isn't this so much fun?" Lucinda cringed, silently berating herself for often being hard on her mother. She made a promise to herself in that moment to go easier on Goldie, throw her a bone and be zany with her on occasion. "I love you, too, Ma," she said, twirling Goldie, who laughed heartily.

Chapter 21

The next day, Jim asked Lucinda to take a break from work and run an errand with him. "Want to go for a ride, get a change of scenery for a bit?" Lucinda agreed, and they drove to the other side of the island, to Hammerhead Wharf, where Sharon's longtime family home was located. Lucinda asked, "Didn't you used to have an uncle who lived over here?" Jim nodded and pulled into a long driveway about a mile and a half from Sharon's place.

The property was run down and stood out like a sore thumb compared to all the others on Hammerhead. It was imposing, almost ominous—like something out of an Alfred Hitchcock film. Once Lucinda got past the initial skepticism, she imagined a couple sitting on the porch drinking sweet tea—back before someone let the place go.

Jim confirmed it was his uncle's place, but no one had lived there since he died a couple of years earlier. Prior to that, Forrester had been in ill health and couldn't keep up on repairs. Lucinda asked Jim if he intended to buy it from Forrester's children but he said his uncle never had kids.

"I'm not going to buy this house," he said, gazing up at the collapsing roof.

"That's a relief," Lucinda sighed, getting out of the truck and walking through the weeds to get a closer look. "This place looks condemnable. No offense."

"Well you see," he muttered, rubbing his chin, "I'm not going to buy it because I already *own* it."

Lucinda apologized and furrowed her brow. "I, uh..." Jim waved her off and laughed. He said his uncle left it to him in his will, but he hadn't planned on doing anything with it since he lived in North Carolina. "I didn't intend to ever move back here, that's for sure," he sighed, kicking at a loose stone from the foundation.

"And now?" Lucinda asked, shielding her eyes from the sun and taking in the scope of the property.

"I can't keep freeloading from the Perrys," he said. "Time to get my own place, right?"

When Lucinda asked if this was where Jim had been disappearing to in his downtime, he nodded. She asked if he was planning to stay on the island, and he mumbled something about there being nothing left for him in North Carolina. Lucinda nodded, recognizing the feeling.

She straightened the mailbox, which was now only affixed to the siding with one rusted screw. "The place is big enough to make some guest rooms in case your kids ever want to visit," she suggested. Jim shrugged, making it clear without a word that he'd given up hope of mending fences with Max and Savannah, which she found incredibly sad.

He unlocked the front door, and they went inside to have a look around. The place smelled vacant, like an old basement after a rainstorm. Jim helped Lucinda unthread the cobwebs from her hair, and they both got a laugh out of the ordeal.

It looked like the place needed gutted after sitting unoccupied for the past two years. It had endured several summer storms, and from the state of things, no one seemed to have assessed the damage afterwards. Rippled floorboards creaked under their weight, and a bird swooped angrily past them when they got too close to her nest in the ceiling fan.

Jim told her what he'd like to do with the place. His eyes lit up as he mentioned hardwood floors, skylights, and a home theater. "To watch old movies on," Lucinda interrupted, smiling. He nodded.

Her phone vibrated in her pocket and she saw a text from Scott telling her he was looking forward to their date later that night. She smiled and put her phone back in her pocket. Jim asked what that was all about. "Huh?" she asked, playing dumb.

"Usually, a smile like that means a person is talking to someone of the opposite sex."

"Oh, well, yeah," she said, blushing. "I mean, it's nothing. One of Ben's friends asked me to dinner."

"Hm, I see."

"Yeah, it's nothing."

"You said that."

"Because I meant it. It's just dinner."

Jim smiled, walked Lucinda through the rest of the house and showed her where he spent the night as a child, the ratty carpeting he tripped on and chipped his tooth when he was eight, and an old leather chair where his uncle would sit and read him *Treasure Island*.

She asked if he missed his uncle, and Jim said that in many ways, Forrester had died years earlier than the date stamped on his death certificate. "Alzheimer's," he sighed, shaking his head.

Lucinda said she was sorry, but Jim reached overhead, grabbing the doorway's frame, and acted resigned to the loss. "When a man can't feed himself or tell you his name," he said glumly, "he ain't really a man anymore, is he? I think Forrester would've considered it a blessing when he died, if he could've considered anything at all by then."

Jim's belly was exposed beneath his shirt as he hung in the doorway. Lucinda felt just as awkward trying to avert her eyes as she had the last time he'd done it. Trying to lighten the mood, she poked her head into a large room and said, "I'd make this one the master bedroom if I were you." When Jim asked why—explaining that it was supposed to be the dining room—she said it would be lovely to wake up to the morning light. "Someone obviously designed this all wrong," she teased. "I mean, if you made this the master bedroom, you could effectively eliminate the need for an alarm clock!"

"So I should put the dining room upstairs where the master is supposed to be, then?"

"Yeah, why not? Buck the system, right?"

Jim wondered aloud if Uncle Forrester's house was too large for him. "It's not as if I'll be having more kids," he said, running his hand along a dusty end table. Lucinda asked him whether there was still a chance to reunite with his ex-wife if they found her. Before he could answer, he saved Lucinda from falling through a hole in the kitchen floor. "Careful," he warned. "That section rotted out from a leaky fridge."

Lucinda laughed, wanting to repeat her question about Camille, but almost afraid of the answer. Maybe it was none of her business anyway.

After the grand tour of Forrester's house, they headed back out to the truck. Jim drove Lucinda past Sea Rock and cut the engine by the curb. They commented on what a beautiful house Sharon had, and Lucinda told Jim about wanting to convince her to rent it out, keep it in the family for the time being.

Then, she turned to face him. She tucked her foot under her leg, took a deep breath, and asked him to tell her about his children. He stammered, made an excuse or two, and finally relented.

He said Max was a travel blogger and had been to thirty countries. He'd run with the bulls in Pamplona, seen the Northern Lights in Alaska, and hiked at Mount Kilimanjaro. "That boy will never settle down. He's rootless," Jim laughed, shaking his head.

When he got to Savannah, he paused, looked out the window and seemed lost in a memory. When he finally started talking, what he said surprised Lucinda. "She's an advanced juggler. I'm talking Cirque Du Soleil level advanced. She can even juggle knives. Can you imagine that?" As Jim spoke, a funny grin spread across his face, conveying pride and awe.

Through her online research Lucinda knew that Savannah Barnes was an impressive young woman. She found it endearing that out of all her accomplishments, her dad was the most awestruck over her juggling skills.

Lucinda's cell phone rang, and Jim motioned for her to answer. It was Mindy at Magic Mirror, who had a last-minute cancelation and could squeeze in a cut and color if she was interested. Lucinda accepted immediately, and when they got back to The Pink Octopus, she wasted no time rushing over to Jellyfish Bay and telling Mindy—who she liked instantly—that she had no idea how good her timing was. "I have a date tonight," she confessed, trying to control her shaking hands. "It's been decades since I've dated. I'll probably screw it all up."

"Nah," Mindy said, painting sections of Lucinda's hair with color and wrapping them in little pieces of foil. "All you have to do is smile."

"That's it?"

"Yeah, someone told me I look mad a lot, even when I'm not. To be honest, it was my mom, and she called it a 'resting blank face.' I'll let you Google it if you aren't sure what the *blank* stands for."

Lucinda examined her resting face in the mirror and was horrified to see that she looked disgruntled, too. She was perfectly happy, but in the absence of a smile, she appeared tired, and even slightly intimidating. "Just smile, huh?" she said. "I hope it's really that easy, Mindy" she added, practicing a smile in the mirror.

"Yeah, just that, and laugh at everything he says. Men like that for some dumb reason. Must make 'em feel important."

Mindy did a fantastic job bringing Lucinda back to life. She no longer felt disheveled with her new chestnut lowlights, as Mindy referred to them. They were shiny and youthful, and made Lucinda feel like a news anchor or a lifestyle model like she'd often seen in yogurt commercials or wristwatch ads.

She drove home practicing her smile in the rearview mirror so many times that the car behind her honked when the light turned green.

Sharon's eyes lit up when Lucinda walked in the door at home. "Va va voom!" she teased, waggling her eyebrows. Lucinda shimmied and they both laughed. Sharon sat at the kitchen table and hot glued seashells to an old-fashioned hairbrush while Lucinda poured herself a glass of iced tea. She held up a barrette with a large starfish affixed to it and said, "What do you think? Does this read youthful glow or older gal trying too hard?"

"I feel like that's a loaded question," Lucinda said, dipping her finger into a jar of peanut butter. Sharon reached over, dug her finger into the jar too, and casually announced, "Jim is still in love with you."

Lucinda's mouth fell open, but she quickly brushed her sister off, and sifted through the jewelry, admiring the smooth shells and well-thought-out details, such as the tiny pearls that adorned the bracelets. When she felt Sharon's eyes on her, Lucinda said the last thing she needed was to get involved in a serious relationship when she was technically still married. "Well, if you don't want to get involved, why go out with Scott?" Sharon asked.

"Did you see those dimples?" Lucinda asked. "He's trouble. He's a fun guy to enjoy a glass of wine with, or maybe take to a concert, but a long-term boyfriend? I don't think so!"

"He's fun for more than a glass of wine. I can attest to that!"

"You're disgusting," Lucinda said, pulling a twenty out of her wallet and handing it to Sharon. "But you make nice jewelry."

Lucinda took a barrette from Sharon's collection and took it into the bathroom to get ready for her big date. She buttoned a white blouse and tucked it into black slacks, touching up her eyeliner and fastening the barrette in her hair.

Standing back to admire her reflection, she recalled Sharon's observation about Jim. What was it with him, anyway? Did he have feelings for her, or did he need some sort of closure? Did he want to prove to himself—and perhaps to Peter—that he could win Lucinda back?

She concluded that maybe Goldie and Sharon were trying to make something out of nothing. They did live on a small island, after all, and watch a lot of soap operas. Maybe they were looking for some juicy relationship drama and creating something salacious out of an otherwise mundane situation.

Lucinda went to the office to search for a bracelet she'd left in the kitchen a few weeks earlier and forgotten about. She was nibbling on a protein bar when her friend, Rachel, called. They said hello, and Rachel asked if Lucinda was going crazy yet. "Oh, it's going fine, other than my mother and sister are trying to set me up with my old high school boyfriend."

Rachel laughed, and Lucinda picked the dried cherries out of her bar and ate them one by one, filling Rachel in on the renovations. "What?" she said, asking Rachel to repeat her question.

"Is he cute?" Rachel asked again.

"Really, Rachel," she said, picking a blackened pistachio from her bar and setting it on the table. "Is he cute? What are we, twelve? Next, you'll be asking me if we're going to get pinned."

"Why aren't you answering the question?"

"Oh, for Pete's sake! Yes, okay? But I wouldn't use the word cute."

"What word would you use?"

"He's more rugged than cute. Weathered, but in a good way," she said, absentmindedly playing with a paper Chinese restaurant menu on the table. "You know how it is, men age like fine wine. Jim's no different."

Lucinda pushed the menu aside and fumbled with the clasp on her bracelet. Suddenly, she heard throat clearing behind her. She turned, shocked to see Jim leaning against the doorway with a devious grin. She jumped, clutched her chest, and told Rachel she had to go.

She ended the call and asked what on earth Jim was doing lurking around the office. He said he wasn't lurking, and that Goldie asked him to replace the old refrigerator in the break room. "Hence, the dolly," he said, pointing to the cart he was pushing.

"What did you hear?" she asked accusingly.

"Nothing, just someone talking, so I came in to announce myself. Nice outfit, by the way."

"Thanks. It's nothing."

"Looks like something to me."

"I better go. I'm running late."

"Well, since we're old friends I probably shouldn't lie. I might have heard more...you know with Rachel?"

"What did you hear, Jim?" she said, blushing. "No, wait! I don't want to know. Text me tomorrow when you're ready to start working on the bathroom in The Green Seahorse. I'll help you install the new sink like I promised."

"I'll try to remember, but us rugged guys aren't so good at storing information in our pea brains."

Lucinda grabbed her purse, threw it over her shoulder, and stormed outside, flipping her bouncy new hair for effect. She was mortified. Just her luck that Jim had heard her talking like that about him to Rachel. She decided the best thing to do was to throw herself into a fling with Scott, to prove to Jim—and her mother and her sister and her brother—that she wasn't pining for him.

Of course, what constitutes a fling these days? Lucinda asked herself. It had been decades since she'd had to know that type of stuff. She Googled "What is a fling" on her phone but deleted it before hitting "Enter." She stuffed her phone into her purse and returned to the house, scolding herself with every step. "You're ridiculous! It's only a date! Just breathe!"

Chapter 22

When Scott picked Lucinda up in his convertible at eight o'clock as promised, she smiled, looked up at the moon, and breathed in the possibility only a first date could offer. It was time to let Peter go—Peter, who was chronically late, even to their wedding—and carve out a new life for herself. He was certainly doing just that back in Stamford. "You look beautiful," Scott gushed, handing her a rose.

"Did you look this good yesterday?"

Lucinda's breath caught in her throat. *What did he just ask me?* Not letting up, Scott continued stuffing his abnormally large foot in his mouth.

"So, what's different?"

"Uh...I got my hair done?"

"Looks great!" he confirmed, satisfied to have the mystery solved. "Want to go to Wing Dings? They have the best chicken wings, if you're into that."

Lucinda nodded, figuring she could browse the menu and pick something less messy than wings. The car ride was pleasant, with no awkward silences. Scott was a chatterbox, which suited Lucinda fine. She'd lost count of how many times she'd fought with Peter to open up to her over the years. For being a lawyer and arguing in court for hours on end, he had very little to say to his wife at home.

Lucinda stared out the passenger window and wondered if Eve had to pry conversation from Peter, too? Once, on a flight from Connecticut to California, she experimented with not being the first to talk. The result was, he sat in his seat and didn't say a word the entire trip. Peter finally broke the silence when the captain announced they were about to land in LAX. "Everything OK? You've been quieter than usual."

Scott was thirty-nine, which Lucinda pretended didn't shock her. He grew up in Texas, but moved to Saltwater Reef to help his uncle with his charter fishing business. His southern accent would have been charming, except that his obvious ladies' man schtick rubbed Lucinda the wrong way.

If she'd had any interest in forming a real relationship with Scott, his obvious ogling of other women in traffic would have been problematic. He proudly shared his intention to remain a lifelong bachelor and added that he had no shame in admitting he lived with his mother to save on rent. Lucinda just smiled, knowing she'd had colds that lasted longer than this relationship was about to, and found a certain freedom in that realization.

She wanted to ask Scott how many women he'd dated on the island but refrained, figuring people who partake in flings—as she was considering doing with him—wouldn't care about their date's romantic history. Besides, before she could say anything, he reached over and looped his fingers through hers, holding her hand as if they'd been dating for months. Shocked, Lucinda turned and stared out her window, trying to avoid her go-to habit when embarrassed: laughter. If this was the speed at which people moved in relationships nowadays, she was fine being unattached.

When Scott's sweaty hand began dripping onto the knee of her slacks, she resolved to give up on dating altogether. If these were the things she'd be expected to endure, she'd join a book club or get a dog for company.

She retreated inward as he prattled on about mundane topics—mostly himself—and realized how badly she wanted out of the car when she began imagining all the places she'd rather be, and her overdue mammogram sprang to mind.

After that night, she would probably accept being alone. She'd had her marriage, raised her kids. Now, she would learn the art of homemade bread making, catch up on her catalog of documentaries, perhaps give Irish step dancing a try. Surely, any of those things would be better than the dating roller coaster.

Scott pulled into the parking lot at Wing Dings, which was nearly full. He got out of the car and stood nearby, texting someone on his phone while Lucinda waited to see if he would open her door. When he didn't, she sighed, closed the visor she'd been using to watch him, and climbed out. *Okay*, she thought.

They went inside, where several people knew Scott and called him Scooter, curdling Lucinda's stomach. She was appalled, as though she was taking a friend's teenage son to dinner as a favor.

They were seated at a corner booth, where Scott tried ordering for her. "Oh, actually, can I look at the menu?"

Lucinda asked Paula, the waitress. She couldn't tell who was more offended by the question, Scott or Paula.

Finally, pressured by Paula's loud gum cracking, Lucinda ordered the chicken tacos and quickly handed her the menu. Paula spun on her heel and disappeared through a sea of other servers, all wearing black-and-white striped shirts with a chicken necktie and red pants. Scott stared at Paula as she sauntered off. "Nice place," Lucinda said, looking around.

"Yeah, I come here a few times a week."

"The waitress seemed a bit put out."

"She always does. She's my sister-in-law."

"Oh, sorry."

"Don't be. Everyone knows she's meaner than cat piss, even to her own kids."

Lucinda flushed, trying to think of how to respond, but didn't have to because Scott started discussing his workout routine, his three unsuccessful attempts to quit smoking, and a tattoo that was too long a story to share on the first date. Lucinda smiled artificially, trying not to slip into her *resting blank face.*

She learned Scott was a Taurus, had a scar on his forearm from wrecking his four-wheeler, and was planning to run for mayor of Turtle Island after he turned fifty. "I figure by fifty, I'll have really lived," he said, flagging Paula down for another beer. "You know? I mean, if you ain't figured things out, seen the world, and settled down by fifty? Come on! That's like, half a century old!"

Lucinda nearly choked on her fried pickle when he got to that part. Scooter was the last person Lucinda could imagine as mayor of the island, and besides, his comments about fifty being ancient felt like acid on a brush burn.

Had Ben not told Scott how old Lucinda was, or was he that sublevel of ignorant? "Will you excuse me while I go to the ladies' room?" she asked, dabbing her mouth with a napkin.

The restroom, which smelled of baby powder and stale cigarettes, was unusually full. Women pushed and clawed to get a spot at the mirror to check their makeup. Lucinda wondered if Wing Dings was a pickup spot or a chicken restaurant because the bathroom was a surprisingly judgmental and competitive place to be. She tucked into a corner and pulled her phone from her pants pocket. She hated to text Jim, knowing he would mercilessly tease her about going out with someone as young and inappropriate as Scott, but she wasn't about to ask Goldie to pick her up.

Lucinda: I'm at Wing Dings on Jellyfish Bay with an ageist male chauvinist named Scooter. Help!

Jim: What do you want me to do?

Lucinda: Anything!

Thirty minutes later, Lucinda was watching Scott devour a plate of hot wings, smacking his lips after licking each finger clean. He talked with his mouth full, recalling the time he was mistaken for Zac Efron by a tourist a few months earlier. Lucinda kept scanning the room for Jim but didn't see any sign of him.

The final straw occurred when Scott—Scooter—Zac—asked Lucinda if he could spend the night at her place. "I can't take you back to my mom's," he said, chewing on an ice cube from the bottom of his water glass. "She said last time was the last time, but we don't have to get into that. Y'all have all those bungalows. Any of 'em empty tonight?"

Lucinda closed her mouth, which had been gaping open, and then opened it again and said, "You know what, Scott? I've silently endured you talking about your family, your health history, even your obsession with German Beer Steins. All this time, I didn't say a word, and you know why?"

Scott shook his head, going back to the discarded wings on his plate and giving them another go. "Because you never asked me anything! Not one question about my job, my dreams, my family! It's like you're on this date alone! The only thing you want to know about me is if you can spend the night? Well, the answer is no!"

Before Scott could respond, Jim approached the table and Lucinda got up, pulled a twenty-dollar bill out of her wallet, and set it down next to her plate. She grabbed her purse, told Scott to delete her number from his phone, and stormed off.

Thinking about Ben, she returned to the table briefly to whisper in Scott's ear. "You're not a useless human, Scott," she said. "Your Ben's friend, so I'm sure we can be friends on some level, too. Just do the female population of Turtle Island a favor and learn how to treat a lady, will you?"

Scott set a naked chicken wing on his plate, grabbed a napkin, and started wiping his hands clean. "Sorry," he said. "I hear you, and that's all fair." Lucinda shook his mostly clean hand and said goodnight.

In Jim's truck, Lucinda complained about how awful the date had been, but said the chicken tacos almost made the entire experience worth it. "We should go back sometime and have lunch," she suggested, looking over at Jim, who kept his mouth shut and his eyes on the road. She added it would be nice to eat the chicken tacos next time without the nausea that accompanied watching Scott make love to his twenty-four hot wings. She shuttered at the still-fresh memory but noticed Jim didn't respond. Not even a chuckle.

The streetlights revealed a bulging muscle in his jaw that grew larger the longer he clamped his teeth together. After a few minutes of silence, Lucinda asked him what was wrong. Jim pulled off the road and into the parking lot of a car wash, kicking up gravel in the truck's wake. He turned the volume down on the radio and faced Lucinda. Her eyes froze in a petrified stare, and all she could do was croak, "Are you OK?"

"Don't you see what's right in front of your face?"

"Pardon me?" she spluttered.

Jim pounded his fists on the steering wheel, letting out a loud groan. "I'm right here where I've always been. Waiting for you to really see me." Lucinda swallowed hard and blinked. She'd never seen that side of Jim, and though she still believed he didn't hurt Camille, his rising frustration was troubling. "Jim..."

"Why won't you let me in? What are you afraid of?"

Lucinda took a minute to consider his question. She wanted him to know she heard him. She leaned her head against the neck rest, closed her eyes, and sighed. She finally explained, saying that all she'd ever known was being Daddy's Girl, and then Jim Barnes's girlfriend, and then Peter's wife. She had no idea how to exist apart from a man. To figure out what she wanted and who she was on her own two feet.

Jim sighed and closed his eyes for a moment. Opening them, he breathed, "Well, you aren't going to find what you're looking for with the Scott's of the world."

"Of course I'm not," she said gently, "but don't you think I should figure that out on my own?"

The corners of Jim's mouth twisted into a tentative smile. He nodded, started his truck, and pulled back out onto the road, tuning the radio. They drove the rest of the way home without speaking. When he walked her to the door, he admitted she was right. She owed it to herself to explore her options.

She couldn't help but think Jim's words sounded like a goodbye but hoped she was misreading him. He smiled sadly, shrugged, and told her to sleep well. She thanked him again for the bungalow signs, telling him they were better than anything she could've picked out herself. Then, he turned and headed back to The Blue Dolphin.

In her bedroom, she lay on the cot with her date clothes still on. Staring up at the ceiling, she was dumbfounded. Sharon was right. Jim still loved her. Her head spun, and all she could do was close her eyes and try to come up with an action plan. *What kind of action plan?* she wondered. It was as if she'd fallen down a hole, and it was too dark to see her new surroundings. *What now?*

A few minutes later, her phone vibrated in her pocket.

Ben: How'd it go with Scooter?

Lucinda: I'm never speaking to you again, just so you know.

Chapter 23

The next day, Lucinda woke up to a text message from Scott, asking if she'd like to go to a movie later in the week, to possibly give him a second chance. He promised not to be a neanderthal, but Lucinda couldn't help but conclude that all he really wanted was a chance to add her to the notches on his belt. *Is it belt or bedpost?* she wondered, petting Ginger, who had mysteriously decided to sleep next to her for the first time since she'd been back on Turtle Island.

She got a shower, toweled off, and went back to her bedroom to get dressed. There was a plate of warm croissants sitting on her pillow with a note.

Lucinda,

Sorry I scared the life out of you the other night in the bathtub and made you ruin your book. I went all the way to Book Nook on Saltwater Reef because they have every obscure book ever written. When I didn't see it on the shelf, I asked a sales associate who had green hair and a nametag that read, None of Your Business, to please look it

up. He informed me that the book has been out
of print since 1974. So, I did what any loving,
loyal, apologetic sister would do: I baked you
chocolate croissants. I hope you can forgive me.

   In the meantime, I thought you might like this
as a replacement book. It's about an unassuming
grandmother-turned vigilante who gets bad guys to
confess to their crimes by threatening to feed
them cyanide-laced sweets. Seemed akin to the
esteemed novel I helped you ruin (wink, wink).

   Love you,

   Sharon

   P.S. After seeing the throngs of toned, pierced,
tattooed cool kids on Saltwater Reef, I'm able to
accept the reality that I'm getting old. I think
I should stay put on Turtle Beach.

Lucinda picked up the tattered paperback that looked
as old as *The Bloomsbury Butcher* and laughed at the title: *Muffin but the Truth.* An elderly woman holding a
plate of baked goods to the mouth of a bound criminal
graced the peeling cover. Flipping to the copyright page,
she smiled when she saw it was printed in 1969. Perhaps
cheesy vintage murder mysteries were another new hobby
for Lucinda to consider, since she doubted she had the
knees for Irish step dancing.

   She packed up a couple of croissants, slid the novel into
her tote bag, and walked to Beach Coffee on the boardwalk. It was a newer café that had a reputation for selling fantastic, prepackaged coffee. She'd ordered individual

bags to put in all the bungalows for guests. She walked, because the place was so close to her mother's house, and she wanted to enjoy the morning breeze on her skin. She'd always been a morning person, but especially on the island. It was the precious window of time before it got hot and crowded and felt more like a tourist trap than home.

On the walk there, Lucinda examined her forearms, admiring the start of a tan—something she had had little of in the past several years. Most of the vacations she and Peter took were to locations that didn't involve sun, sand, and bikinis. She'd had enough of that growing up, so when he or the kids wanted to take an Alaskan cruise or go skiing in Aspen, she was the first to pack her puffer coat.

Inside the coffee shop, Lucinda made her way to the counter to pick up her order. The barista, a friendly young man named Phil, asked if she'd like to try the "Flavor of the Day." She shook her head politely, but Phil wouldn't take no for an answer.

She couldn't be mad at Phil. He had floppy hair and chocolatey eyes that reminded her of a Goldendoodle. "Um...," she said, biting her lip. Phil gave her a crooked smile, the hope in his eyes extending all the way up to his hairline. "Oh, come on," he nudged cheerfully. "What could it hurt?"

"OK, sure."

"What size would you like?" Phil asked, grinning broadly. "We have Itty-bitty all the way up to Obscene."

"Wow, okay, how about something in the middle?"

"Ok," he said, flatly, the light in his puppy dog eyes dimming just a little. "Name?" Lucinda told him her name, which he wrote on a white paper cup.

Then, Phil set the cup on a counter behind him and called back to his helper, "Boring, Lucinda!" Lucinda untucked her hair from behind her ear and tried to hide behind it. Suddenly, she had flashbacks of Sharon chiding her about the beige nail polish and personal uniform idea and told Phil to make it Obscene.

While Phil scanned her debit card, Lucinda reviewed the menu on the wall and saw that he wasn't joking about the sizes. They were *Iitty-bitty*, *Boring*, *Ginormous*, and *Obscene*. Lucinda laughed, marveling over what lengths businesses go to to stand out from the competition. Still, it made her smile, and *that*, she figured, was the whole point.

She sat at a wrought iron bistro table outside and sipped her cup of Chocolate Fudge Brownie coffee, which didn't taste much like chocolate, or fudge, or brownies. She retrieved her new book from her bag and began reading. It was gloriously cheesy, reading like a teleplay of *Scooby-Doo, Where are You?* which was also released in 1969, much to Lucinda's amusement.

When Jim walked past her carrying a newspaper, she called after him. He turned and saw her, smiled, and asked what she was doing. "Well, I'm supposed to be setting up the coffee stations at the bungalows," she confessed, sipping her drink, "but there's a very persuasive barista inside who insisted I try the flavor of the day."

Jim held out his hand and asked to try a sip. Lucinda was taken aback. In high school, they used to share drinks all the time, but this felt strange, intimate. Lucinda handed him the paper cup and he smiled when he took a drink. He handed it back to her and said to wait right there.

After a few minutes, he returned holding a cup similar to hers, but smaller. Perhaps it was the Ginormous size. "Guess you liked it," she said as he took a seat across the table from her. He shook his head. "Nope, this is something else. That was revolting. No offense." Lucinda laughed and bent the top of the page of her book so she'd remember where she left off next time she picked it up.

She reached for her tote to put the book away, but Jim held out his hand. When Lucinda gave him the book, he examined the cover before turning it over to read the back. He looked up, licked his lips, and then pressed them together, looking like the cat that ate the canary. "Oh, just say it," she sighed.

"Jinkies," he said.

Lucinda laughed, grabbed the book, and stuffed it in her bag. Jim sipped his coffee and talked about the jellyfish he'd seen floating on the shore when he took a walk on the beach at sunrise. "Hope this place isn't turning into Jellyfish Bay," he said, leaning back in his chair.

"If they're migrating here, it's not for the coffee," Lucinda said, pushing her cup across the table for good. "And I bought three-hundred dollars' worth of their coffee for the bungalows. Nice, huh?"

She pulled a croissant out of a paper bag and placed it on a napkin before sliding it across the table to Jim. He took a bite and held up his newspaper, saying that so far, he'd avoided being listed as a wanted fugitive on the island. "How long do you think it'll take for Internet detectives to find out I'm here?" he asked, wiping his mouth.

Lucinda smiled, assured him there'd be a break in the case soon, and asked if his coffee was any better than hers. He said the coffee was good, but the croissant was phenomenal, and that he might have to go inside and order some to go. Lucinda told him Sharon made them, and he joked that he may have picked the wrong Perry sister.

Lucinda swatted his arm and stole the entertainment section of his newspaper. She missed *The New York Times* and made a mental note to have the address changed on her subscription to her mother's house. Jim sat back in his chair and laced his fingers behind his head. A coy smile stretched across his face, and Lucinda asked him what he was thinking. He cocked his head, squinted as if trying to figure out a puzzle, and said, "Grown-up Lucinda drinks coffee, huh?"

She snorted, shook her head, and replied, "Not really." She explained she liked the *idea* of coffee. She said that movies and books made it seem so cozy, so comforting but in reality, she'd tried it every way Jim could imagine. "Iced, frothed, black, loaded with flavored creamers and sugar. I've tried cappuccino, lattes, mochas. I even made a coffee bar in my kitchen and bought a $2,100 espresso machine...and guess what? I still hate coffee."

"Well, I'm relieved to know you're still you."

"I'm still me because I still hate coffee?"

"Yep, but you've changed in some ways."

"Like what?"

"Well, Miss Goodie Two-Shoes in high school would never have dogeared a book. Tsk tsk," he joked, sweeping one of his forefingers across the other.

Jim stood up and asked Lucinda to follow him. He took her unfinished coffee, dumped it in a nearby trash can, and said, "Come on." When Lucinda said she had things to do, he told her to relax, and hoisted her box of coffee onto his shoulder.

They walked back to The Pink Octopus and dropped the order off in the lobby before climbing in his truck. When Jim tuned the radio to a George Strait song, Lucinda couldn't help herself. "Grown-up Jim likes country music?" she observed, feeling witty. He shrugged, looked in her direction and said, "Grown-up Jim might still have some surprises up his sleeve."

Lucinda reclined her head on the neck rest and hummed along to the song, though she'd never heard it. After a few minutes of driving, Jim noticed Lucinda smiling. He almost asked why but preferred to imagine his own reasons for the content look on her face. How he'd missed riding along country roads with Lucinda Perry as his passenger.

When they were teenagers, they would drive for hours, sometimes in circles around the island, talking and daydreaming and listening to the radio. His car would smell like strawberry perfume long after she got out. How he'd missed that scent. A few years earlier, before Jim left Camille, he'd torn a perfume sample out of one of her magazines. It wasn't exactly as he remembered Lucinda's but close enough. He stuck it to his dresser mirror and when Camille questioned it, he did something he seldom did: lie. "It was my mother's favorite perfume," he said, smiling sadly.

"You must really miss her, huh?" Camille asked, putting clean socks into his drawer while he stared at the ad. "Yes, I do," he replied. "It never gets easier."

Jim wanted Lucinda to give him another chance. He understood she needed time to figure out what she wanted, who she was on her own two feet without a man in the picture. But he hoped with everything he had that when she was finally done searching, she'd end up back at his door, back to the one person who never stopped loving her. They'd already lost so much time. He thought it a shame to waste another day.

When Jim pulled his truck into the Turtle Beach Port and cut his ignition, Lucinda raised an eyebrow and asked what he was up to. He shrugged, slid his keys into his pocket, and told her to follow him. They boarded the ferry and headed to Pelican Harbor.

Lucinda looked around and noticed most of the seats on the boat were empty. The ferries ran from four o'clock a.m. until midnight seven days a week, but most of the early morning travelers were headed away from Pelican Harbor, not to it. Anyone ferrying this early was usually a local on Pelican Harbor, heading to their tourism-related jobs on Emerald Isle and Angel Shores.

Ten minutes later, they were in the welcome center, a place she'd certainly never spent much time in before. There'd been no reason to. There was a huge push for people to visit Turtle Beach, where the island's most notorious legend supposedly lived. Lucinda wondered why her parents never capitalized on the myth. They could've put up signs or had boat excursions where passengers could search the waters while her father recounted the tale.

She made a mental note to ask her mother why she hadn't thought to cash in on the myth—though she could picture Goldie getting upset if she referred to Herc as a myth. Goldie not only considered him real, but one of her dearest friends.

There were racks upon racks of brochures on the various attractions the island had to offer. Tourists could visit the lighthouse on Turtle Beach, rent Jet Skis on Saltwater Reef, and get custom breakfasts at Waffle Schmaffle on

Jellyfish Bay—which might be the only reason a tourist would ever visit Jellyfish Bay since its beaches were notorious for the jellyfish overpopulation. "Maybe you guys could offer something like this," Jim said, pointing to a coupon for a free dinner at a nearby restaurant with a two-night stay at a hotel on Saltwater Reef. Lucinda liked the idea, and said she'd reach out to a few restaurants and see if any of them wanted to collaborate.

When they'd taken the ferry back to Turtle Beach Port, Jim tuned the truck radio to a pleasant station that played eighties soft rock, and asked Lucinda if she remembered the legend of Hercules. She rolled her eyes and reminded him that she'd grown up on Turtle Beach just like he had. "Yes," he said, waggling a finger, "but all our fathers told us different stories about Hercules so there isn't really just one legend. It's more like dozens. I'm curious what version *you* heard."

Once back at The Pink Octopus, Jim cut his engine and they walked down to the water and sat next to each other on the sand. "Well?" Jim said. "Tell me your story!"

"You first," Lucinda said, pretending to button her lip.

Chapter 24

When Jim was about six years old, his father, Angus, took him out on an old boat to fish for grouper. While they were eating bologna sandwiches wrapped in waxed paper, Angus asked Jim if he thought he was brave enough to hear the tale of Hercules: the biggest sea turtle who ever lived, a turtle bigger than a blue whale, and with magical powers. A turtle who, legend had it, was still alive and well in the waters off Turtle Beach. Jim sat up straight, and assured his father he was brave, not even afraid of the dark anymore like his younger sister, Cindy.

Angus handed his son a bag of salt and vinegar potato chips and said he'd tell him the legend on one condition. When Jim said, "Anything, anything!" his father put his hand on his shoulder and said, "You must promise to pass the legend along to your son someday. It's the only way Hercules can continue to live after all this time. If islanders stop passing the story down to their children, Hercules will go away forever." Jim nodded, crossed his heart, and dug into his potato chips while his dad regaled him with the story of the great and magical Hercules.

Many years ago, Turtle Island was uninhabited by people. There were no roads or pizzerias or T-shirt shops. No tourists, and not even a single person living on this island. Maybe no one ever would have lived here, except that when a ship was traveling from Italy to America, a fire onboard caused the vessel to explode, killing almost all the passengers. Only three men and their families survived. One was a good man with a kind wife and respectful, hardworking children. Another was a wicked man who stole his way onto the ship by killing another family of passengers prior to boarding the ship. He gave the tickets of the victims to his wife, his children, and himself, assuming a new identity to continue his deceit. Finally, the third was an indifferent man, mealy-mouthed and weak of spirit.

When they reached the shore after a hard night clinging to rubble at sea, the good man took charge. He assigned the survivors tasks, some gathering materials to build shelter, others scavenging for food. The wicked man didn't like being told what to do, even though the good man had all the survivors' best interests at heart. The wicked man was greedy and hoarded what little food his wife and children could find, keeping the indispensable provisions to himself. He built a shelter for his family, and was a great builder, but would help none of the others with their dwellings.

The indifferent man, wanting to be liked by all, agreed with the good man when he was with him, and agreed with the wicked man while in his presence, never wanting to upset anyone more powerful than himself.

The wicked man's son found a nest of sea turtle eggs and waited for them to hatch. As the tiny turtles were making their journey to the ocean, the little boy snatched them all up, and took them to his father's camp, where they boiled and ate them. The good man's son sat on the beach crying when he saw the travesty. He didn't want to believe anyone as young as himself was capable of such cruelty, for there was plenty of food on the island such as berries, fish, and wild boar to sustain everyone without harming the beautiful baby turtles before they'd had a chance to live.

Out of the corner of his eye, the boy saw something moving. He turned and saw a single baby turtle floundering in the sand. He'd fallen out of the arms of his captor, injuring his leg. The boy scooped the baby turtle up, gently cupped him in his hands, and ran back to his camp, showing his father the tiny survivor. His father, the good man, compared the baby turtle to the little boy, saying, "He's a survivor, just like you." When the boy pointed out that the baby turtle wasn't like him because the turtle had no family, his father said, "That's not true. He has us. We will be his family. We'll call this small cluster of islands Turtle Island, and everyone here will be his family."

The wicked man and his sons tried at every turn to take the turtle from the good man's son, especially as he grew larger and meatier. They wanted to cook the turtle and have a feast, for he grew the size of a motor vehicle after only a year. The good man knew he must intervene, as he was tracking the growth of the turtle and could see that he was still growing every single day. There was no way to hide him, but he needed protection. He was not a mere animal. To the good man and his family, the turtle was one of them—cherished and adored. Some islanders even claimed the gentle giant had healing powers, and shared miraculous stories of his love and power.

The good man, seeing a need for order among the community, called a meeting among the survivors and suggested a vote to elect a leader among the group. Everyone over age ten was eligible to vote, and the results showed a clear win for the good man. "As mayor of Turtle Island," he announced, "I only have one rule. No one is to hurt Hercules. If you do, you will be banished from the island. All other laws will be modeled after the laws from our homeland, simple laws that every civilized society enforces, no more, no less.

Over time, the wicked man grew greedier and more disgruntled about having to live under the control of the good man. The indifferent man continued to play to the other men's affections. When the good man and the wicked man both noticed the indifferent man's disloyalty, they decided to banish him from the island. "We do not agree on much," the wicked man said, "but we can agree that a man must stand for something. All the indifferent man does is say what we each want to hear, often with disastrous results." The good man nodded and said, "I disagree with what you say and do most of the time, but I can trust that your word is true. That is more than I can say for the indifferent man. A man who cannot be trusted has no place in our world."

By now, Hercules was the size of a blue whale. He lived off the coast of Turtle Beach, as they'd named the good man's section of the middle island. Hercules visited every day, taking the children out for rides, helping men fish, and was better than any boat when it came to protection during a storm. He saved all the men's lives on several occasions, even the wicked man. The good man and the wicked man made a secret pact: they would remove the indifferent man from the island. Hercules carried that family hundreds of miles away, through storms and gales, dropping them off somewhere too far away to ever find the island again.

The good man and the wicked man eventually parted on good terms, the wicked man heading to the mainland to seek opportunities not available to him on the islands. As Hercules continued to grow, so did his magical powers. He continued to heal the sick, brought rain during droughts, and saved shipwrecked survivors, who he brought back to repopulate the island.

Hercules is over a hundred-and-fifty years old
now and is almost as big as this entire island.
Legend has it, he created a family of his own
underwater, much like Atlantis. He is the king
of the sea turtles and assigns his soldiers to
protect the sea surrounding Turtle Island. That
is why we have never had a hurricane, even when
the news shows one headed straight for us.

If you're ever lucky enough to be on the
water and see Hercules, and he approaches you,
do not be afraid. He rarely interacts socially
with islanders anymore, but when he does, he
distributes blessings beyond measure. It is said
that if he allows you to touch him, you will live
to be a hundred years old, and die happy and loved
and at peace in your bed.

When Jim's father finished the story, Jim asked him
whether he believed the legend of Hercules. Angus nodded, and said, "There are three kinds of people, Jimmy.
Good ones, bad ones, and ones who stand on the line
between right and wrong and wait for a strong wind to
blow them in one direction or another. It's important to
stand strong in your beliefs, or your word won't mean a
thing."

"So, I should believe in Hercules?"

"I didn't say that. I said you should decide what you
believe in, and then stand firm in that decision, and never
waiver."

"Why do you believe in the legend, Dad?"

"Because no one has ever disproved it."

Jim thought that answer made good enough sense for
him. Each time he recalled the story over the years—espe-

cially as he became a father himself—he realized his dad's advice was layered with many other meanings. The heart of it, though, was that he didn't want Jim to waffle in the things that mattered most in life. "You've got to stand for something, or you'll fall for anything," he'd once heard in a song. That, too, seemed reasonable to Jim.

Jim looked at Lucinda, who was smiling and seemed to enjoy the story. She asked him what he decided: Did he believe or not believe? He shrugged and said, "It's far-fetched, but I'm a hopeful guy. So, I'm going to believe it until someone proves it a farce."

"Just like your dad," she replied, smiling.

Lucinda reclined in the sand, using her arm behind her head as a pillow. After a minute, she turned to Jim, who had settled in beside her. She asked if he'd ever shared the legend with Max, as Angus had instructed? Jim shook his head, and when Lucinda asked why not, he said he thought he'd have more time.

He had envisioned taking Max out on a boat and eating bologna sandwiches and sharing his father's story with him. "It's not too late," Lucinda encouraged, squinting against the sun. Jim smiled, sat up, and opened a bottle of water. After he took a sip, he replied, "Your turn. What's your Herc story?"

When Lucinda was ten years old, her father, Tom, asked if she had ever heard of Hercules the sea turtle as big as the island. Lucinda laughed, and said, "Daddy, I heard he was the size of a whale, not the entire island!" Tom said whoever told Lucinda that story was wrong. When she asked how he could be so sure, Tom laid his hand on Lucinda's shoulder and looked her square in the eye, saying, "Because I saw Hercules with my own two eyes. He saved my life, and let me tell you, he was so big that he makes blue whales look like herring!"

Tom pulled an ear of sweet corn from a bag and handed it to his daughter, promising to tell her all about Hercules if she'd help him shuck the corn for supper. Lucinda nodded and sat behind the house husking ears of corn-on-the-cob while her father told her about his run-in with the great and mighty Hercules: the turtle who saved Tom's life when he first came to the island.

When your mother and I came to the island, we were strangers. I'd played a lucky hand in poker and walked away with a beachfront resort on some island named after a turtle. The guy I beat at cards put up for collateral an inherited bungalow business he described as paradise. I didn't care that I'd never heard of Turtle Island, or that I had no idea how to run a business. I just knew it had to be better than Duluth in January. All I could think of was sun and sand and fishing in a little boat all day. It sounded like heaven, but I needed someone to help me run it,

I was drinking coffee in a diner one day and saw a beautiful woman in a wedding dress, crying and eating every item on the menu. She was telling the waiter that she left a man at the alter on her wedding day because she knew he could never give her the adventure she craved. Well, to make a long story short, I tricked her into coming to the island with me, promising that no matter what happened, she'd get plenty of adventure.

When we got here, though, it was both of us who were tricked because the property—what you now know as The Pink Octopus—was in shambles. It was a lemon, as they say. We took a year just to get it to where we could rent out the bungalows and have running water at the main house.

Eventually, your mother and I fell in love, the kind that is better than any fairytale or movie you've ever seen. We married, and soon she was expecting her first baby: you. One day, I was out fishing, trying to catch us some dinner since there weren't many options on the island back then. A squall came in, and my boat capsized. I was taking in a lot of water and thought I was going to die. Suddenly, I saw a giant eye come out of the water and look at me. It was too large to be a whale. I didn't know if I was hallucinating, or what. The head raised out of the water and a mouth that looked a mile wide opened and said, "Do you want to live?" I said, "Of course! Please help me!"

The enormous turtle—which I soon learned him to be—said he could grant me one wish, but only one.

I could touch him, and live to be one hundred, or he could right my boat and nudge me back to dry land. "If I do that," he said, "I won't count that as your wish. You may use your one wish to grant someone else the one-hundred-year life." I gasped for air and told him my wife was expecting a baby, and asked if I could use the wish on both her *and* the unborn child. He smiled. "Your selfless love is honorable, and I will grant your wish. Your wife and baby will live to be one hundred years each. In exchange, I ask that you tell your children about me and raise them to love and respect all my descendants."

I nodded, and he righted my boat and pushed it back to land, where your mother was waiting at the shoreline for me. She saw the giant turtle and, rather than be afraid, she walked right up to him, kissed his nose, and said, "I will be eternally grateful to you for saving the love of my life."

The turtle, who said his name was Hercules, smiled, turned, and swam away. I've never seen him again, but Goldie has a few times. She takes the boat out at sunrise sometimes, before any of us are up, and calls for him. Sometimes he comes, but other times he's busy somewhere else on the island and cannot hear her. When he does come, they have wonderful conversations. She tells him about you, and he promises her that no matter where you go or what you do with your life, you'll always return to the island, because you'll be drawn here by love.

When Lucinda was finished, Jim shook his head in awe. He laughed, and said, "Well, two things: One, it makes total sense that Hercules would have long talks with Goldie, of all people. Out of all the islanders, no wonder she's one of his closest friends. Two, I guess it was always in the cards that you were going to return to Turtle Island, huh?"

"Guess so," Lucinda said.

"Because of love," he said, handing her a fresh bottle of water from his backpack. "Love brought you back, Luce."

Lucinda shifted uncomfortably, and Jim let her off the hook by putting the focus back on the legend. He said that those were only two of the many versions of the Hercules legends he'd heard, and Lucinda nodded, agreeing that every friend she had while growing up had his or her own story, too.

Jim said that Hercules might not be as popular as Nessie, but he could most definitely draw more of a crowd than The Pink Octopus had seen in the past several years. "Your family isn't capitalizing on old Herc, Lucinda! Can your daughter put some stuff on the website that will intrigue people? Maybe invite them to come and see if they can glimpse him out on a charter expedition with Ben?"

"The Hot Fisherman," Lucinda said, laughing. "That's not a bad idea, actually."

"Don't sound so surprised. I'm full of them! And why does Ben get to be the hot fisherman? I'm back in town now."

"You don't fish."

"But we both agree I'm hot, right?"

Lucinda swatted at Jim's arm, giggling. After a few minutes, he asked if she wanted to get dinner the following evening and discuss some ways to work Hercules into The

Pink Octopus's marketing plan. She used her finger to draw a heart in the sand, not realizing what she was doing, and said, "Can't, sorry."

Jim didn't have to ask. He knew she had another date. He hoped it was with a new guy, and not a second date with Scott. In fact, he hoped there would be no second dates of any kind. *Let her have her fun*, he thought. *Eventually, she'll figure out what she really wants.*

Chapter 25

Lucinda admired herself in the mirror. She'd been working hard to lose some weight and her efforts were finally starting to pay off. She was down ten pounds and liked the way her waist took shape in the wrap dress Sharon had picked out for her. She wasn't going to wear it, but after staring at it every day hanging on the back of her closet door, she'd decided it was time to try it out.

She brushed her hair and looked at the clock. Fifteen minutes until Brad would be there to pick her up. Why had she agreed to allow Sharon to arrange a blind date so soon after her disaster with Scott? Now it was too late to back out. She hoped her sister was a better matchmaker than Ben.

Brad rang the doorbell ten minutes early, which Lucinda didn't care for but decided to let slide. She'd watched so many movies with fun montages about women her age starting over, going on dates, and rediscovering all the fun things they'd set aside to raise children. She needed this to work. Brad didn't have to be Mr. Right, but she hoped to end the evening with fewer regrets than she'd had with Scott.

When she opened the door, Brad handed her an enormous bunch of wildflowers. "Thank you," she said, blushing. "They're beautiful." It had been years since anyone brought Lucinda flowers. Peter thought them a waste of money, saying they died after a few days, anyway. "They weren't cheap," Brad added.

"Oh," was all she could say in response.

"Yeah, it's no big deal. I'm just saying they *should* be beautiful for the price."

Lucinda sighed, invited him in while she put the bouquet in water, and listened while he talked about the restaurant where he had scored an exclusive reservation. It was a new Italian place that served what was supposed to be the best eggplant parmesan outside of Rome. When Lucinda's eyes brightened, Brad said, "I'll pay this time since it's the first date." Although Lucinda was rusty with dating, she was certain Brad broke a critical rule by mentioning money twice in the first five minutes.

Brad drove a nice car that smelled like pine and had soft, ivory-colored leather seats. He held the door and was polite apart from his miserly comments. They both liked home design shows on television, Carol Burnett, and bamboo pajamas. They each had two grown children. In some ways, Lucinda saw a glimmer of hope that she and Brad could have a nice relationship, but it was too soon to tell.

Ciao Spaghetti had a line out the door, which, thanks to their reservations, Brad and Lucinda bypassed altogether. Strangely, it was the only Italian restaurant on the whole Island, according to Brad. A pretty hostess named Ava seated them at a quiet corner booth and complimented

Lucinda on her matte red lipstick. Brad handed Lucinda a menu and said, "You can order whatever you'd like." *Gee, thanks Brad*, she thought.

The restaurant offered an extensive menu, which made Lucinda question how they kept so many foods fresh. She remembered an episode of a reality cooking show that went behind the scenes of popular restaurant kitchens and uncovered roaches, rotting food, and filthy ovens full of mouse droppings. The host, a famous chef, scolded the restaurant owners and devised a much simpler menu that allowed for easier preparation and less waste. With a menu the size of Ciao Spaghetti's, Lucinda thought it safe to avoid the clams just in case.

When Stephan, the server, came to take their order, Lucinda picked the Fra Diavolo, which Brad later questioned with raised eyebrows. "Why would you order lobster?"

"Why not?" she asked, confused.

"Well, think about it. We don't have lobster in this part of the world, you know? So, that means it's frozen."

"I don't mind."

"Suit yourself," he said, nervously rearranging his place setting. "I mean if it were me, I couldn't justify paying for lobster that I knew wasn't fresh."

Lucinda excused herself and went to the ladies' room to call Jim. She apologized for doing this a second time but said she couldn't get ahold of Ben, and she didn't want to ask Goldie to drive at night. When Jim asked what was wrong, she hissed, "I'm on a date with Ebenezer Scrooge!"

Jim said to sit tight and that he'd be there in twenty minutes. "Hurry!" she whispered before hanging up. She put her phone into her bag and checked her lipstick in the mirror. She'd been self-conscious about wearing it, but she figured it must be on-point if someone as young and beautiful as Ava admired it.

She went back to the booth. Stephan brought their meals, and part of her felt bad for having Brad pay for a meal when she planned to dip out well before dessert. If he'd even spring for dessert at all. The next comment quickly dispelled any guilt. "They're supposed to have good desserts here," Brad said, buttering a slice of bread. "Maybe we can split one." Lucinda smiled, tucked her napkin in her collar, and dove straight into her lobster.

She was nearly finished when Jim walked up to the booth. Ava was with him, apologizing to Brad and Lucinda. "I told him this was inappropriate," she said, her long lashes blinking double-time. Jim pounded his fist on the table and said, "Look, Lucinda! You may be giving up on this marriage, but I'm not." Lucinda's face grew hot, her eyes like saucers. Motioning toward her handbag, Jim continued. "Now, grab your bag and come on home, baby. The kids miss you. I'm sure we can work something out."

"You're *married*?" Brad gasped, nearly choking on his pasta.

Lucinda bit her lip to keep from laughing. The whole restaurant was watching. She apologized to Brad and said that she didn't mean to mislead him. She offered to pay her half, which seemed to perk up Brad's ears for a minute, until he looked up at the vein still throbbing in Jim's forehead. "No, no. It's all right," he said, throwing his hands up in surrender. "Just go on home and work on your marriage, I guess."

Outside, Lucinda climbed into Jim's truck, turned to him, and said, "Impressive performance. Too bad I'm probably banned for life at Ciao Spaghetti now!" They began laughing, the kind of laugh that seemed to lift pounds of cumbersome weight from Lucinda's shoulders.

Jim commented that Brad looked like he was going to cry, and Lucinda said it probably had more to do with paying sixty dollars for frozen lobster than it did anything else. When Jim asked how she met Brad, Lucinda slapped the dashboard. "Sharon!" she said, groaning. "My family is officially forbidden from setting me up again. *Ever!*" Jim smiled, tuned the radio, and said, "Except Goldie. She knows what you need better than Ben and Sharon."

Lucinda wasn't sure she liked Jim sneaking that comment into an otherwise light conversation. She imagined all the times she called her mother over the years to say that Frankie lost a tooth or Jill was voted Homecoming Queen or Peter's mother and father were in a car crash. How many of those big life events did Goldie break her neck to share with Jim? "Why did you keep in touch with Mom over the years, Jim?" she asked. Jim shifted awkwardly in his seat and stared at the road.

"She's a nice lady," he finally said. "I always thought of her as a second mother."

"But we broke up three decades ago. Surely there must be a reason you'd keep in touch with your ex-girlfriend's mother for so long?"

Once the words came out of her mouth, Lucinda finally understood. He didn't talk to Goldie because he wanted to hear about The Pink Octopus or about Ben's latest fling, or even Sharon's health. He didn't take her mother's calls because he was bored or lonely or liked the sound of Goldie's chirpy voice. He stayed in touch with her because it was the only way keep Lucinda in his life.

She looked over at Jim, who was stopped at a traffic light adjusting the sleeve on his jacket to stay busy. She bit her lip, unsure how to proceed without embarrassing him. Coming up with nothing, she turned her eyes to the road ahead, too. It was a warm, clear night. Clear in more ways than one now.

Back at home, Jim went around to Lucinda's side of the truck and helped her out. He smiled, shrugged, and said goodnight. "I hope your next date goes a little better for you," he said, walking backwards toward his bungalow. "Maybe Grandma Helen has someone she can set you up with at Whispering Pines?"

"Very funny," Lucinda said, smiling. "Goodnight."

Two hours later, Lucinda was tossing and turning on her horrible mattress when she finally shot up, pulled on a robe, and headed for the door. She marched over to Jim's cottage, having no idea what she was going to say when he answered the door.

Chapter 26

Lucinda stood silently on the porch of Jim's bungalow, trying to figure out exactly what she was doing there. Her lips were moving a mile a minute, rehearsing what to say—though no sound came out. She knew she couldn't start dating him again. There was too much water under the bridge, too many years apart to simply pick back up where they left off.

Regret quickly filled her lungs with cotton, making it hard to breathe, and she turned to leave. To go home and sleep on it. But she heard the door creak open. "Lucinda?" Jim whispered, "What are you doing here? Another terrible date already? A midnight showing at the cinema gone bad?"

He stepped onto the porch. His hair was tousled, and he'd somehow grown a five o'clock shadow since she'd last seen him an hour ago. She'd woken him up, and should apologize, but instead, she turned to face him directly. His eyes were warm, sleepy, waiting. "I'm sorry," she whispered, turning to leave. "I shouldn't have come here. Go back to sleep." Before she could step off the porch, he gently took her by the arm and turned her to face him. Taking her face in his hands, he leaned down and kissed her.

Lucinda had kissed no one but Peter in decades. Those moments with her husband had lacked passion for too long to remember. Normally, they'd only give one another a quick peck upon coming or going. She felt her body relax and didn't rush things. She simply allowed Jim to take over and do what he'd wanted to do for thirty years. She knew he'd earned the kiss and didn't want to rush him.

Feeling his warm hands cupping her face, his lips on hers, she thought perhaps it's what they both wanted all this time, not only Jim. When he backed away and looked her in the eyes, he said, "There. Now we got that over with and we can go about the business of figuring out what we are to each other." He took her by the shoulders and spun her back toward the steps so she could go home and sleep on it.

Halfway down the stairs, she stopped, turned around, and said, "I don't want to hurt you. I'm not put back together yet." Jim scratched his chin, looked up at the moon and then back at Lucinda. "Well," he said, "I don't want you to hurt me either, but it's a chance I'm willing to take."

She climbed back up on the porch, leaned against Jim and rested her head on his shoulder. After a few minutes, she backed up, straightened her posture, and said, "I want to date. I want to take it slow, be wooed, and feel like a lady." Jim extended his hand and shook Lucinda's, telling her it was a deal. When Lucinda descended the stairs and started walking back to her mother's house, Jim said, "Hey

Luce?" She turned back, and he whispered, "We're really doing this?"

"We're really doing this," she said, smiling. "It'll either be the best or worst thing we've ever done, right?"

She jogged the rest of the way home, feeling like she was bouncing on clouds, and texted Sharon when she got back to bed.

Lucinda: You up?

Sharon: Yep, reading a book that lists one hundred and one things to do when you're bored, but I find the whole thing boring. What's up?

Lucinda: Can you meet me in my room?

Sharon: Good date with Brad?

Lucinda: Even better...

Chapter 27

The next morning, Sharon, Lucinda, and Goldie were having breakfast before a big furniture delivery was scheduled to arrive. They'd ordered new beds, dressers, and lamps for all the bungalows. "Mom, did you hear the news?" Sharon said with a scheming twinkle in her eyes as she buttered her toast.

"What news?" Goldie said, setting her fork down.

"Sharon, you're such a gossip!" Lucinda wailed, swatting her with a cloth napkin.

"The suspense is killing me," Goldie begged, her eyes alight.

"Lucinda and Jim got back together!" Sharon squealed.

Goldie got up and did a little dance, clapping and singing, "Praise Jesus, Praise Jesus!" Lucinda and Sharon giggled, and Ben walked in asking what was up. Sharon told Ben the news and he yawned dramatically, saying it was hardly news. He took a muffin, turned to head outside, and told Lucinda not to screw things up this time. She jumped out of her seat, grabbed his muffin, and said, "You don't get to eat today!"

Two large purple delivery trucks pulled up outside the office, and everyone got their shoes on and headed outside. Jim came out to greet them and Ben started making googly eyes and saying if Jim and Lucinda were going to make out, to please go inside so he didn't have to watch. "Excuse my brother," Lucinda said to the delivery men. "He was born without a prefrontal cortex and is prone to uncontrollable outbursts."

The delivery men unloaded the furniture into each cottage, directed by Lucinda and Sharon. There were six Xander's Furniture delivery men in total, and they put the beds together in no time. Goldie and Lucinda plugged in the lamps and arranged vignettes of sculptures, coffee table books, and candles in each bungalow. That process took longer than assembling the beds because they couldn't agree on décor placement. One would position a vignette or flower arrangement, and the other would rearrange it, a process that went on for hours.

When they were wrapping things up, it was late into the afternoon. Jim asked Lucinda if she wanted to go get a late lunch, but she said it was family dinner night at the Perry house, so she had to get cooking. "I found a recipe online for Cincinnati Chili, and it made me nostalgic for *WKRP in Cincinnati*, so I looked up the song," she said dreamily. "I dare you to listen and try not to sing along. You simply can't do it! So, yeah, now I'm making Cincinnati Chili, which is really just chili over spaghetti noodles and topped with shredded cheddar, and someone please tell me to shut up!"

Jim told Lucinda her mind was a complex place to be, and Goldie took her by the shoulder and said, "Why don't you invite your boyfriend to join us for supper?" When

Lucinda groaned, Goldie winked at Jim, who blushed and tucked his hands in his pockets.

Lucinda laughed at how much it felt like high school dating again, and not only because Jim was her former boyfriend, but because she was living under her mother's roof, getting teased by her siblings, and cooking in the family kitchen again. "When do we get to actually grow up?" she asked Jim.

"On *this* island?" Ben yelled from the boat. "Never!"

"Amen, brother!" Sharon agreed. She struggled to carry a stack of paintings to hang in The Peach Squid.

Lucinda rushed to help her, and Goldie told Jim he was welcome to come for dinner and be her guest if nothing else. While she was inside the bungalow helping Sharon hang a picture of a little girl building a sandcastle, Lucinda got a text. It was from Jim's daughter.

Savannah: I thought I'd touch base. There isn't much to report, but I wanted to ask how my dad's doing? I haven't connected with him in a while.

Lucinda: He's hanging in there, Savannah. I know he's worried about you and your brother. Are you OK?

Savannah: I guess. I wish we could get some answers, though. Tomorrow is Mom's birthday, and I don't even know what to do about it. Anything I come up with feels morbid.

Lucinda: I'm so sorry. If there is anything I can do, please let me know. Also, pass along any news, big or small. I'm trying to follow the case as closely as I can, but it's hard from so far away.

Lucinda went back to hanging the painting, and when Sharon asked who was blowing up her phone, she sat on the edge of the bed. "It was Jim's daughter, Savannah.

The police are no closer to solving the case than they were on day one, it seems." Sharon shook her head. "What a shame. That must be awful for her, not knowing where her mother is. Mom drives me crazy, but I can't imagine her vanishing into thin air!"

After they finished hanging the last painting, Sharon backed up and checked to see if it was straight. "Man," she said, admiring her work. "I'm good, aren't I?" She looked at Lucinda and stuck out her tongue and crossed her eyes. "Yes," Lucinda agreed, "and humble!"

"The truth is, it felt amazing to hold a brush again," Sharon said.

They went back to the house and prepped dinner for later. Lucinda couldn't believe how well she'd been getting along with Sharon since she'd been back on the island. They weren't ones to fight, but they'd never been close either. Sharon browned the ground beef and Lucinda chopped tomatoes and measured scoops of ground cinnamon, swatting Ginger off the counter twice. It felt good to cook with Sharon. Neither Jill nor Frank took to cooking, and Peter never met a takeout menu he didn't like, so meal planning was always left for Lucinda. She hummed her favorite song while she minced garlic, feeling content to have a cooking partner.

Once everything was prepared, Lucinda grabbed a banana and told Sharon she'd see her later. She went to her room to look up the story on Camille, hoping to find any minor detail that police and web sleuths may have somehow overlooked. When she reached the doorway, she saw the cot was gone. In its place was a pretty four-poster bed with a floral quilt and fluffy pink pillows. It looked like something straight out of a Martha Stewart magazine.

After sleeping on the world's lumpiest cot, this bed was better than a million dollars in Lucinda's eyes. She clasped her hands to her chest, screamed for her mother, and flung herself onto the pillowy mattress. It felt divine, like resting on a cloud.

When Goldie came running, Lucinda jumped up, hugged her, and thanked her for the surprise. Goldie shrugged and said, "I don't know what you're talking about. I had nothing to do with this."

"Are you serious? Then who..."

"Girl, you're not that thick, are you? At this point, if you don't want him, I'll take him!"

"Classy, Mom."

"Hey, next time complain about the air conditioner. It's almost as old as Grandma Helen!"

"I'm telling her you said that!"

"Go ahead! I've said worse to her face!"

Lucinda sat on her new bed and scanned the latest media coverage on Camille. It seemed she really did vanish into thin air. She hadn't used her credit cards since the day before she'd last been seen alive, and she didn't reach out to her children, her workplace, or even her elderly mother. There was no sign of her anywhere, and Savannah did an interview on the news where she'd said Camille would never have left her cat to fend for herself.

Lucinda closed her laptop and freshened up for supper. When the doorbell rang, she greeted Jim, raised an eyebrow and joked, "Had I known dating you came with a brand-new bed, I'd have pounced on you my first night here!" He hugged her, and said she deserved a good night's rest, and they sat down at the table with Ben, Sharon, and Goldie. The doorbell rang again, and everyone looked at each other, confused. No one could figure out who was still missing from the table.

Goldie jumped up, pointed at her children, and warned, "Don't any of you dare make a stink about this. It's only supper." She answered the door and let Sal in, which made everyone smile. "I brought wine and saltwater taffy because no native islanders ever actually *eat* saltwater taffy," he said in his thick Italian accent." Lucinda laughed, and Ben told Sal he had a good point.

Over dinner, Sharon passed around a sampling of her jewelry for everyone to see. The collection turned out beautifully. Each piece was unique, encrusted with pearls, rhinestones, abalone, and tiny shells. Most of it was up-scale enough for even a wedding party. Some pieces were meant to be casual—to appeal to city folk who wanted to lean into island life with a starfish barrette or a sand dollar charm bracelet, but mostly it was quite luxurious. "How much you askin' for this stuff?" Sal probed, tearing a piece of garlic bread off the loaf with his bare hands.

"Sal, don't be crass," Goldie said, playfully smacking his hand.

"No, Mom," Sharon said, "I want everyone's opinions on what to charge. I'm not sure how to price all of this."

"Sharon," Lucinda said, beaming, "I had no idea you were this talented."

"I'm more than just a pretty face," Sharon said, framing her face with her hands.

"Don't joke," Lucinda said. "This is incredible. Where did you learn all of this?"

"Online tutorials, mostly."

Everyone marveled at the intricate details Sharon put into the pieces. The gold necklace with the pink half scallop shell and pearl inside, the Abalone shell flower pendant, the turquoise and Cowrie shell earrings. Sharon must've stayed up nights working on these, Lucinda thought. Goldie held up a pair of spiral shell drop earrings and said, "I'll give you fifty for these!" Sal pulled his wallet out of his back pocket so quickly that he knocked over his wine. He apologized, sopped up the spill with wads of napkins, and handed Sharon a crisp fifty-dollar bill. "Let me get them for you, sweetheart," he said, gazing at Goldie admiringly.

Ben bit his lip, snorted, and mouthed, "Sweetheart?" Goldie slapped him on the back of the head. "Oh, Sal," she said, "you're too good to me." Ben rubbed the back of his head and said it's a wonder he didn't have brain damage from how many times Goldie smacked his skull over the years. "You're a queen," Sal gushed, batting his eyes at Goldie. "You should be treated as such."

"Thanks, Sal," Sharon said. "But I'm not sure guests will pay fifty for the earrings."

Ben said a purse designer he used to date once told him it was perfectly all right to set premium prices on merchandise if you kept all the items priced higher than average. "In other words," he said, "You can charge fifty for the earrings, but don't ask five bucks for the picture frames, you know? Consider the entire collection more of a luxury."

Goldie suggested that Lucinda and Sharon go shopping for display cases for the jewelry. Sal waved a stocky hand across the air in front of him and said that Sharon should name her collection "Sharon's Island Treasures." Smiling broadly and revealing his gold crowns, he added, "I see it in neon lights."

Sharon thanked Sal and said perhaps she'd paint a simple sign that read, "Sharon's Treasures." Sal nodded, pleased with himself. Lucinda pulled a photograph from her back pocket and placed it on the table. Everyone began passing it around and Ben pointed out the thing Lucinda had most wanted him to see: the old T-shirts Tom and Goldie used to sell in the lobby. They were white ringer tees with pale pink trim. "The Pink Octopus" was screen printed on the front in wavy-looking font, and had a large roller-skating pink octopus on the chest.

Lucinda said she'd found the picture under her cot and wanted everyone's opinions on selling the shirts at the front desk again. Sharon piped in, reminding her that there were already at least a dozen successful T-shirt shops on the island. "But none with our business's name on them," Lucinda protested.

While everyone debated, Lucinda grew quiet, a silly grin on her face. Goldie asked if the cat had gotten her tongue, and Lucinda shook her head. "No," she said, examining her nails. "There's no point in arguing, though. I already ordered two dozen in every size so deal with it." When Goldie's mouth fell open, Lucinda laughed.

Ben, who had been checking his phone throughout dinner, threw a napkin at Lucinda and said she was the most Machiavellian Perry of all, but added he wore a Large, and to set one aside for him. He started taking his dishes to the kitchen, and Goldie asked if he had a date or some place important to go. He leaned down and whispered, "Don't any of you dare make a stink about this. It's only dessert," before kissing the top of his mother's head.

Just then, the doorbell rang, and when Ben answered, a pretty girl holding a plastic cake carrier stepped inside the house. Sharon asked why Ben didn't invite her to dinner, but the girl answered for him. "Oh, I had to work. I just got off a little while ago, but I made this last night. I hope you all like Black Forest Cake!" When she spoke, Lucinda recognized her voice. It was Ava, the hostess from Ciao Spaghetti.

Ava sat down, and they all laughed Lucinda's crummy date with Brad. Ava said that after Lucinda left, Brad asked the manager to remove the meal from his bill, but the manager refused since the lobster was almost gone. "Why did you set me up with a miser?" Lucinda asked Sharon. "Are you trying to tell me something?"

Sharon's cheeks flushed, and she busied herself slicing the cake. "I was hoping he'd changed," she finally admitted sheepishly.

"Wait, Brad was one of your cast-offs?" Lucinda screamed, covered her face with her napkin, and the entire table burst into laughter.

By nine, everyone was drinking coffee and playing cards. Lucinda motioned for Jim to go outside with her, and they took a stroll along the beach. The conversation turned to aging, and all the things no one ever told them about it such as the aggressive push from doctors to get colonoscopies and mammograms, and the loud, creaky knees, and how everyone suddenly seemed younger than them—from doctors to salesclerks.

They discussed their gratitude over having such a long history, avoiding the whole getting to know one another bit. Every so often, Jim would stop, take Lucinda's face in his hands, and kiss her. It was a beautiful, warm night, and Lucinda thought it probably couldn't get much better. "Would you like to go on a breakfast picnic tomorrow and watch the sunrise?" Jim said, bending down and picking up a sand dollar. He handed it to her, and she brushed it off and kissed it.

"I'd love to," she beamed.

"Goldie will have to light an extra candle for me over missing church, but that sounds nice, Jim. Oh, hey, I promised Sharon that I would take her to physical therapy at eleven. Think we'll be back by then? They do Sunday appointments once a month and apparently, they're hard to come by so I'd hate for her to cancel."

"We'll be back well before that," he said, kissing the back of her hand. "I promise."

Lucinda turned and started walking back toward the house, flattered at Jim's creative date invitation. When he asked if she wanted to go back to his place, she shook her head and reminded him that she wanted to take things slowly. He laughed quietly, nodded, and agreed. He made a joke about not knowing how much slower they could take it than thirty years, but said he respected Lucinda's wishes.

She kissed his cheek, agreed to meet him at his truck at six a.m., and jogged barefoot back to Goldie's. If her knees creaked, she couldn't hear them over the sappy ballads playing like a record in her head.

Chapter 28

Lucinda woke up at five-thirty the next morning and rinsed some fruit to pack for the picnic. She'd never been on a breakfast picnic, and with short notice, wasn't sure what to bring. She looked through Goldie's cupboards and found breakfast pastries, but not much else. She put some into a tote bag, along with the fruit, a container of yogurt, and two spoons.

She put on a bathing suit under her clothes but cringed at the thought of Jim seeing her stripped down to nothing but a clingy piece of blue spandex. Maybe it wouldn't come to that, she thought. It was only breakfast, after all. She grabbed her sunglasses and purse and went outside to wait beside Jim's truck. He opened his door shortly after she got there, and carried a large cooler outside, loading it onto the bed of the truck. "When did you get all this?" she asked incredulously. He told her he had a few secrets up his sleeve and that he, like Sharon, wasn't just a pretty face. Lucinda laughed when he awkwardly tried framing his face the way her sister had the previous night.

Jim drove them to Turtle Beach Port, parked, and they ferried to Angel Shores—to a private beach that required an exclusive members-only beach permit. Lucinda had heard it was a thousand dollars for a permit and needed renewed in person every even year. When Lucinda asked Jim how he had a permit, he winked and said, "I told you, I have secrets, woman!"

They took a taxi to the beach. Lucinda helped him lug the cooler to the water and they spread out a blanket she'd brought from home. Jim opened the cooler and lifted out a feast. He had croissants, fresh jam, real butter, and even bacon. "It won't be hot, but do you really need bacon to be hot to enjoy it?" he asked. Lucinda grabbed a piece, took a bite, and said, "Definitely not!" He had bottles of orange juice, chocolate pastries, and banana muffins. Lucinda nervously pulled the fruit and Pop Tarts out of her tote bag and shrugged. "Sorry," she said, laughing. Jim waved her off and said he didn't expect to ask a girl to breakfast and make her do the cooking.

They watched the sunrise, and it surprised Lucinda that they were alone on the beach. She asked why more people didn't stop to appreciate things like sunrises or a mother duck and her ducklings or even a rainbow. He shook his head and said that in his experience, most people spent their time overextending themselves to afford their lifestyles, but then complained about being too busy to enjoy what mattered most. "Sometimes you need to stop and take a minute to appreciate what's going on around you," he said, popping a grape in his mouth. "That's my two cents, anyway."

"I believe the kids today call that a 'hot take,'" she said, taking his cue and eating a grape. Jim joked that anymore, he felt like he needed a millennial dictionary to get through life. Lucinda looked in the distance and saw that a child must have forgotten his sand toys after a day at the beach. She pointed them out to Jim, who suggested they build a sandcastle. Lucinda rolled her eyes and groaned, "Get serious." Jim nudged her with his knee and asked when she'd last built one. "A sandcastle?" she asked, picking at a pastry. "Who knows? Forty years?"

Jim asked Lucinda if she had ever noticed that so many "lasts" in life had come and gone without announcing themselves. When she asked what he meant, he took a swig of orange juice, put the cap back on, and lay in the sand. Looking up at the clouds, he explained that people never know when it'll be the last time they search the skies on Christmas Eve for Santa and his reindeer or the last time they'll climb a tree. "Then one day," he said, sitting up and looking at her, "you're a middle-aged dude who takes blood pressure medicine and gets up four times a night to pee."

"No, I get it," Lucinda said, laughing.

"I wish I knew to savor the last time I ate Count Chocula cereal."

"I wish I knew the last time I rocked one of my babies—it would've been Frankie—and fed him a bottle. Oh, how I would give my right arm to go back and have just one more time doing that."

"We could always have a baby together?" Jim said, chuckling.

Lucinda shook her head. "First, absolutely not at my age! Ugh, can you imagine? Second, it wouldn't be the same. I want Jill and Frankie to go back to being babies, to go back to needing me. A new kid wouldn't fill this hole."

Jim stood up, grabbed Lucinda by the hand, and said, "Let's go play! I can't help you rock your baby again, but I can damn sure help you relive building a sandcastle!" She smiled, blinked away the tears her memories had drummed up, and looked around as if someone might be secretly judging two adults playing in the sand. Finally, she stood up.

They each took a bucket and shovel, and started filling them with sand, and packing it down tightly before turning the buckets over on a flat stretch of beach. The child who left the toys behind must have been heartbroken because this wasn't *any* set of sand toys. This was a deluxe set with flags and leveling tools and various shaped and sized buckets. It took about forty minutes to get the details right, and as the sandcastle took shape, the sky lit up with reds and pinks and purples and oranges that almost made Lucinda cry again. It almost looked like the sky was dawning on not only a new day, but a whole new life for her.

When they finished, they returned to the blanket to drink their orange juice and admire their work. "That's some sandcastle, mister," Lucinda told Jim, patting his knee. He nodded proudly and leaned over to kiss her. He joked they should start entering nationwide sandcastle contests. "We could make a living by traveling the globe and winning sandcastle contests. How cool would that be?"

Lucinda fished through her purse, looking for her phone to take a picture. She wished she had a tripod so they could both get in the frame. By the time she found her phone, Jim had moved the cooler across from the sandcastle and stacked some logs on top of it that someone had left behind from a bonfire. He motioned for Lucinda to hurry over so they could capture the sunrise in the photograph. She put the camera on the logs and set the timer for ten seconds.

They stood in front of the sandcastle and took a few pictures until Lucinda got one she approved of. They sat back down and talked a while longer. The tide washed in and began to level their creation. "Oh no," Lucinda cried. "All our hard work down the drain!"

"Literally," Jim said, laughing.

"Now I remember why I stopped making sandcastles," she huffed. "All that work and they're wiped out in a single wave! It's so unfair."

"That's the thing, Luce," he said, putting his arm around her. "We can put all our hopes and dreams into building something, only to have it leveled right before our eyes."

Lucinda sniffed, wiped her eyes, and asked, "When did you become a philosopher?" He stroked her hair and hummed an old song they danced to at their senior prom. She giggled, and they sang the lyrics together—out of tune—remembering it word for word.

After a few minutes, when the sandcastle was almost completely gone, Jim asked if she regretted putting all the hard work into it, and she shook her head. "I had the time of my life, truth be told. I forgot how much fun it was to just *play*, you know?"

Jim reached for Lucinda's phone, pulled up the picture they'd decided was the best shot, and suggested they frame it for the lobby of The Pink Octopus. She agreed and apologized for hurting him all those years earlier. "I appreciate your apology, Lucinda," he said, brushing her hair out of her eyes, "but I don't regret our relationship one bit. I know I got hurt, but it's a lot like these sandcastles that kids build. Everyone knows falling in love is a risk, that a tide could come out of nowhere and wipe the whole thing out. But we do it anyway, because while we're in the thick of it? It's *magic*!"

"I'm sort of thinking that what we built *did* last forever," Lucinda said, touching Jim's cheek. "We're here aren't we? We survived, and we still care deeply for one another."

"I more than *care* for you, lady. Don't you get it? I love you. More than you'll ever know."

"I love you, too," she said, sniffling.

He used his thumb and finger to zoom in on the picture of the two of them in front of the sandcastle—the splendid sunrise paling in comparison to their bright smiles—and held the camera up for Lucinda to see. "We could caption it 'Sandcastles and Second Chances,'" he said, smiling. Lucinda rested her head on his shoulder and whispered, "Sandcastles and Second Chances. I love it."

When they were waiting for the taxi to head home, Jim asked Lucinda what she thought of the two of them fixing up his uncle's house and living there together someday. When she looked surprised, he said, "What? I'm done wasting time! We've gone long enough without each other, and I want to spend every single second of whatever time I have left within arm's reach of you." She smiled so broadly that her cheeks hurt and nodded. "I could handle that."

On the drive home, Jim's phone buzzed in his truck's cup holder several times, but he never let go of her hand to check it. Finally, when it was clearly not going to stop, Lucinda said, "You better get that."

Jim waited until he got to a stoplight and read the message. His face didn't reveal whether it was a good text or a bad one. He placed the phone back in the cup holder and cleared his throat but didn't take Lucinda's hand back. When she asked if everything was all right, he replied, "That was Chief Fox. They found Camille."

Chapter 29

Lucinda felt as though she'd been holding her breath from Turtle Beach Port to The Pink Octopus, almost as if the wind had been knocked out of her. Camille was found, but was she alive or dead? Was it foul play? Would Jim be called back to North Carolina? Arrested? She felt dizzy with questions, but there was no one to ask. Jim was also in the dark.

When they got back to the house, Jim went inside The Blue Dolphin to call Chief Fox. He told Lucinda she could come too, but she declined, figuring he needed privacy. She hugged him and said goodbye, reminding him she was leaving at ten-forty-five to take Sharon to her therapy session.

Inside, Goldie was icing cupcakes to take to church. She asked Lucinda if she wanted to go to the potluck after the service, after Sharon's appointment. Lucinda shook her head, sat on the sofa and began to cry. Goldie asked what was wrong, and Lucinda told her that she'd had the most amazing morning with Jim, but that right before they got home, the police called to say they'd found Camille.

"Is she dead or alive?" Goldie asked breathlessly, opening her laptop to search the headlines. She typed in "Camille Barnes found," and shook her head after a minute or two of scanning the latest news. "Nothing yet."

"They probably won't put it on the news until they've notified all the family," Lucinda said, picking at her cuticles. "I wonder if Max and Savannah know. Those poor kids!"

Goldie closed her laptop and knelt beside Lucinda's chair. She tried to comfort her, but anything she said was simply a guess. Until Jim talked to Chief Fox and reported back to them, whatever happened with Camille would remain a mystery. Goldie couldn't assure Lucinda everything would be all right. She couldn't guarantee that if Camille were alive, Jim wouldn't have a newfound appreciation for her and want to go to marriage counseling. It was one thing to have a relationship sour, but another when someone presumed dead popped back into the picture.

Perhaps Jim would see her in a new light, assuming she was still alive! If she were dead, that might open a new can of worms.

Suddenly, despite Camille being located, everything felt upside down in Lucinda's world. Her stomach hurt and her head throbbed with uncertainty. Goldie fixed her a cup of peppermint tea, and Sharon walked into the living room rubbing her eyes as if still waking up. "Who died?" she said, yawning, but immediately regretted it when she saw her sister crying. Goldie told her that Jim's ex-wife had been found and they were waiting for answers. "Is she dead or alive?" Sharon asked.

"Gosh, Sharon!" Lucinda hissed. "We don't know yet, okay?"

"Okay, sorry!" Sharon said. "Excuse me for caring!"

Lucinda gathered her car keys and told Sharon to get a move on. Sharon saluted like a military soldier and slid on her sandals. They went to the car, and it didn't take long for Lucinda to apologize, saying she didn't mean to snap at her sister but that the stress was killing her. "I just had the best morning of my life," she said, sniffling, "but now I don't know what's going to happen. Jim might leave Turtle Island forever, depending on what the cops have found."

Sharon tried to assure her sister that no matter what happened, Jim wouldn't leave Lucinda hanging. That didn't help, and Lucinda was spiraling into panic mode, finding it hard to get in a deep breath. She waited in the car listening to sad songs on the radio while Sharon had her physical therapy appointment.

Sharon's physical therapist, Joni, suggested she start using a cane—"a real one," she said. "Not the makeshift one you bring in here sometimes. That thing is enough to put an eye out!"

Joni said the cane might not be forever, but that until Sharon got her sea legs—which Joni explained would come with proper medication, supplements, and physical therapy—it might be a good idea. She suggested Sharon bedazzle the cane the way actress Selma Blair had done with hers. Sharon liked the idea, even though she worried what Matt would think about dating a girl with a cane. She cringed at the idea of having the dreaded MS conversation with him. She was really starting to like him and didn't want to scare him off.

While Lucinda was tuning the car radio, Jim texted.

Jim: She's alive. I don't know much, but Savannah called and wants me to go home.

Lucinda: OK, well it's good that Camille's alive! Do you know how long you'll be gone?

Jim started to text back and deleted whatever he was saying several times. Lucinda was holding her breath, hoping he wasn't going to say he was leaving the island for good. She felt a bit selfish for being jealous that Jim was rushing home. If only for Max and Savannah, it was the right thing to do.

Finally, he answered with a short, "I'm not sure," and Lucinda felt her legs turn to jelly. She asked if she could see him when she got home. He said yes, but that he didn't have much time. He'd found a cheap flight into Wilmington National Airport but had to leave in a couple of hours.

Lucinda felt her world spinning out of control. How could their timing be so off? She was foolish to leave Jim in the first place, she thought, grinding her teeth, and fighting back tears. Then, it took her thirty years to come to her senses and get him back. Now, after only a short time as a couple, they'd be saying goodbye again. She couldn't help but wonder whether Jim was rushing home to clear his name officially, or because he was relieved the actual love of his life was found in one piece.

The thought of Jim tearfully reuniting with his real soulmate, a woman who seemed erratic and unfeeling to Lucinda, was too much to bear. She buried her head in her hands and choked back the tears. "Not again," she whispered. "Please, don't let me lose him again."

She sat up straight, took a deep breath, and resigned herself to whatever was coming next. She knew that if karma were real, she had a penance to pay after the way she'd broken Jim's heart all those years earlier. Regardless of whether she was a good person now, she crushed him like a bug on the sole of her shoe the day she left him for Peter.

Back at home, Lucinda helped Sharon to a chair, filled Goldie in on the very little bit she knew about Jim's situation, and left to go speak with him. He was already packing a duffel bag when she got there. He said little, only that the police weren't telling him anything beyond the fact that they'd found Camille. Lucinda wanted desperately to ask Jim if he was scared, relieved, or some other emotion she couldn't put a name to. She didn't, though, feeling it wasn't her place to push too hard when she'd only recently let down her own guard with him.

She sat in a chair and watched him pack, stopping to text someone or another now and again. She ran her fingers through her hair and waited patiently for Jim to shed some light on his plans. Finally, he sat down beside her and said, "I know you want to know what I'm planning to do. All I can tell you is that I am itching to go home and clear my name. That's all I know for sure right now."

Lucinda stood and paced the kitchen floor. She wanted to beg Jim to come back after he'd wrapped up his family affairs. She wanted to promise she'd do everything she could to give him a good life if only he'd return, if only he'd pick her instead of Camille. Instead, she placed her hand on his shoulder and whispered, "Do whatever you have to do, Jim. If I can help in any way, let me know."

She asked when he was going to Pelican Harbor to board his first plane, and he told her his taxi would be picking him up in less than an hour. Things were moving so quickly. Lucinda felt a headache coming on. The room was spinning, and she felt flushed. Jim noticed her rubbing her temples and got a cold cloth to put on her head. "Let's lie down and try to get rid of it," he said, pointing to her head.

Lying on Jim's bed with his arm around her waist, Lucinda imagined getting on the plane with him. She could go back and help him tie up loose ends, clear his name, and then help him pack his belongings. They could move back to the island, live in his uncle's house, renovate it together.

She couldn't leave, though. Her mother and sister needed her. The Pink Octopus had a grand reopening she couldn't miss. There were vendors to contact, a news piece scheduled, flyers to put up around Turtle Beach. She couldn't miss Grandma Helen's 100th birthday for anything. How many more would there be?

She let a few tears fall silently onto Jim's pillow, hoping he wouldn't notice. When he felt her shoulders shuttering, he whispered in her ear, "It's your turn to tell me about *your* kids." Lucinda closed her eyes, comforted by Jim's warm breath on her neck. She wasn't sure what Goldie had already told him about Frank and Jill, but her best guess was nearly everything. She didn't know what she could reveal that he wouldn't already know.

She sniffled, smiled, and took a cue from his descriptions of Max and Savannah. "Jill rescued baby animals all the time as a kid. I'd be cleaning her bedroom and find a turtle in the hamper, or a baby bird nestled in her sock drawer. When she learned that the little bunny symbol on skin and hair products meant the company didn't test on animals, she went down...well, a rabbit hole, scouring the Internet for everything she could find on the subject. Horrified, she vowed to start her own organic skincare business. She was just eleven.

Last year after college, she launched Pure Love 4 Life, a cruelty-free brand of makeup, skincare, and nail products that donates a percentage of its proceeds to animal welfare organizations around the world."

"Sounds like a sweet girl."

"She is," Lucinda said, proudly.

"And Frank?"

"Frankie is straight edge all the way, not quick with the warm and fuzzies, you know? But every Mother's Day he sends me somewhere beautiful for a weeklong vacation. He pays for my friend Rachel to go, too. We've been to Africa, Europe, and Ireland, plus a lot of U.S. destinations."

"Where's your favorite place you've ever been?"

Lucinda's pillow was cold and wet from her tears, and she knew she must look affright. She desperately wanted to roll over, touch his cheek, and say, *Right here. Right here beside you is my favorite place I've ever been*. But without knowing where his heart was, she sighed, and told him Banff, Canada in winter was breathtaking.

Despite her best efforts to stay awake for their little bit of time together, sleep took hold and Lucinda woke up two hours later to an empty cottage. When she went back home, she found a note on the kitchen table that said Sharon and Goldie went to the potluck and would be home by suppertime. Lucinda poured herself a glass of water, took a sip, and dumped the rest down the drain. She loaded her dirty glass into the dishwasher and went to her bedroom. Feeling helpless, she texted Savannah and said she was happy for her that she got her mother back.

Savannah: Thanks, Lucinda. I'm glad she's alive and fine, but we'll have a lot of repair work to do as a family if we're ever going to move beyond this crazy mess.

Lucinda tried to compose a text several times but didn't quite know how to respond. What did Savannah mean by "We'll have a lot of repair work to do as a family?" Did Camille need hospitalization? What did she mean by "family?" Was she including Jim in that family unit? Her head started to throb again. Squinting, she punched the keys on her phone.

Lucinda: Oh, goodness. Well, I hope everything works out. Let me know if I can be of any help.

Savannah: Will do. I was hoping to meet you someday, but if my dad's coming home, I guess that won't happen. Take care, though. You've been really sweet.

Lucinda began to cry when it sounded like Jim wouldn't return to Turtle Island. She'd lost him once, but that was her choice, foolish as it may have been. Now, though? She was losing him again, and it was Jim who decided. *I guess I deserved this one*, she thought, closing her eyes and pulling the covers up. *Turnabout is fair play.*

Chapter 30

Channel 6 news, WTIX, sent field reporter, Tasha Trenton to interview the Perry family for a piece on Grandma Helen's 100th birthday celebration which was quickly approaching. Tasha was new, and had only been officially on the job for a few months after a college internship at the station led to a full-time gig. The powers that be assigned her the puff pieces such as the twentieth anniversary of The Turtle Beach Birdwatchers Association and the Jellyfish Bay Chili Cook-Off.

Tasha made small talk with Lucinda as Tyrone set up the cameras and microphone. "So," she said, looking around at the freshly painted cottages, "why aren't you guys all booked up? The place is adorable!"

Lucinda explained that The Pink Octopus was closed for renovations and would be hosting its grand reopening over the weekend to coincide with Helen's birthday party. Tasha asked if she could mention that in the news piece and Lucinda nodded, thrilled that she didn't have to be the one to bring it up. All the publicity would be wonderful for business, especially after the cost of paint, repairs, fixtures, decorations, linens, and upgrades had taken hungry bites out of her budget for weeks.

Tasha went live, and asked questions such as what food would be served at the party, who was invited, and what state of mind Helen was in at nearly one hundred. Goldie told Tasha to go to Whispering Pines and ask Helen herself. "She's sharp as a tack, that one," Goldie snickered.

Tasha came to life on camera, looking the part of a typical field reporter, and wrapped things up with her signature sign-off, "That's the news, and I'm outta here!"

When the camera stopped rolling, Tasha became a regular, somewhat insecure millennial again, biting her thumbnail and asking Lucinda what she thought of the sign-off. "I've tried a couple of different ones, but I think this one makes me sound breezy. Sometimes if I don't concentrate on sounding breezy, I have a resting bitch face." Lucinda laughed and said she knew exactly what Tasha meant.

Tasha was a sweet girl. She'd grown up in Texas, attended a prestigious college on a cello scholarship, and moved to the island when she landed the internship at WTIX.

When Goldie horned into Lucinda's conversation with Tasha and asked if she was single, Tasha blushed, and showed her a picture in her phone. "My fiance's name is Boston. He's a search and rescue diver." Goldie, smiled tightly, and pretended she'd forgotten something in the office. Once she realized there would be no matchmaking with Tasha and Lord-knows-who, she lost interest immediately.

Lucinda chewed the inside of her cheek when her mother dismissed Tasha, quickly making a joke about looking into whether or not she might've been adopted. "We're so different, my mom and me. I don't get it," she stammered. Tasha laughed, said she thought Goldie was adorable, and began telling a funny story about her own mother.

Ben asked Lucinda and Sharon to meet him at his place for lunch, which they thought was odd, but agreed to nonetheless. He served his famous barbeque ribs, corn on the cob, and watermelon. They talked about sports, and what to get Grandma for her birthday. Ben showed his sisters the sexy firemen calendar he got Helen, saying, "I get her one every year. I think that's what's kept her alive so long!"

When the question of whether to get a new charter boat for the business came up, Ben shifted in his seat, not saying much. "What's going on?" Sharon asked him.

"Nothing, why?"

"Come on, Ben," Lucinda said, "you've been acting out of sorts for a while."

"Did you bring us here to tell us something?" Sharon prodded. "You finally joining the circus or what?"

"Don't tell us you and Fawn got back together and are engaged?" Lucinda joked.

After a few minutes of coaxing, Ben finally admitted that he didn't necessarily want to commit to working at The Pink Octopus forever. Lucinda said he didn't have to, but this upset Sharon. She said that if Ben quit, and Lucinda went back to Connecticut, she'd never be able to leave the island. When Ben asked where Sharon wanted to go, she snipped, "That's not the point! Everyone gets to just leave? I'll be left here alone to deal with Mom and make sure Grandma's okay, and the business. It's a lot, Benny!"

Lucinda squeezed Sharon's knee, and said that first, the three of them were all adults. Anyone could freely leave whenever they pleased. She added it wasn't anyone's job to be the glue of the family. Ben and Sharon exhaled when Lucinda said that. "What do you want to do, Ben?" she said, sitting back and taking a deep breath. He shrugged. She asked again, and his cheeks grew red. "I want to become a massage therapist and get a job on Angel Shores, OK?

"At the spa?" Sharon asked.

"Why do you seem embarrassed about that?" Lucinda asked.

"I want an actual profession, not just taking people out to catch fish and fixing stuff around The Pink Octopus, you know? I don't want to die in a charter boat."

"Who's dying?" Sharon asked sarcastically.

Ben said he had been looking into classes on the mainland and thought about enrolling, but he was afraid their mother would be upset if he left the island. Lucinda asked how long it would take Ben to get his certificate. He said it would be twelve months, and Lucinda asked for the school's website and wrote it down. "Ben, what if you can take the classes during the day, do some evening fishing excursions to keep guests happy, and then, once you get your certificate, we could offer massages for an upcharge at The Pink Octopus? You wouldn't have to leave to pursue your dream, but you also wouldn't have to spend all day fishing."

Ben thought about it for a while and said he didn't think massages for tourists of The Pink Octopus would be enough to live on. He said he couldn't imagine doing fishing excursions to make up the difference and trying to massage guests when he smelled like low tide. Sharon suggested he offer his services by appointment to people all over the island, such as in clients' homes, at hotels, or even do a day a week in downtown Turtle Beach where he could offer ten-minute walk-up massages. "Kind of like a street performer," Lucinda joked.

"Exactly!" Sharon said, smiling. "But instead of wearing a red nose and making balloon animals, you'd get to rub cute girls' shoulders."

"Wow, I sort of thought you guys would laugh at this," Ben said, running his fingers through his hair.

"We're not jerks," Sharon said. "Well, maybe Lucinda is, but I'm not."

Lucinda threw a couch pillow at Sharon. Ben handed each of them a cold beer from the refrigerator, and they toasted. "To Ben's new endeavor," Lucinda said, clinking her bottle on Sharon's and then Ben's.

"Not to sour the good mood," Sharon said, "but did you hear from Jim yet?"

Lucinda shook her head. Ben sipped his beer, and then looked at Lucinda seriously and said that if Jim had half a brain, he'd tie up loose ends to hurry back to put a ring on it. Lucinda laughed, and said she wasn't even technically divorced yet. "Please," Sharon said. "I just ate! You're going to make me sick thinking about you being with Peter the Aardvark."

Marry me, thought Lucinda, while Ben and Sharon amused themselves, drawing comparisons between Peter and an anteater. *We've only been together a couple of days. Well, thirty years and a couple of days, but still*.

She casually checked her phone, but there was nothing from Jim. She wondered if he was busy or if it was something more? Maybe he was finally back where he considered to be his real home, maybe in Camille's arms. The scariest thought of all was wondering how she'd deal with the scenario of never hearing from him again.

Chapter 31

Goldie and Lucinda were in the kitchen that night baking lemon brownies. Goldie agreed to share her secret recipe with Lucinda—only after swearing her to secrecy—so they could find the most economical and fast way to make them in large quantities. Their plan was to put a small box of them in each bungalow, enough for one per registered guest, and when they wanted more, they'd find them for sale at the front desk.

Goldie went grocery shopping the day before and bought the ingredients, carefully itemizing and calculating the cost per brownie. "If we cut each pan into nine brownies, "she said, chewing on the tip of her pen, "then our cost is eighty-nine cents per square."

Lucinda did some math of her own and suggested they sell the brownies individually and in packs of six, assuming no one would pay for a dozen at the price they needed to ask. "Now if we leave off the glaze, we could make them for seventy-nine cents per brownie," Lucinda suggested, pointing to a plain brownie.

"Bite your tongue!" Goldie hissed. "My glaze is legendary. I won't omit it, so if that's what we have to do to make this happen, you can forget it!"

"Calm down, Mother. We'll keep the glaze."

Goldie asked if they should offer a variety of brownies, such as chocolate, coffee, and blondies. After some thought, Lucinda decided it might be best to avoid becoming a bakery. "I think we should be famous for one brownie, and let it end there," she said. "People will come from all around to get a taste." Goldie beamed as though imagining "Goldie's Famous Lemon Brownies" in lights.

Lucinda grated the lemon zest while Goldie whisked the powdered sugar glaze. "Mom?" Lucinda said. When she had Goldie's attention, she asked if all that stuff about Hercules was true, and whether he'd really granted Lucinda and Goldie a hundred-year life? Goldie nodded, said that people could call her crazy all they wanted, but sometimes she went out on the water and visited the giant turtle. "How come no one else still sees him?" Lucinda asked, closing her eyes and breathing in the invisible lemon cloud floating overhead.

Goldie shrugged, and said she didn't know but maybe the people who did, didn't sound a horn about it. "Probably don't want folks calling them crazy!" she said, winking at Lucinda.

"So, we're really going to live to be one hundred?"

"Between us having my mother's genes, and Hercules giving us the blessing? I think we stand a pretty good chance."

"Well," Lucinda mused, licking her finger and wincing from the sour lemon juice, "guess I'll take up skydiving, since there's apparently no danger in it for me. I can also add to the list snake handling, chain smoking, and drag racing."

"Are you waiting for a reaction?" Goldie asked, rolling her eyes. "Is that what you need? Me to beg you to continue playing it safe?"

"I didn't know opening my heart up to love again—which is akin to walking through downtown naked thanks to Peter—is playing it safe? Besides, laying it all out there didn't pan out too well for me, did it? There are worse things than keeping your head down and staying in your own lane. Some of us just aren't meant to find our happily ever after."

Lucinda waited for Goldie to protest, but she didn't. She cleaned up the kitchen, wiped the counters, and straightened the dish towel hanging on the oven door. It reminded Lucinda of being a little girl sitting at the counter and watching her mother gracefully navigate baking a complex dessert or cooking dinner for a crowd.

Despite Goldie's indifference to homemaking, she was a natural at it in every way. "Mom, do you remember the time I begged you to make your cinnamon roll cake for my third-grade class?"

Goldie continued to clean, almost as if she had no recollection of the memory. Lucinda continued, "It was the last day of school and Miss Jacobs picked three of us to bring desserts for the party. I wanted you to make your cinnamon roll cake, but you made peanut butter cookies instead. I cried the entire way to school. Did you know that?"

Goldie lit a candle, as she always did when she finished cleaning the kitchen, and folded a dish towel in thirds, hanging it neatly on the oven door. She was done cleaning and seemed uninterested in Lucinda's story. "I wish you remembered, Mom," Lucinda said. "I wanted to ask why you wouldn't make the cake I asked you to bake?"

"Who said I don't remember?" Goldie said, flipping the light switch off.

"Well, if you do, then will you explain why you made peanut butter cookies instead of my favorite cake?"

"Tammy Freemont. Tammy Freemont is why I made peanut butter cookies."

"Huh?"

"She loved that cake, remember? She always asked for it when she came over to play with you."

"I remember. We were best friends until Michelle Scott moved to the island. Then, they both turned on me. Why can two girls be friends, but never three? Did you ever notice that?"

"I think you just answered your question about why I wouldn't make the cinnamon roll cake," Goldie said, kissing Lucinda on top of her head.

"Mess with my daughter, mess with me." She winked at Lucinda and disappeared into the living room to watch a game show on television. She turned back once to say Lucinda's theory on love sucked and that her love life wasn't over until the fat lady sang.

Lucinda shook her head and managed a smile. Suddenly, she felt her phone vibrate in her pants pocket. It was Jim, asking if she could talk for a few minutes. She texted "Yes," and went to her bedroom and shut the door. When he called, she breathed a sigh of relief, but that relief quickly turned to stomach knots when she heard him speak. He was polite but sounded a million miles away, almost guarded. He let out a sigh, and explained what happened to Camille, or at least the story she told police.

When Jim got back to North Carolina, he went straight to the police station, where Max, Savannah, and Camille were waiting in an interrogation room. Savannah's arms were crossed, and Max was texting on his phone when Jim arrived.

No one got up to greet Jim, but Savannah started crying. Before Jim could ask what was going on, Chief Fox knocked on the door and entered, offering for Jim to sit down. "Camille was picked up in San Diego for trying to cash a bad check, weren't you there Camille?" All Camille said in response was that she wasn't speaking until she was appointed a lawyer.

Max slammed his cell phone on the table and said, "I'll fill you in, Dad. Mom skipped town with a guy she met online who promised her a beachfront apartment and free modeling photos, if you can believe that." Jim looked at Camille, who picked her chipped nail polish and rolled her eyes. "It seems," Chief Fox said, clearing his throat, "that she wanted to go missing for a while and watch you squirm while the police fingered you as the prime suspect in her disappearance."

"Well, it worked, Camille!" Jim yelled. "The entire country thought I murdered you and hid your corpse!"

Camille snorted, and Chief Fox told her to wipe the smile off her face. He wiped it off for her when he informed her that she'd committed a slew of crimes during her weeks on the run. "Crimes that'll put your rear end in prison, lady!" He tugged at his collar, apparently as annoyed with Camille as Jim was, and explained that Camille had wasted police dollars in the search, written at least a dozen bad checks, and assumed the identity of a woman whose purse she stole from a movie theater. "That's how we caught her," Chief Fox told Jim. "Using the poor victim's credit cards. But, those charges are nothing compared to lying to police."

"What lie did she tell, sir?" Savannah asked, using a tissue to apply pressure to a fingertip she'd bloodied biting her nails.

"She made an anonymous call three days before we apprehended her, saying that your father was seen disposing of large garbage bags the night she went missing. That's a crime, Ms. Barnes. You lie to cops, you're going to jail. Period, end of story."

"She insinuated I was disposing of a body?" Jim yelled, running his fingers through his hair.

"Yes, and through some good old-fashioned detective work, we traced the call to a Robert T. Callum of San Diego."

Chief Fox told Jim, Max, and Savannah that Mr. Callum was a known criminal with a rap sheet longer than his greasy, stringy hair. Jim fought a smile when the chief said that part.

A few minutes later, everyone was dismissed, and Camille was led to a cell where Jim assumed she'd be for a while, though he didn't care enough to ask.

Before leaving, he asked Chief Fox if he was now cleared of suspicion and able to go about his business. Chief Fox nodded, shook his hand, and apologized for the inconvenience. "In our defense," he said, "it really is the husband most times."

In the parking lot, Max and Savannah apologized to Jim and they went to an ice cream stand Jim used to take them to as youngsters. They sat at a picnic table discussing what to do about Camille. Savannah was furious, especially because in all her mother's plotting and planning to destroy Jim, she'd allowed her own kids to believe she was dead, and that their dad was a cold-blooded killer. Max blurted out, "I'm done with her," and shook his head. "You do whatever you want, Savvy. I know you'll end up feeling sorry for her and caving, but I'm done."

"I'm nearly done, too," Savannah argued, "but I'll make sure she gets a decent lawyer."

"We're sorry, Dad," Max sighed. "Mom's been telling us for years what a miserable jerk you were, and I guess eventually we started to believe it, especially when she went missing."

"Can you forgive us?" Savannah cried, wiping her eyes with a paper napkin.

That was where Jim left off on the story, and Lucinda realized she'd been holding her breath most of the time he'd been talking. She let out a long sigh and asked what happened next. Jim said Max flew to back to Chicago and Savannah asked Jim to stay in North Carolina and help her get their old family home ready to sell before she had to return to New York.

Lucinda nodded, forgetting Jim couldn't see her. When he asked if she was still there, she said yes, and then, "I hope everything works out for all of you, Jim."

He told her he'd had a wonderful time reconnecting with her but that he felt he needed to stay in North Carolina for a while and help Savannah process everything. Lucinda opened her mouth to ask for clarification on the words, "a while," but closed it again, not wanting to push.

When they hung up, Lucinda got the feeling that might be the last time she would speak to Jim Barnes for a long time, which felt worse than if she'd never reconnected with him in the first place. Wondering what had become of him all those years was better than knowing full well he was still warm and funny and loyal and handsome, that the years didn't harden him. Because all those things only made her regret the choice to pick Peter over Jim that much more.

Scott texted while Lucinda was in the bath and asked if she'd reconsidered going out on another date with him. She texted a quick, "Sorry, Scooter," and then deleted his number from her phone.

When she climbed into bed that night, she touched the spot on the mattress beside her and thought, *I may as well accept that I'm meant to be alone. I've blown multiple opportunities, and it's looking like love just isn't in the cards for me.*

Chapter 32

The next morning, Grandma Helen called and asked Lucinda to stop by Whispering Pines for a visit and bring her some snack items and a bottle of hand cream she'd run out of the previous week. "Maybe some mauve nail polish for my birthday party, too, sweetie," Helen suggested.

While sitting at a stop light, Lucinda saw two young girls, somewhere around fifteen, she guessed, riding bicycles. One was turquoise and one was lemon yellow, and the girls were holding hands as they rode down main street. Lucinda smiled and remembered being a teenager—back when her friends were her entire life and she still believed anything was possible with enough hard work and dedication. She dialed Ben's number while keeping her eyes on the road.

It took a while for him to pick up, and when he did, he answered with his mouth full. "What are you eating?" Lucinda thundered. Ben didn't answer for a long minute, only continued crunching. Lucinda sighed loudly into the phone and said she didn't have all day. Finally, Ben said, "Lucky Charms, sheesh! Didn't your mother tell you not to talk with your mouth full? Mine did. Even at thirty-six I don't utter a single word with food in my mouth, afraid Mom will slap me upside the head. What'd you call for anyway?"

Lucinda told him about the girls riding bicycles and asked why he'd never thought to rent them out at The Pink Octopus. He asked why he'd rent girls out when people were looking for bungalows, and Lucinda groaned loudly. Seeing she was in no mood for jokes, he sighed and said what Goldie, Sharon, or Ben always said when Lucinda questioned why they hadn't gotten on board with the rest of the hospitality industry on Turtle Island: "Money."

"Well, what would cute bikes cost? Something in the realm of $200?"

"I promise you I'm the last person on the island to know about cute bike prices."

"Ugh, look into it and if you can find them for about two hundred or so a pop, pick up six of them. I'll text you my credit card number."

"With what vehicle am I to pick up half a dozen cute bikes?"

"Ask Jim to use his truck. Oh, wait. Never mind. Gosh, Ben, just figure it out!"

She ended the call, and her nostalgic, sweet, summery mood was gone just like that. She looked for the girls on the bicycles, but they were gone too. When she got to the nursing home, she had a text from Ben, saying she was moody and that the best remedy was to call Scooter.

Ben: Also, it's not the bikes that'll be pricey. Do you have any idea how much bicycle racks cost? And locks? And baskets? Because you know all the tourists need a flowery basket to complete their aesthetic, or whatever it's called.

Lucinda: The budget is $2,000. Knock yourself out. Hurry, though, because I want this to be available at the grand reopening. I've gotta go. I'm visiting Grandma. Remember her? Would be nice if you'd visit her from time to time, you know?

Ben: Call Scooter. You need a man!

Grandma Helen was sitting in a lavender-colored TV room that smelled of urine and beef gravy, and yelling at Edna Clarice for sleeping through *The Price is Right*. Lucinda walked up behind her and kissed the top of her head. "Hi, Grandma," she said, kneeling next to her.

"Let's sit outside, honey," she said, unlocking the wheels on her wheelchair and rolling her eyes. "I'm tired of listening to Edna Clarice snore! So rude!"

Lucinda stifled a laugh and walked her grandmother out to the veranda. They picked a shady spot, which wasn't difficult to find since Whispering Pines was careful not to risk any of their residents getting sunburned if they fell asleep outside. Lucinda unpacked the bag of nuts and chocolate covered raisins and popcorn and magazines. "Did you get the lotion, too?" Helen asked, concerned. Lucinda held it up, and Helen smiled and asked how she got so lucky to have such a smart, attractive granddaughter.

They visited a while, and after the second round of checkers, Lucinda realized Helen hadn't called her to Whispering Pines to discuss something important at all. She was lonely.

Lucinda understood that feeling all too well. Before moving to Turtle Island, she'd spent most of her time alone. The kids checked in occasionally, and she played Bunco with her girlfriends once a month. She volunteered at the library weekly, and had lunch with Rachel after church sometimes, but in general, she'd been lonely, too.

When Helen asked how Lucinda was doing since Peter left, she shrugged and made a joke about *Who needs a man, anyway?* Helen gave a sad smile and said she missed her late husband, the grandfather Lucinda never knew, Stu. "If you could find a man half as wonderful as my Stuie, you'd be better off than most," Helen said. Lucinda smiled, and asked what was so wonderful about Grandpa Stu.

Helen went on to describe meeting Stu when her father took her with him to buy chickens from a farm on the other side of town. "Was this in North Dakota, Gram?" Lucinda asked, leaning in closer and resting her hand on Helen's. She nodded and continued. "I was nine and Stu was eleven. We played with the farm animals until my dad finished talking to Stu's father. Oh, I suppose it was only an hour or so, but that's all it took. After that, we were inseparable. My dad would drop me off on Saturdays to help Stu's family with the farm chores. I milked goats and cows, fed the chickens and gathered eggs, and had a grand old time."

"So, you two eventually dated?"

"Yes, it was called courting back then. I went to school, but Stu's family couldn't afford it, so I taught him to read. Do you know he went on to have the largest farm in Bismarck?"

"No, I had no idea," Lucinda said. "I'm embarrassed that I don't already know this, but how did Grandpa die?"

Grandma Helen took her time getting to Stu's death. First, she talked about how he delivered two of their four children at home, even with Aunt Eileen being breach, how he was a wonderful father, and that every Valentine's Day he made Helen a chocolate cake that tasted awful, but what she wouldn't give to have a slice now.

After a few minutes of sitting with her eyes closed, probably imagining the chocolate cake, Helen opened them and said, "It was Christmas morning. The kids wanted to open their gifts, but Stu said he needed to check on the laboring mare. He was gone a while, and finally your uncle, Kevin, went out to the horse shed to look for him. He came running back inside, hysterical, saying Pa was hurt."

"What happened?" Lucinda asked, her eyebrows knit together.

"The mare was in distress and kicked Stu in the head. He died almost instantly."

"Oh, Gram, I'm so sorry. How old was Grandpa when he died?"

"Forty-two," she said, wiping her nose with a tissue she pulled from her sleeve. "But the mare and her baby lived. I never blamed her. Anyone who's gone through labor wouldn't blame her."

Lucinda felt incredibly sad and had to remind herself that this had all happened over sixty years earlier. She wanted to ask Grandma Helen why she never remarried, but the timing didn't feel right. Instead, she asked how Grandma came to the island.

Helen recalled it was after Ben was born. Goldie needed help to manage three little kids and the hotel, as Helen referred to The Pink Octopus. Lucinda shrugged. "I think everyone on Turtle Island believes you've lived here all your life."

"Let 'em think that," Helen laughed. "It makes me something of a celebrity! Of course, I'll never be as famous as Hercules!"

After their visit, Lucinda was back in the car driving home and listening to a slow song on the radio. She thought of her grandmother's life, and how, even though Stu and Helen loved each other deeply, it was really more of a tragedy than a love story. After all, it was cut short when Stu was very young—younger than Lucinda was now. Poor Helen never remarried, out of loyalty, most likely.

Lucinda bent the rearview mirror to look at herself. She brushed her bangs out of her eyes, sat up straight and made a promise to herself. If Jim was gone, and Peter had moved on with Eve—the sting of which Lucinda wondered if she'd ever really get over—then perhaps it was time for her to move on, too.

Whether starting afresh meant finding a man or diving into a new hobby or getting a Cocker Spaniel, Lucinda resolved to live her life to the fullest, not become the ninety-nine-year-old sweet woman in a nursing home recalling a love so old, even the memories had cobwebs.

She loved Helen more than anything, but she looked at her as a cautionary tale. Lucinda knew she had more adventures to go on, more stories to rack up, and she was going to start immediately.

Chapter 33

Lucinda spent the afternoon navigating the new website, with Jill on the phone guiding her through its pages. She'd done a magnificent job making The Pink Octopus appear the perfect blend of tranquility and entertainment. The cottages lined up on the beach looked like a row of dollhouses, and the pink umbrellas opened beside all the beach chairs looked like they'd been plucked from a life-size Barbie doll house.

Calls were already coming in, much to Goldie's annoyance over trying to keep up with the new reservations system. She wondered why people needed to call when the site had a feature to book cottages online.

Sharon was setting up displays of her handcrafted jewelry, hair clips, and picture frames and let out a long sigh. "Mom, people are bound to have questions. It's not like the new website will eliminate the need for a telephone!" Goldie slammed a stapler on the counter, grumbling under her breath, "Well, what good is it, then?"

Lucinda held up her hands and motioned for her mother and sister to relax, take a deep breath, and try to have fun during the process. "Go do a handstand or something, Mom. Try to find your Zen place."

Ben and his friends unloaded turquoise bicycles from the backs of two trucks, along with a bike rack, and parked them behind the office building. Lucinda smiled when she saw little white baskets on the fronts of each bike.

Goldie disappeared into the office kitchen, returning a few minutes later with a pitcher of instant iced tea and a sliced peach.

They all sat down and collected themselves, drinking tea and imagining where the business might be in a year. "Sharon," Lucinda said, leaning toward her sister and biting her lip, "have you ever thought about renting Sea Rock? I mean rather than allowing it to sit vacant?"

"Why not just sell it?" Goldie chimed in.

"Because it's her home, Mom," Lucinda growled. "What if her situation changes someday and she wants to move back in there?"

"You don't have to put the word 'situation' in air quotes," Sharon sighed. "I know you mean what if I find a new husband?"

"I'm sorry, Sharon," Lucinda said, sliding back in her chair. "I didn't mean..."

"I know what you mean," Sharon said. "Why do you guys think I date so many randos? It's because I don't want to replace Alan. I feel funny about it. I had one marriage. It would be so strange to start over with a brand-new husband. Thus, the randos."

Lucinda didn't understand what "randos" meant, and Goldie rolled her eyes and said, "Random guys, Lucinda. Get an urban dictionary, will you?" This made everyone laugh, a deep, cleansing belly laugh.

When Ben walked into the lobby a few minutes later, Lucinda asked if he knew what "randos" meant. "Random dudes?" he replied, hiking up his shorts. Lucinda groaned, and soon everyone got back to work. There were only a couple of days until the party and still lots to do.

Lucinda thought a test run in the cottages might be a good way to ensure everything ran like clockwork. As it was, they blocked off the rest of the month to iron out the kinks, but to be certain they needed guests.

Lucinda asked Sharon and Goldie if they'd be willing to sleep in one of the cabins the following night as something of a test run. They agreed, and Lucinda said to conduct a proper experiment, they should fill all thirteen cabins. "I want The Lemon Jellyfish," Sharon said. "It has the best water pressure." Goldie called dibs on The Peach Squid because it had a mini-library and she planned to add to it with her collection of Harlequin romances, saying guests come to the island to be swept away.

Lucinda thought about it and considered taking The Blue Dolphin—Jim's cabin. She felt her eyes well up with tears at the memory of lying in bed spooning with him. The memory was so strong she could almost smell his cologne. She pretended she had something in her eye so Goldie wouldn't make a big deal out of it, and penciled herself in at The Great White, the largest bungalow on the property.

Goldie asked why she needed the honeymooner's cottage when she'd be staying there alone? When Lucinda gave her a dirty look, Goldie threw her hands up in surrender. "I didn't mean anything by it!"

The truth was, Lucinda had dabbled in *The Secret* years ago. It was a book based on the law of attraction. Rachel gave it to her for Christmas one year, but she'd never read it. Finally, while packing for a trip to Paris with Peter, she'd tossed it in her carry-on bag for something to read on the airplane.

She read it back-to-back twice on the flight. Peter studied his notes for a conference he was scheduled to speak at, so he wasn't much company during the plane ride. The book theorized that nearly everything in life is determined by a person's attitude, specifically whether they believe they are worthy of miraculous things. The contributors to the book claimed that an unwavering faith in life turning up roses was tantamount to attracting everything from a good parking spot to a million dollars.

The idea was to start small, so Lucinda attracted a cup of tea, which arrived when Rachel unexpectedly stopped by after a walk with her latest rescue dog. "Tom Cruise thought you might like a Raspberry Milk Tea," Rachel chirped in a high-pitched baby talk as the enormous Bernese Mountain Dog climbed her leg. Lucinda was so taken aback that *The Secret* might work, that she never asked why Rachel named her dog Tom Cruise?

Wanting to further test the theory, Lucinda tried again by attracting an orchid, which Sharon sent her a month later. The card said, "I saw one of these in a movie, and for some reason I thought of you. Don't kill it!"

Deciding to dream bigger, Lucinda visualized a new car. She even sat in Peter's recliner in her living room and pretended it was the driver's seat of a sporty SUV—just as the book instructed. Lo and behold, Peter gave her his Land Rover, when he grew tired of it after only six months. "Take it," he said casually over a dinner of pork chops and new potatoes one night. "I'm getting a Thunderbird."

Lucinda thought it was the universe telling her that anything was possible, but later learned that Eve expressed interest in a blue Thunderbird convertible, saying she'd fallen in love with them years earlier after watching *Thelma and Louise*. That small jab to Lucinda's ego was enough for her to become distracted and forget about *The Secret*.

Then, as she picked a cottage to spend the night in for the test run, she thought, *Maybe, just maybe, if I visualize myself as a newly married woman—happy, in love—the Universe will bring it to me.* She booked the honeymooner's cottage but doubted *The Secret* would work to bring her a new love when she couldn't let go of the old one.

She texted Ben and asked what cottage he'd like, and he picked The Pink Octopus, the business's namesake. "Guys," she said to Sharon and Goldie, "that leaves nine cabins we'll need to fill on short notice."

"Sharon, hand me that notepad," Goldie said. "Let's make a list of influential people on the island. Let's make it VIP-only."

"That makes good sense, Mom," Sharon said, scrolling through the contacts on her phone. "Maybe we can strike up a deal with them where we refer business to each other!"

"How about Glenn the Coffee Guy?" Goldie said, referring to the owner of Beach Coffee."

"Well, he certainly can't complain about the coffee in the morning!" Lucinda joked.

Soon, they'd added Mindy, the hairstylist from Magic Mirror, Evan from Kiss My Tees, Bibi from Bibi's Cupcakes, and Doctor Richards, the family's dentist since Alan died. After more brainstorming, they compiled a list that was full of more retailers than friends, which made the most sense from a business standpoint.

Sharon tore the list in half and offered to make calls after she ate lunch, saying she felt like a girl boss. Goldie started making calls immediately, and Lucinda put her hands together in thanks and blew her mother a kiss goodbye.

As she washed her face before bed, Lucinda made a mental note to make some new friends on the island. She'd long ago lost touch with her high school classmates, and, besides, it was time for a fresh start. She'd thought it would be with Jim, but maybe the universe was telling her it wasn't a man she needed, but some good old-fashioned girlfriends.

By the next night, The Pink Octopus was practically glowing in the setting sun. The bungalows stood out with their fresh pastel paint. The landscaping was lush and full, the sidewalks swept, cottages decorated and stocked with snacks and fresh towels. Even the restored pink octopus statue from Mack 3 had been delivered, as good as new. "We rock!" Ben said, eating a carrot stick and watching the men carefully lower it to the ground from the crane. "The Pink Octopus looks better than ever!"

Goldie smirked, swallowing the urge to say, *Well it should for what we paid for it!*

Sal was proudly manning the grill, serving up steaks and burgers from his butcher shop, and sporting an apron that read, "It's not only my steaks that sizzle!" Ben was taking small groups of guests out for boat rides, asking them to share their Hercules stories. Lucinda bought a new dress—a red number that made her feel like Sela Ward—and was playing hostess, feeling good about being down twenty-two pounds, even though the last five or six were from being too depressed over Jim to eat.

She handed out the room keys, fielding questions about the bungalows. She was straightening her necklace when a man walked into the lobby and introduced himself as Ted the Magician. Lucinda smiled and searched for his name on the reservations list. She didn't remember Sharon, Ben, or her mother mentioning collaborating with a magician, but thought it a brilliant idea. "I believe I'm booked for one night in The Tangerine Clam," he said, thumbing delicately through Sharon's jewelry. Lucinda liked the way Ted showed respect for her sister's creations, treating them with care so as not to break anything.

She was confused, not finding anyone named Ted on the list. Her eyes darted outside at Goldie, who was busy striking a Warrior pose to promote her yoga classes. Lucinda cleared her throat and began sweating, figuring she could always sleep in her own bed if necessary, and put Ted in The Great White.

She touched a finger to the computer screen and said, "Sir, I'm sorry, but we have a different guest booked in that cabin." As she reviewed the name slotted in The Tangerine Clam—Dr. Theodore Magesto—she laughed. "I get it. Theodore—Ted, Magesto—magician. Clever."

The man giggled, and Lucinda liked the sound of his laugh. It was masculine, and confident, but not over the top. "Your mother calls me the magician, but really I'm the resident plastic surgeon on Trinity." Lucinda smiled, and then, connecting the dots, she gasped. "Wait, my mother's had plastic surgery?"

Ted pretended to zipper his lips shut, and Lucinda looked back outside at Goldie, who was throwing her head back and laughing. All eyes were on her, as they always were at parties. It'd been that way all of Lucinda's life. Goldie had a way of sucking up all the oxygen wherever she went.

She handed Ted his key, noticing an uncanny resemblance to the Tom Selleck poster on her bedroom wall. "Wait," she asked, her eyes flickering, "I've heard Trinity is a spa-like retreat. I've also heard it is celebrity rehab. Are you telling me it's a ruse for a plastic surgery outfit? Is that the real reason people come back looking well-rested?" Ted laughed and told Lucinda Trinity offered both spa services *and* cosmetic surgery. "And rehab?" Lucinda asked, cocking her head. Ted smiled and shrugged.

He shook his head when she asked him to divulge a few celebrity guests. "HIPAA, and all," he said, pretending to zipper his lips again. Ted the Magician was handsome when he zippered his lips. He asked if Lucinda would be joining the festivities outside, and she nodded. "I think I will." She had a few more guests to check in but found herself looking forward to chatting further with Ted. He tipped his hat, exited the lobby, and was immediately charged by a screaming Goldie.

Lucinda sat down on the stool behind the front desk and smiled. No one had ever tipped his hat to her. She thought it was something only men like Cary Grant did, and even then, only in movies. *Could this be The Secret hard at work?* She rolled her eyes, sighed, and checked her cell phone to see if there was anything from Jim. There wasn't.

Chapter 34

When all the guests had checked in, Lucinda joined everyone on the beach where Ben had a beautiful bonfire pit hollowed out, complete with a circular bench, all made from sand. Lucinda heard him telling Goldie about it but had no idea it would look so picturesque, so dreamy. It was filled with various sized candles and reminded her of one of those viral videos where a supposedly hidden camera captured a man dropping to one knee and proposing.

Though she always felt things like that were staged, she admitted that Ben's homemade bonfire pit would serve as the perfect backdrop for just such an occasion.

He caught her looking, and she waved him over. She gave him a hug, handed him a beer, and said, "This totally puts to shame the adorable sandcastle I built recently. Thanks a lot!"

"Maybe I'll decide to forego massage therapy training and become a professional sand artist," he said, sipping his beer. "What would that be called? A sandscaper? A sandscape architect?"

"You won't."

"Won't what?"

"You won't forego massage school."

"Oh, really?"

"I paid your tuition in full. Happy next twelve birth-days!"

Ben picked Lucinda up and spun her around in a bear hug. He thanked her profusely, and she brushed him off, saying it was part of the "Peter's a Lousy Cheating Scum-bag Scholarship Fund."

Ben offered to pay her back, but she shook her head and said you don't pay back scholarships. "I could offer you free lifetime massages, but the idea of touching your bare skin gives me the heebie-jeebies," he said, shivering. They both laughed, and Lucinda said he could pay her back by being happy. He agreed and suggested she dig into that concept herself.

Lucinda nodded and motioned to the crowd, saying things looked to be going well. Ben agreed, and then asked what they were going to do about Lucinda's situation. She shrugged, and said she was going to keep moving for-ward—to whatever "forward" meant. When Ben suggest-ed another friend of his, Lucinda covered his mouth with her hand. "Bite your tongue!" Ben laughed, raised his beer, and said, "To new beginnings."

"To new beginnings," she said, winking. She took a sip of her drink, the champagne bubbles fizzing on her tongue, and wondered how she could look forward to a fu-ture without Jim. Ben kissed Lucinda's cheek and made his way to the band—Cheeseballs in Paradise, the new on-staff entertainers at The Pink Octopus—and whispered in the bandleader's ear.

Chuck hushed his band, summoned Goldie to the stage, and put his arm around her. Feigning shyness, Goldie shifted on her feet and covered her mouth with one hand. "The next song is a gift from your son, Ben," Chuck said into the microphone. Ben blew Goldie a kiss. "It's his way of saying thank you for all you and the late, great Tom built here on Turtle Beach—a grand accomplishment and veritable treasure here on the island."

Goldie gazed at Ben—his hands in his pockets, feet bare, disheveled hair. He was tousled and his white suit wrinkled, but somehow, he never looked more effortlessly elegant than he did on that stage. When Chuck finished speaking, Ben fist bumped him, and motioned for the microphone.

Chuck obliged, and Ben tapped it, sending a screech through the night air. Everyone giggled. Goldie kept her eyes fixed squarely on her son.

Ben cleared his throat and began speaking. "A lot of folks on the island wonder why I haven't settled down yet." He looked around the crowd, pointing at a few people and playfully accusing, "You know who you are when you're over at Food Basket on double coupon day or at Clive's shooting pool. Y'all are discussing if and when I'll get hitched!" More laughter from the crowd.

Lucinda sat in a chair beside Ted the Magician and took a bite of coconut cake. Ben looked her way and winked, always at ease before a crowd of people—a lot like his mother that way.

Sharon was sitting at an adjacent table with Matt, and already wiping her eyes. Ben continued, "Well here's the thing, guys. No matter how beautiful The Pink Octopus is with its newfangled makeover..." Everyone clapped and cheered. When they quieted down, he continued, "Nothing will ever be as beautiful as my parents' love story. They set one hell of a bar in the love department, and, well, I just don't want to settle for anything less than that type of magic!" By now, the guitarist began strumming a familiar song, and the crowd was on their feet cheering.

Ben kissed Goldie on the cheek, hugged her, and spoke into the microphone one last time, saying, "In case any of you have given up on love, let us draw inspiration from Tom and Goldie's wedding song. Hit it, guys! Give it all you've got for my ma!"

He returned the microphone to Chuck, who started singing an acoustic version of Elvis Presley's *Can't Help Falling in Love.* Ben outstretched his hand to invite his mother to dance, and she happily accepted.

They danced in the moonlight, and Lucinda's heart ached at how much Ben looked like their father. When he slipped into shadow on the dance floor, Lucinda thought it may as well have been Tom twirling Goldie around with his hand on the small of her back. A tear slipped down her cheek, and she let it remain there.

She didn't want to pretend anymore that she was fine. She missed her daddy, plain and simple, and she missed Jim. That she had an exceptionally handsome, single doctor within reach was completely wasted on her. She took her phone out of her handbag and texted Jim.

Lucinda: I hate to make assumptions, but I'm thinking you got your closure with me and are good to move on with your life. I just wanted to say that I understand, but it still hurts. Very much so, as it turns out.

She put her phone back in her bag, and sipped her champagne, remembering her elopement to Las Vegas, and how Tom never forgave her for not letting him walk her down the aisle. She wished she could turn back time and not marry Peter, not break up with Jim, hug her father...but then she wouldn't have Frankie and Jill. She blew her nose, unconcerned with whether she looked tacky.

Ben motioned to Sal, who cut in and took Goldie in his arms. It didn't matter that Sal was several inches shorter than Goldie because in that moment, they looked like royalty, twirling in the moonlight. When Ben walked off the stage and into the night, it was as if Tom was walking away, having extended his blessing to his wife and children. *Time waits for no one*, Lucinda thought, as she pushed the remnants of her cake around on her plate.

She shook her head, recalling that in her short time on the island, her mother, grandmother, and sister explained how they'd had one love in their life. A love so great that they hung up any hopes of allowing lightning to strike twice. *Not me*, Lucinda resolved, looking at the accomplished man beside her. *I'm too young to be done with love*.

Ted noticed her watching him and leaned over, whispering, "Would you care to dance?" Lucinda shrugged, accepted his invitation, and was on her feet. Ted had strong hands, and was a capable dancer. *Of course*, she thought. The band played more songs, including some that would even have an uptight librarian twisting and shouting.

Besides being ridiculously handsome and light on his feet, Ted wasn't a half-bad conversationalist. He talked about interesting topics such as politics, animal preservation, and his charity, which provided free plastic surgery to children in Guatemala one month a year. Lucinda let him speak, closing her eyes and resting her head on his shoulder during a slow song. The band played, and Ted talked, and the moon painted everyone in the most flattering light. Lucinda breathed in the moment, eyes closed, and hoped tomorrow she could pick herself up, dust herself off, and start all over again. *If only it were that easy*, she thought.

Sharon invited Matt to the party, but not to sleep over. They'd only had a few dates and were hitting it off, but she still hadn't told him about the MS. Soon, she wouldn't have a choice. Lucinda wondered what Matt thought was the reason behind Sharon's cane, but she forgot to ask her sister. Anyway, he didn't seem like the type to shy away from a wonderful woman with a health condition. He appeared to be pretty great in Lucinda's eyes. Even Ben and Goldie commented that he was a catch.

He arrived early at the party, carrying an old sailboat on the back of his truck. When Sharon asked what it was for, he said, "Just wait and see." After dark, he parked it in the sand and brought a projector to show old black and white films after dark, the sail acting as a movie screen. Lucinda smiled as she watched Sharon lying on Matt's lap while Frank Sinatra serenaded Grace Kelly in *High Society*.

She found herself hoping Sharon would rent her house because she had a feeling she'd remarry someday and want to move back into it.

As the night went on, guests eventually made their way to their assigned bungalows. Someone would find Lucinda or Goldie and ask where a light switch was or if they had a first-aid kit, or whether smoking was allowed in the cottages. By eleven, Ted said goodnight to Lucinda, mustering the courage to ask if she was seeing anyone. She hadn't expected a question like that, and it made her palms sweat. She shook her head and said, "I don't think so."

Ted smiled, and said, "You don't think so? Whew, I'm glad you cleared that up." Lucinda laughed, seeing that Ted was only joking.

She blushed when he kissed the back of her hand and waved goodnight. Goldie swooped in when he walked away, and her mouth twisted into a grimace like she'd stumbled upon a rotten egg. "Ted the Magician?"

"Why not? He's good looking!"

"Because you're going to marry Jim. That's why."

"Mother..."

"How did Ted say we knew each other?"

Lucinda did as Ted had done earlier and pretended to zipper her lips. Goldie raised her eyebrows, stood up straight, and said, "I'm all natural," for your concern. "A little Botox here and there hardly counts. It was more for my migraines than anything."

Lucinda smiled, made the OK symbol with her thumb and index finger, and said she wasn't sure when Goldie had ever experienced migraines, but all right.

She walked back outside and sat on a beach chair listening to Cheeseballs in Paradise wrapping up their set. They ended the evening with *Come Monday*, and Lucinda couldn't help but wonder what her "Monday" would look like now that she was back to being alone.

After a minute, she craned her neck to see The Tangerine Clam and wondered if Ted slept in plaid or striped pajamas, figuring if this were a movie, she'd slip into his door and spend the night with him—whether she was over Jim or not. She never understood how casually the movies had divorcees hopping into one new bed after another. They sure made trysts look fun, though.

She looked up at the moon, checked her phone one more time, and noticed that Jim hadn't responded to her text yet. She scrolled to her last text with Eve, which said, *I'm hoping we can eventually be friends again, Lucinda. I always considered you a sister.* She deleted the text thread and blocked Eve's number.

Goldie was wrong about Jim coming back and marrying her, Lucinda thought. She rubbed her feet together, enjoying the natural exfoliation from all her time in the sand. The loneliness crept over her like strangling vines, and for a split second, she considered showing up at Ted the Magician's door after all.

She glanced at his bungalow again just as his light clicked off. Standing up, she brushed the sand from her dress, took a deep breath, and exhaled. She began walking and wound up on her mother's porch instead of Ted's. "This is not a movie," she whispered to herself, looking up at the paper moon. "And I'm not that girl."

Walking inside, she made her way back to her bedroom and stared at the beautiful gift Jim had given her. It seemed like a long time ago. She slid out of her dress and fell into bed alone. She patted the pillow beside her, wondering if anyone would ever share her bed again.

Chapter 35

A couple of weeks later, Grandma Helen's 100th birthday bash was finally at hand, and the vendors showed up early to prepare. There were food trucks and carnival rides and two clowns, one to paint faces, and one to make balloon animals for the children. The Perry's little section of beach was hopping, and The Pink Octopus was in full splendor.

Sharon's legs were acting up, and she was upset because she had hoped to make it through the relaunch without a deep conversation about her MS with Matt. She passed off her symptoms as neuropathy, somehow feeling he might digest that diagnosis more readily than multiple sclerosis.

Lucinda suggested she take him aside early on and explain everything so she could get that stress out of the way and enjoy the day. "Then he can help you get around today, since we'll all be so busy," Lucinda said. Sharon didn't like the idea, wanting to wait until Grandma Helen's day went off without a hitch. "Today's about Grandma," she said, wiping her eyes, "and the business, or course."

"OK, but if you need anything, please let me know."

"I do need one thing."

"What is it?"

"Tomorrow let's talk about renting Sea Rock. I think you're right. Someone may as well live there just in case I ever want to move back. You never know what the future holds, right?"

"Let's plan to discuss it tomorrow, then," Lucinda said, squeezing Sharon's hand. "This is good stuff, Shaz."

Lucinda helped her up, and they went into the kitchen where Goldie had just brought Grandma Helen in to wait for the party to begin. Lucinda sat at the table doing Helen's makeup, and Sharon took pictures, wanting to remember every detail of the day.

There was a knock at the door, and in walked Jill and Frankie, along with their cousin, Kelly—Sharon's daughter. Lucinda and Sharon squealed, scurrying to hug all their kids and crying. "Did you arrange all this, Sharon?" Lucinda asked, sniffling. Sharon shook her head and said she was about to ask Lucinda the same thing. Ben followed behind everyone and complained, "Why does it always have to be one of you who arrange all the great stuff around here?"

Sharon and Lucinda sandwiched Ben into a bear hug, and Helen demanded everyone kneel so she could get a better look at them. Jill, Frankie, and Kelly took turns hugging their great-grandmother and taking pictures. Helen cried with joy, and Goldie told her to knock it off, or she'd destroy her makeup.

Soon, everyone was discussing logistics. Jill could stay a week, but Frank had to return to work, so he'd be leaving in a few days. Kelly, upon seeing her mother's difficulty getting around, said her return flight was flexible. "I can stay awhile, Mom," she said, laying her head on Sharon's lap. "I've missed my mommy."

"I thought you had no more vacation time at work, honey?" Sharon questioned.

"They'll understand, Mom. Family comes first, right? I've really missed you!" Kelly said, removing a roller Sharon had missed from her hair.

Channel 6 News sent Tasha Trenton again, and this time, she was happy to meet Helen, whose spunk lived up to the hype. Lucinda whispered to Sharon that Tasha seemed sincere, and Sharon nodded and asked if they should try to set her up with Frank. Lucinda laughed, and Sharon added, "Hey, if he fell in love with her, he might move to the island! You can stay, too, then we'd just have to work on Jill!"

"What about Kelly?" Lucinda asked.

"Nope," Sharon protested, shaking her head. "When she got her Harvard acceptance letter, I wanted to declare it a national holiday. All I've ever wanted was for her to get off this island, have a career, and see the world. She's too good for this place."

"And my derelict children aren't?" Lucinda teased.

"Jilly can run Pure Love 4 Life from anywhere, right? It's mostly online. And Frankie? Well, come on! He's the Jeff Bezos of real estate, but younger and cuter. He can buy up all the hot listings from his sofa, he's so good! Kelly can't be an engineer on the island."

Lucinda considered everything Sharon said but knew Frankie and Jill would never move to the island full-time. Though much of their family were native islanders, it was never their life. They were New Englanders through and through.

She listened as Grandma Helen answered Tasha's questions about how the island had changed since she was young, and whether she planned to ride the Ferris Wheel that was set up by the water. Helen was in good spirits, and played along, cracking jokes and hamming it up for the camera.

The afternoon carried on seamlessly. There were at least a hundred and fifty people, but thankfully, Sharon and Lucinda planned for a crowd, and two dozen food trucks served free and discounted food to everyone. The vendors were gracious, handling the never-ending lines of people with patience and courtesy, probably knowing how much new business they could gain from a crowd that size.

Goldie stood up to make a speech and thanked everyone for coming. She talked about how Helen sacrificed for everyone all her life, and the party was a fraction of what she deserved. Ben nudged Lucinda and said, "This is the first time I've ever heard Mom say something nice about Grandma. I feel like the world might end now because some strange ancient prophesy has been fulfilled."

Goldie told her mother she loved her and that, "Obviously, a lot of other people do, too, Mom."

Then, she plugged The Pink Octopus and announced they'd be offering coupons to local restaurants, free breakfast in the bungalows, paddle boarding, bicycle rentals, shuttle service, and, best of all, yoga classes. "If you want legs like this," she said, hiking up her skirt, "be sure to sign up for one of my sessions before you leave. They're not just for guests!" The crowd applauded when Goldie showed some leg, and she shimmied off stage, glowing.

Sharon and Lucinda laughed, and Ben said he needed bleach dumped in his eyes to clear the image of his mother hiking up her skirt on live television. Everyone was having a good time. The children were building sandcastles, and couples were dancing on the beach. Cheeseballs in Paradise were hilarious and did a great job keeping the momentum going by asking if anyone remembered dances like the Running Man, the Moonwalk, and the Electric Slide. When someone in the crowd was the first to demonstrate, Chuck rewarded them with a band T-shirt he fired from his cannon.

Lucinda watched her grown children dancing, mingling, and having fun. She loved everyone being in the same zip code again, even for an afternoon. The ordinarily buttoned-up Frank let his hair down and was having a good time. Lucinda remembered some scary times early in his life when doctors didn't know if Frank would ever play sports, run, or do things like other children. She shook her head in awe, watching him twirl Grandma Helen's wheelchair around the dance floor.

Tracing hearts on the table with her finger, she felt the day was almost perfect. Her phone vibrated in her pocket, and she pulled it out and looked at the message. It was from Jim. She hadn't heard much from him after texting that she missed him. He replied, but only a brief message saying he was working some things out and would be in touch soon.

Jim: Hey, how's the party going? It's today, right?"

◻Lucinda closed her eyes and tried to control her emotions before replying. The truth was, she had lost hope when it came to Jim. He was in North Carolina trying to mend his relationship with his daughter. She couldn't deny him the chance to repair his family. She was a day late and a dollar short of winning him back.

Lucinda: Yes, it's going well, thanks.

Jim: Helen is a vision in pink. I can't wait to watch you age that beautifully, too.

◻Lucinda swallowed hard. How did Jim know Grandma Helen was wearing a pink dress? She stood, looked around, and walked toward the dance floor, where Helen was taking a break from dancing. Frank was handing her a glass of iced tea.

As Lucinda neared the band, Chuck stopped singing and spoke into the microphone. "Sorry everyone, but I was supposed to stop singing the minute I saw this beautiful lady step onto the dance floor." Lucinda froze in place, feeling her cheeks flush.

The couples all stopped dancing and parted to reveal a dapper Jim, wearing a light beige linen suit with a white shirt, partially unbuttoned. Her hand shot up to cover her mouth. She'd never seen Jim in a suit, only a tuxedo at the prom thirty-some years earlier. He handed her an enormous bouquet of pink lilies and red roses and spoke into the microphone Chuck had given him, saying, "Hello everyone. I'm sorry to interrupt Grandma Helen's birthday party, but this couldn't wait another minute."

The buzz from the crowd began to decrease, falling into a deafening silence. Someone's balloon popped, and Lucinda jumped, eliciting giggles from the crowd. Jim continued, "A long time ago, I let a beautiful girl go a little too easily. I guess it all worked out since neither of us would have our wonderful kids if I'd fought harder for her."

Lucinda glanced at Frank, who was looking on, confused, and over to Jill, who was smiling. She turned her hands palms up, like *What's going on?* Tasha grabbed the cameraman's lens and pointed it directly at Jim and Lucinda. "Well, anyway, I found the beautiful girl a while back, and seeing her took my breath away. I had to choke back tears when I witnessed the lovely woman she'd become. She commented she didn't know why her mother had secretly kept in touch with me for thirty years, as if Goldie was the one initiating things. The truth is, *I* couldn't let go. *Me*. I was the one who needed to know that she got through labor all right or that she moved into a safe neighborhood in Connecticut or that her son, Frankie, had recovered from his heart surgery. I let Lucinda go because it's what she wanted, but I selfishly held on by keeping tabs on her. Maybe that makes me a stalker. I don't care."

□The crowd was riveted, and Lucinda was tearing up, breathing deeply, and biting her cheek to avoid ugly crying. Sharon stood, walked over to her, and put an arm around her shoulders. Lucinda gripped her hand, fighting back tears. "I had to go home to North Carolina recently," Jim said, sighing, "and prove I wasn't a murderer." He looked over at Helen, whose eyes were wide. "It's a story for another day, Grandma Helen, but I promise I'm a teddy bear."

The crowd giggled nervously. "When I got there," he continued, "I realized it wasn't home anymore. I'm not sure it ever was, really, because Lucinda wasn't there. And if I know one thing after all these years, it's that my home is anywhere I'm close enough to touch Lucinda May Perry. *She's* my home."

Jim dropped to one knee, and the crowd let out a collective gasp. Lucinda could hear her heart thumping in her ears. Sharon gripped her arm and whispered, "Do you need my cane?" Lucinda laughed through tears, and Goldie stuffed a tissue in her hand. Lucinda mouthed, *thank you*, and winked at her mother. "Lucinda," Jim said, presenting a canary diamond ring. "We let too much time get away from us. Please, from the bottom of my heart, put me out of my misery and just marry me already."

Lucinda's cheeks hurt from smiling so broadly. She immediately searched for her mother in the crowd, wanting to see the joy in her eyes from succeeding at her matchmaking schemes. Goldie's arms were extended straight over her head, a victory pose if there ever was one. Lucinda called out to her, "It only took thirty years to get your way on this, Ma!"

"Does that mean it's a yes?" Jim pleaded, placing a hand on the floor beside him to steady himself. "Because my knees are buckling!"

Lucinda nodded, and the crowd erupted in applause. Sharon wiped her eyes, and Ben shook his head as if to say, *What took you idiots so long?* As if on cue, fireworks shot into the evening sky, and Tasha high-fived the cameraman, congratulating them on capturing the moment. She winked at Jim, who tapped his nose, two conspirators congratulating each other for pulling off the big surprise.

Everyone cheered, and the band played Jim and Lucinda's prom song, which made her cry. She helped him to his feet, and he winced. "Thanks," he said smiling. "It's difficult to be debonair while wincing." They laughed, and

Jim took Lucinda's face in his hands just like always and kissed her lips.

"This time you're not getting rid of me," she whispered.

"This time, I won't be so quick to let you go," he said, his voice breaking on the last word. "I'm never spending a single night away from you again, Lucinda. I'm yours, and you're mine, and that's all that needs to be said."

When someone tapped her on the shoulder and said, "Lucinda?" she didn't need to turn around to know who it was. She smiled, spun on her heel, and extended her arms. "Savannah! It's so nice to meet you!"

"My family calls me Savvy," Savannah clarified, embracing Lucinda. "I think it's safe for you to call me that after all we've been through."

"Welcome to Turtle Beach, Savvy," Lucinda said, smiling.

Jim twirled Lucinda around the dance floor, and rather than feeling self-conscious about what the heat was doing to her hair, or whether her lipstick was still on, all she could feel was gratitude for life's twists and turns. She and Jim took a long detour—and it led to four beautiful children—but now she was back where she belonged, on Turtle Beach and in the arms of the only man she'd ever truly loved.

Introduction to Saltwater and Serendipity

What if the stranger in the seat beside you happens to be your destiny?

When a beautiful woman he's never seen before approaches uptight businessman, Frank Flowers, professing her undying love, he's immediately compelled to learn more about her. He follows her onto the Turtle Island ferry, where she admits the grand gesture was a dare: *Say "I love you" to a stranger.*

When Frank learns why Rose is visiting the island—to honor her friend's bucket list—he takes a detour from his busy day to help her check some items off the list. The adventure—which has the pair blowing bubbles, picnicking on the beach, and riding a tandem bicycle—has Frank feeling like a kid again. No one has ever made him feel as at home, at ease, and excited about life as this mystery girl.

He's prepared to sidcline his entire summer, if need be, to spend every day with Rose, checking the bucket list items off one by one. But, when they lose track of each other before exchanging last names or phone numbers, Frank fears his best chance at true love has just slipped through his fingers.

Remembering that Rose must go home—wherever that is—in two weeks, Frank sets out on a mission to track down the most beautiful, interesting woman he's ever encountered, promising himself he'll drop to one knee and propose if he finds her. His entire family, along with most of Turtle Island pitch in to help Frank find his soul mate before she's gone forever!

As the search unfolds, Frank continues to find himself one step behind Rose, but is regaled with enchanting stories of islanders who encountered her. Through the stories, Frank becomes more and more smitten by this stranger, who seems to sprinkle a little magic wherever she goes.

As the clock ticks on, Frank is losing hope that he'll find Rose before it's too late. However, what keeps him going are the continual signs everywhere that the universe is aligning and carving a path for the two of them to meet up again—if only he can find her before she leaves Turtle Island forever!

Goldie's Famous Lemon Brownies

Ingredients:

1 store-bought box of yellow cake

1 box of lemon instant pudding

2 eggs (room temperature)

1/3 cup lemon juice (fresh or bottled)

1 ½ tsp. lemon zest

Glaze:

1 cup powdered sugar

1 tablespoon lemon juice (more if preferred)

Lemon zest for garnish (optional)

Instructions:

1. Spray an 8" or 9" baking dish (8" for thicker brownies) with parchment paper and spray with cooking spray.
2. Preheat oven to 350 degrees.
3. In a bowl, beat cake mix, pudding, eggs, lemon juice, and zest.
4. Pour into baking dish.
5. Bake for 24 minutes, or until fork comes out clean.
6. Mix glaze by whisking all ingredients in a bowl. Set aside.
7. Once brownies are completely cooled, drizzle with glaze, slice, and wait for your applause!

Like Free Stuff?

To receive a **FREE** novella, *Seabirds and Saying Good-bye*-the story of how Goldie and Tom met and started The Pink Octopus, sign up for my newsletter here:

https://dl.bookfunnel.com/1ednvobowk

If you liked *Sandcastles and Second Chances,* book 2, *Saltwater and Serendipity,* is available for pre-order on Amazon and will be released July 11, 2024

Thanks for reading! If you loved this book and have a moment to spare, I would really appreciate a short review as this helps new readers find my books!

About the Author

Lianne James writes clean, dreamy stories to remind people that true love exists at any age and stage of life, if only you believe in it. In her books, you'll always be guaranteed characters who enjoy all things food-related (especially if it involves carbs) and never make you feel bad about skipping your walk to read another chapter.

Lianne lives with her husband who she found later in life on a dating website. The two of them sprinkle a little magic love dust on everyone they meet, hoping that all the world will find the special kind of relationship they did. Lianne's biggest message she'd like to share with her readers is that romance is not just between a book's pages! It exists for every single person, because no matter what you think is wrong with you, someone out there is looking for your brand of weird. That's a promise!

Visit her website at liannejames.com or drop her an email at liannejameswriter@gmail.com

Made in the USA
Columbia, SC
08 August 2024

40130876R00181